FINDING TIEGAN

HANNA PARK

BAISONG PRESS

Finding Tiegan

Cover Art by *Niki White* www.nikiawhiteart.com

Visit Hanna Park at www.hannapark.ca

Baisong Press, PO Box 291, Port Carling, ON P0B 1J0

Second Edition, 2025

Digital ISBN, 978-1-0689975-5-6

Paperback ISBN, 978-1-0689975-4-9

Published in Canada

First Edition, 2021, by The Wild Rose Press

PRAISE FOR HANNA PARK

HANNA PARK HAS A TALENT FOR WRITING UNFORGET-
TABLE CHARACTERS DEALING WITH INSURMOUNTABLE
GRIEF. EMOTIONAL, HEART-WRENCHING PROSE TAKE THE
READER ON A JOURNEY OF SELF-DISCOVERY, PASSION,
AND ROMANCE. HIGHLY RECOMMEND!

— N.N. LIGHT'S BOOK HEAVEN

FINDING TIEGAN IS A RIVETING NOVEL THAT CAPTIVATES
READERS WITH ITS BLEND OF ROMANCE, SUSPENSE, AND
PARANORMAL ELEMENTS. PARK MASTERFULLY BALANCES
THE THEMES OF OVERCOMING DARK PASTS AND
EMBRACING LIFE, CREATING AN ENGAGING AND
THOUGHT-PROVOKING NARRATIVE. LOVERS OF ROMANCE,
ESPECIALLY THOSE WHO APPRECIATE A MIX OF EROTI-
CISM, PLOT TWISTS, AND PARANORMAL INTRIGUE, WILL
FIND THIS NOVEL COMPELLING.

— BOOK REVIEWER

PRAISE FOR HANNA PARK

A solid five stars for Hanna Park's debut Finding Tiegan. The setting and the characters are as vivid as they are sexy. Suspenseful, mythological, and very sexy.

— SUE JASKULA, AWARD WINNING AUTHOR

Finding Tiegan by Hanna Park is a must-read! With highly engaging dialogue and perfect narration, there was never a dull moment in the book, and once I started reading it, I could not put it down. The characters were well-developed, and readers will also appreciate the seamless flow of the plotline, which leaves no room for confusion for the reader.

— READERS' FAVORITE

For Tiegan and Tomás, who deserve a second chance

1

*"Life status: currently holding it all
together with one bobby pin."*—Unknown

Tiegan

"Tiegan!" Vera launched forward, flinging her arms around me. "You're finally here!" Tones of honeysuckle, rose, and musk filled my nose, replacing stale airport air with her go-to scent, Burberry. It had been three years since I had seen my best friend, and I'd missed her. I had missed this. I dropped my backpack on the floor and grinned, hugging her back—hard.

She gripped my shoulders, her gaze running away from my face. "Jesus, girl. What's going on with you? You're too damn skinny. Have you been eating? Did you sleep on the plane?"

"I'm okay, Vera, I'm fine." But on the weight point? Vera was right. I was not casting much of a shadow these days. I had lost twenty-six pounds since Aaron died.

"Are you sure? You don't look fine. You look, I don't

know…ghostly. Are you still having those nightmares?" Her gaze searched mine.

"Vera, I'm fine." I gazed at my friend, into a heart-shaped face framed by cascades of white-blonde hair and eyes of cerulean blue—eyes that could see right through you or hold you frozen in time.

"I worry about you, you know. And the funeral. I feel so bad I couldn't make it to the funeral." Her eyes shadowed.

"It's okay. I didn't expect you to come." I tilted my head, reassuring her with a smile.

Three long months ago, my world shifted and came crashing down, to be exact. Aaron, my one love, my husband, had an affair—a lengthy romance with a woman he worked with—not something I could accept or forgive. It was the reason I let him go, a perfectly good reason. At least, that's what I told myself. At first, I couldn't breathe. And then I was heartbroken. Why would he do that to us? Our life together was perfect, or so I thought. How could I have been so wrong?

"Aaron…where are you?"

"Working late, babe— Be there soon, babe— On my way, babe."

Yeah, right, babe.

All those unanswered messages and the excuses made no sense. I suppose I didn't want to see.

Aaron expected I would forgive his indiscretion. He had apologized, and I had cried. I should have told him to leave, but my heart clung to him, refusing to accept the truth despite his heartbreaking revelation. We'd gone to bed, but I couldn't sleep. Moonlight filtered through the panes of the lace-covered window, and for a time, I lay there, staring at a crack in the plaster ceiling, a minute fracture that grew bigger and bigger the longer I stared at it. How I hated him then, lying in bed next to him, my throat tight with unshed tears, my mind a spool of unraveled thread. Still, I hungered for his touch. I straddled his body, brushing his lips with a teasing tongue. He had moaned under a blanket of sleep, and I wondered if he dreamed of her. He responded as I knew he would: his shaft hardened, ready to please. His fingers, always so agile, had squeezed my breasts, and he had kissed me with a driving tongue. I remember the hard press of his hands on my hips, the sweet ache of orgasm, and the hot, pulsating jet of Aaron's seed. We had used each other for the last time. In the cold light of morning, it was clear, to me anyway, that our marriage was over.

Four weeks later, Aaron died. And I blamed myself. I didn't pull the trigger or drive his car off the road, which was what happened. But now, I couldn't sleep. I couldn't eat. I stared at the food on my plate, and I saw horrible things: maggots crawling in and out of dead flesh, splintered bones, and darkness—empty holes filled with darkness. I swallowed the lump in my throat and said the words that have haunted me for weeks—I confessed.

"Vera? Aaron's death was my fault." I held her wrist, stilling her escape.

"What? What are you talking about?" She looked at me.

The whirr of wheeling suitcases, the cacophony of voices, the melodic ding of the elevator; all those sounds faded away. I shared the only secret I had left.

"He wanted to come home, and I told him no. Then he crashed the car." I closed my eyes, remembering the sounds amplified through my phone's speaker: the horror in Aaron's voice, the rising crescendo of disbelief, and then the silence. In heavy rain and dense fog, Aaron's car had left the highway and rolled three times down the side of an embankment.

"What? No, you can't think that." She shook her head, refusing to blame me for Aaron's unfortunate demise.

"When I close my eyes…I see his face." My eyes burned. I hung my head.

"Tiegan…" She cupped my shoulders.

"I can't help it. It's like an explosion in my brain—the glass smashing and the car. It rolled three times. Did you know that?" It was such a relief, telling someone—I'd been holding my breath for such a long, long time.

"Tiegan, it was an accident. It was the weather. It was Aaron, being Aaron. I'm sorry, but no. None of it was your fault." Her voice filled my mind, replacing Aaron's.

"I guess you're right." I pinned my lips into a tight line.

"Of course, I'm right. Come on." Vera hooked her arm around mine, guiding me through the long halls of the airport. Her silence was comforting.

Hiking my backpack higher on my shoulder, I exhaled a long breath. Vera was right—Aaron left me long before he died. It was time I left Aaron—in the past, where he belonged.

"I love your car!" I gasped, my gaze wandering over the cream colored convertible.

"This is Lola." She lifted her shoulders and grinned.

"Lola?" I tossed my pack into the backseat of the vintage bug.

"Yep, I take Lola everywhere!" She handed me a white headscarf and a pair of cat-eye sunglasses and then pressed a button, dropping the retractable soft top.

"Put these on, girl. We're going topless." Vera covered her head with the scarf, wrapping the ends around her neck, tied them in the back, and then slipped on dark sunglasses, completing the Audrey Hepburn look.

I followed her lead, flipped down the sun visor, and preened into the little mirror. "How do I look?"

"Marvelous, darling! Absolutely marvelous!" She grinned.

I giggled at the full-on English accent.

Within moments, we were cruising along a quiet coastal highway. I breathed in warmth and sea salt. I could almost smell the sunshine. The road curved along a sweep of never-ending ochre cliffs and offered a blue sky and a big ocean view. What I had admired in photos did not compare or do justice to the real thing.

"Wow, Vera. I can't believe you live here. Look at those cliffs…" I said as Lola swung around another breathtaking bend in the road.

"You brought your paintbrush, right?" She sent me a side-glance.

"Yes, ma'am, I plan to find my muse again." And I meant that. While I was an artist—one of the lucky ones who made a living drawing inspiration from the sea—I had painted nothing since Aaron. When I stared at the canvas, I saw nothing but an empty blank space.

"I'm glad, Tieg." Vera reached out and gave my fingers a gentle squeeze.

"Oh my God, these cliffs are freaking insane. Just look." I gazed up and then up again. I loved rock climbing. Back home, the rock faces of the Cape Breton Highlands were my favorite haunt. This cliff's face, sheer limestone, was a wall of nooks and crannies, a climber's paradise. But Aaron was my climbing partner, my safety net. How many weekends had we spent together? My rope tied into his—my stomach fluttered with a nauseating sense of unease.

"Have you been doing any climbing?" I cocked my head, admiring Vera's look—the dark green swing dress with a stand-up collar, complementing five-inch red plaid stiletto heels.

"I took Steve to *Albufeira* to do some bouldering, but he wasn't into it. We should go—maybe next week."

"Oh, how is Steve?" In all my self-absorption, I forgot about Vera and her life.

"He's good. His practice is doing well." She kept her eyes on the winding road.

I knew all about Vera's latest love: the veterinarian from Lisbon, from her social media posts, and the many rescue events they attended. The latest, a tea party to raise money to sterilize stray cats and dogs. "Hmm, that's good. And how's it going with you? What's new on the farm?" Vera's passion—the re-homing of strays—hence the farmyard of animals she owned: five dogs, six cats, two donkeys, and one iguana.

She wiggled her fingers, and the light caught on a solitary sapphire. "We got engaged."

"What? You said nothing? You didn't tell me?" My heart leaped. How could it not? My best friend was getting married?

"We are. Well, that's the plan." Her hand tightened on the steering wheel and her lips pressed together.

"I'm so happy for you, Vera. This is wonderful news." I twisted in my seat, unable to contain my excitement. I was a sucker for love—I loved love. I loved Christmas and puppies and sleeping in late. And chocolate, everything chocolate.

"Thanks, hon." Vera shot me a quick glance.

"When do I meet him?" I was not worried about Vera; she wase the careful one. Me, myself, and I—eyes wide shut kind of girl. Something I needed to work on. Soon.

"He's at a conference in Lisbon for a few days, but we'll make plans after that." She nodded once and then twice.

The sonic scream of a street bike shattered my newfound sense of euphoria.

"Holy hotfoot! What was that?" My gaze followed the blurred haze of exhaust. I scanned the horizon, searching for evidence that what had passed even existed.

"Hath heaven met hell is more like it," Vera said in a wry voice, her lips pursed in a thin fine line.

"What do you mean? What's wrong? You know that guy?" I said in a quick voice.

"Yeah, I know him." She selected a rockabilly station—toe-tapping lyrics playing on the radio.

I tapped my fingers on the dashboard and grinned. "Tell me more. Tell me more."

"What's that?" She lowered the volume.

"Who is he?" I stretched my voice, arching my eyebrows.

"No one." Her shoulders lifted and her brows creased.

"What do you mean, no one?" I sat back in my seat and studied her.

"Okay. All right. That was Tomás. Tomás Ferreira—he owns a restaurant in town. It has a five-star reputation. He does not." She huffed and shook her head from side to side.

"Hmm, so...an excellent prospect?" I settled into the leather seat. The last thing I wanted, or needed, was a relationship with a man, fallen angel or not, but teasing Vera was just so easy.

"No, Tieg, he's anything but." Vera tilted her chin in my direction, her lips in a severe line. Her face broke into a smile, and she laughed.

It was infectious. I giggled, overcome with the urge to join in her laughter.

We arrived in the small tourist town of Carvoeiro, my home, for the next three months. The town was spectacular and so very Mediterranean: purple and pink bougainvillea walked over low-slung stone walls, a stunning accent to a never-ending terrace of white stucco buildings and a lace of ironwork. The focal point was the beach: an expanse of golden sand and butterscotch cliffs, sponge toffee pitted by the winds of time. A red and white fishing sloop leaned on its hull in search of safe harbor from the merciless pull of the ocean tides.

My stomach lurched as Lola rounded the next corner. Vera punched the accelerator, tossing me backward, as Lola grumbled her way to the crest of the summit. Vera shifted gear, coming to a hard stop behind a vintage car in mint condition with the logo Vila Algarve painted on the driver's door.

I squinted into the sunshine, struck by the simplistic beauty of the boutique hotel with its shifting waves of white stucco and flower boxes overflowing with tendrils of color; its rooftop chimneys—stylized sentinels on the lookout still for hostile Moorish invaders.

"I still don't understand. Why did you rent a place? You know I have plenty of space." She looked at me, her expression filled with questions.

This was a rehash of an ongoing conversation, one we've had since the early stages of my holiday planning. Vera offered I stay with her, but thanks to the sizable chunk of money I inherited from Aaron's estate—well—let's just say this holiday was a goodbye present from Aaron. And I intended to make the most of it.

I stuffed the shades and the scarf into the glove box. "Stuck in between two almost newlyweds? All that head-banging wild sex? I don't think so." I blew a kiss over my fingers and climbed out of the car.

"Yeah, right. I'll see you tonight, okay? Don't forget." She waved her hand in the air, her new sapphire ring sparkling in the sunshine.

———

A brass bell tinkled as the door swished shut behind me. The foyer of Vila Algarve was a cozy space of whitewashed plaster. A man, as ancient as the cobwebs hanging from the cast iron chandelier, sat behind the counter tapping his fingers on a keyboard. The fragrant scent of aftershave tingled in my nose. A moment came back to me—my grandfather slapping on the Old Spice—the three lines running across his forehead, the long face, and an enormous nose, the wrinkles on either side of his smile.

"Can I help you, lass?" An unexpected Scottish burr scraped my eardrums. The man peered at me through circles of steel, resting halfway down a straight nose.

"Yes, please, I have a reservation. I'm Tiegan, Tiegan Moss." I straightened my shoulders.

"Aye, Miss Moss, welcome to Vila Algarve. I'm Derek, your concierge." A warm smile touched sharp denim-blue eyes. My grandfather had blue eyes and bushy eyebrows, just like Derek. "How was your trip, lass?"

"Great. Thank you. It's so nice to be here. It's so warm." I signed the reservation while Derek inspected my passport.

"Aye, it is that. You're from Canada?" He peered over the rim of his glasses, his eyes wide.

"Yes, I am, from the east coast. Cape Breton." I nodded.

With the formalities complete, Derek walked through a swinging half door, the kind you saw in old cowboy movies. He motioned me to follow, but not before grabbing the strap of my backpack, which he lifted off the floor with the strength of a much younger man. I walked behind Derek, into bright rays of sunlight, insisting all the while that I could carry my bag.

"I hope you dinna' mind the steps, Miss Moss? We have you on the third floor, in the Pelican suite." He walked down the sidewalk, past the vintage car to the side of the three-story building.

"No, I don't mind, not at all. But please, Derek, call me Tiegan." I rested my hand on his forearm.

"And what brings you to Carvoeiro, Tiegan?" He looked at me.

"I'm visiting my friend. Maybe you know her, Vera

Pearce? She owns a boutique in town." I pictured Vera's questioning gaze. I recalled her concern—for me.

"Aye, I know Vera. A bonny lass she is." He followed the winding staircase, hugging the sidewall, winding its way to the uppermost peak.

From that vantage point, I had an inland view of the town and the neighborhood—a carpet of red tile rooftops flowing downhill and then uphill again. A schoolyard: the hurrah, the whoop and holler of shrieking children, the clamor of ringing bells. A delivery truck blocked the main street. Cars honked.

The stairs ended at a narrow, green, painted door—a copper plate with a lion's head decorative knob mounted in the center of the door.

Derek unlocked the bolt and wiped his brow with the back of his hand. My heart staggered, and I peeked sideways, hoping he was not about to keel over.

"Not to worry, lass. The key sticks a wee bit." Derek dipped his head and threw me a sly grin.

The hinge creaked, the door swung wide. I followed him inside, admiring the open design, the vaulted ceiling, the curved ribs running from the top of each wall in a high, sweeping arch. Porcelain tiles in a warm butter shade ran through the entire apartment. The kitchen took up one corner, an overstuffed couch and a matching chair—the entire living room. A dangling rainbow of multi-colored beads—a gem from the sixties—separated the bedroom.

The pièce de résistance, a set of antique French doors, crackled with layers of old paint, swung open to a Juliet balcony. Drawn to a frame of blue sky, I leaned over the intricate damask of a cast-iron railing, astonished by the beauty of raw ocean and a view that goes on for days. A warm breeze ruffled my hair. I lifted my face into the sunshine, closing my eyes.

Derek walked through the apartment, opening the shutters, exposing the apartment to a surge of salty air. "It would be best if you let the water run a wee bit, miss. We havnae had anyone up here in quite a while."

"Derek, it's perfect." I turned at the sound of his voice, my face one big smile.

"Aye, you'll let me know if you need anything?" He smiled as he walked out the door.

"I will, for sure. I promise." I grinned, closing the door after him.

And then I was alone. I basked in the solitude, running my hands over what would be mine for three glorious months.

A floor mirror leaned against the bedroom wall, and I saw what Vera saw: 'gaunt' was an excellent way to describe my current look—more like a zombie than a ghost. Too skinny, too pale, cheekbones jutting out of my face. I liked my eyes— the eyes of a chameleon: sometimes green, sometimes gray, sometimes a vibrant shade of teal—spooky eyes. Sometimes, I scared myself.

I changed out of my too-warm traveling clothes into an oversized white shirt and black leggings. I tied the ends of my shirt into a knot, emphasizing the one womanly feature I had—my hips. Circling, I decided I was happy with the look.

One task remained—email Mom and Dad. I set up my laptop on the kitchen table, logged into the Wi-Fi, and opened mail: "I have arrived, the flight was good, the Algarve is beautiful, the apartment is perfect, and Vera says hello."— hit send.

I hopped off the couch and stretched my arms over my head. I yawned—I don't dare lay on the bed. Nope, what I wanted to do was explore. I slipped into my sneakers, closed the green door behind me, and hid the key underneath the closest flowerpot. Halfway down the stairs, I stopped. I forgot to close the shutters. The sky was blue, and the sun was shining bright. What could go wrong? I raced down the remaining steps.

The narrow street Vera's Lola climbed not more than an hour ago was the road I followed. I expected a sidewalk, but found wide steps descending the steep slope.

Wafting on a current of breeze was the flavor of street food: the hard crack of candy apples and the tang of salty pretzels. I had arrived in Carvoeiro on November one—All Saints Day—a national holiday in Portugal, and the town square was alive with celebration. Children raced from one shopkeeper to another, calling out *Páo-por-Deus*, asking for sweets. Their eyes danced with excitement as they compared treat bags filled with goodies.

Benches, decorated with pretty pieces of blue and white Valencia tile, lined the town square and were where people, young and old alike, lingered. I joined them, out of breath from the sprint into town. I stifled a yawn. I couldn't sleep on the plane. I have never slept on a plane. Why? Because I might do something embarrassing, like snore or drool—or something even more disastrous, like walk in my sleep, which was something I did. Maybe I walked in my sleep to run away from the nightmares?

Just like Vera said, I had nightmares. The walking in my sleep part? Yep, another horror story—it was not the usual wander around your living room and wake up on the couch kind of wandering. No, I went for a trek—outdoors, to the ocean, to the harbor, to the end of the pier, which was a good five kilometers from where I lived. I stared, a glazed-eyed zombie in kitty-cat pajamas, into the wide maw of the wild Atlantic Ocean.

I woke, too hot and so very thirsty, my mind racing too fast—a machine gun that never ran out of ammo. Kiss and run, crash and burn. Top that off with a panic attack, and yeah. Welcome to my world.

———

Tomás

They say time heals all wounds, but that's a lie. For me, time is a life sentence filled with memories. I buried my face in my hands and allowed my heart to bleed. I missed you every day, my sweet Sylvie—but today of all days was the hardest—the day you left me. Thirteen years —I can't believe it was that long ago. I missed your smile. And the babe; the life we almost had.

Stop. Get out of your head. Sylvie is gone, and she's not coming back. Her life ended because of you. Sorry doesn't cut it, and there's no such thing as forgiveness.

My cell phone sat on top of my desk, chirping, vibrating —I glanced at the text message before it disappeared.

—Hey? You there?—

My sister—Anca—a lengthening thread of dots appeared, then disappeared.

"Mr. Ferreira, we're running out of green peppers and onions." Catarina poked her head into my office. She gazed at me with dark, knowing eyes.

Catarina was the lead server at Casa Rosalia; she ran the kitchen and managed the staff. It was safe to say if Catarina left Casa Rosalia, this restaurant of mine would fall apart. Not something I wanted to think about. Not today, anyway.

"Are you sure, Cat? We had a delivery two days ago, didn't we?" My brow furrowed—I reached for the latest purchase orders, if only to appease myself.

"Want me to send Joe?" She studied me with lifted eyebrows.

"No, I'll go later." I looked up and then down.

—*Tomás????*—

My phone chirped—vibrating across the desk.

"Oh, and Mr. Ferreira? That new girl? The blonde? She quit." Catarina's eyes widened, and she smirked.

"Another one?" The green peppers and onions were not the reason for this interruption. I blew a whistling breath between my teeth and tapped my fingers on the desk. "Okay. What do I owe you this time?"

"Ten euros—I told you she was too pretty." Catarina slipped away, her laughter following her down the hallway.

—*Hellooooo? Tomás? Where are you????*—

I grabbed the cell. Ankles crossed, legs outstretched, I leaned back in the chair.

—*Hi. What's up?*—

—*Hey! Where've you been?*—

—*Where do you think?*—

—*I miss you, irmao.*—

—*What is it, Anca? Is something wrong?*—

—*xoxoxoxoxoxo.*—

—*Yeah, okay. What's that for?*—

—*Come to Lisbon. I found this great bar.*—

—*Sorry. Not my thing.*—

—*Oh, come on. Don't be such a bore. And guess what? I have a friend who wants to meet you.*—

I rolled my eyes and grinned. If anything, Anca was predictable, and she had too many friends.

—*We'll have such fun. Come to Lisbon—I want to show you off.*—

The conversation was going nowhere. I reached for my glasses and today's newspaper, flipping each page until I found what I was looking for—the classifieds and the help wanted ads.

—*Astrid.*—

—What's that?—

—My friend. Her name is Astrid. She's fucking hot.—

—Thanks, but no, thanks.—

A blind date? With a woman called Astrid? No—not in the cards. Not for me. I made a promise long ago, and I intended to keep it.

—Oh my God, Tomás. Move on. How long has it been?—

I tapped my fingers on the desktop, glancing at the clock. A loud bang drew my attention to the rear of the restaurant. Inside? Outside? I rose from the chair, my curiosity piquing.

—Hey? You there? I didn't mean it like that. I'm sorry.—

—I'm busy, Anca. I have to go.—

—Oh, guess what? I got a gig at the Lighthouse. I'm super excited.—

—That's great.—

I plowed my fingers through my hair, huffing a breath.

—Will you come?—

—Sure.—

—You promise you won't forget?—

—I promise. I'll be there. When is it?—

—Next week. And you'd like Astrid.—

A rumbling engine caught my attention. I cocked my head, picking up the bleeping back-up alarm, the hissing brakes, the screech of metal on metal.

—She's funny, smart...she's got a nice ass.—

—Goodbye, Anca.—

Could I imagine it? My mind wandered—to the last blind date Anca coerced me into. How many years ago was that? Astrid—a woman named after a flower. I shook my head back and forth. So not happening.

—Tchau, Tchau, Tomás :-).—

"Mr. Ferreira?" Catarina stood in the doorway, twirling strands of her ponytail around her index finger.

"Yes, Cat?" I rubbed my forehead.

"The beer truck's out back. Want me to deal with it?" She smirked.

"No, it's okay. I'll see to it." I had the distinct impression she felt sorry for me. A raise—it was time to give Catarina another raise. I would see to that next week.

2

---

*"If you stumble, make it
part of the dance."*—Unknown

Tiegan

Leaving the din of voices behind, I followed narrow alleys passing gated estates, courtyards, and bursting orange groves, sprawling branches heavy with fruit. The citrusy scent tickled my nose as I ascended one hill after another, but a pang of hunger put an end to my explorations, turning me back toward town.

I found what looked like the real deal, a step above a greasy spoon but a classic diner just the same—the kind of restaurant people just know about. We had one back home: The Blue Dog on Main put our little town on the map with its Friday special: the double bacon cheese mushroom melt—an ungodly mouthful of homemade goodness.

This place was called Casa Rosalia. Outdoor tables sat under an awning of blue stripes, the pages of a menu scotch-taped to the entrance door. Parked on an angle in front of the restaurant was a Ducati: not just a motorbike, but a big black fire-breathing monster. My pulse kicked up a notch, my fingers itching to touch the shiny handlebars, the bulbous tank, the hard leather seat. Could this be the home of the bad boy Vera warned me off? I ran my fingers through my hair and pushed the door open.

Casa Rosalia had a familiar, homey feel—muted walls, painted orange, a plank floor, the color of beat-up coffee beans, a ceiling beamed with heavy timber. A refrigeration unit sat at the entrance, displaying today's catch—beady black eyes pierced mine, silver scales glistened. The kitchen was visible through an open window. A man in a black skullcap chopped vegetables, and a girl with a pink ponytail polished cutlery, but the place was empty. Had I made a bad choice? I turned to leave when a voice stopped me dead in my tracks.

"I'll be there in a moment." A smooth rumble resonated through the empty room. It was melodic, almost lyrical. The voice echoed in my mind, overwhelming me with bewilderment—a sense of déjà vu. I knew that voice. A man dressed all in black appeared on the far side of the dining room.

"Can I help you?" His scent hit me first, sandalwood with an undertone of musk.

"Yes, please, I was hoping for lunch. Are you open?" My mouth dried. My throat closed.

"No, we open at six, for dinner, if you'd like to come another time." His voice, that velvet murmur, wrapped around me like a soft blanket.

"Oh, I'm sorry. The door was open." I gazed into razor-sharp, intelligent eyes—two bottomless pools of chocolate flecked with gold. His hair, a mass of black ink curls, framed high cheekbones, a square jaw.

"I'm Tomás Ferreira, the owner of Casa Rosalia. Who are you?" He offered his hand. His firm lips curved into a smile, and his eyes pierced into mine—a woman could get lost in those eyes.

"Tiegan…Tiegan Moss." I offered mine.

His eyes burned with gold fire. More intriguing—the liquid heat racing through my veins. Vera's review of this man was bad, all bad. In the back of my mind, warning bells clanged. I ignored them.

"You're new around here." With outright arrogance, he turned my wrist, holding my fingers within his. He brushed the palm of his thumb along the ridge of my knuckles.

"Yes, I just arrived. I'm visiting a friend for a few months." My breath caught, and I forgot to breathe. A daring question? No, not a question, a statement. I realized Tomás Ferreira was a man used to getting what he wanted. I wanted to jerk my hand away. I wanted to trail my fingers along the underside of that square jaw and taste those wide, luscious lips.

"And where did you come from?" His eyes narrowed, leaving me with the impression he was confused.

"From Canada—Mabou, Cape Breton, to be exact." I wished I were five inches taller. Damn.

"You've traveled a long way for lunch." He studied me.

"Yes, I guess I have." I chuckled. "It's nice to meet you, Tomás, but as you said, the kitchen's closed. I should be on my way. I'll come back, maybe another day," I said, in a voice too quick. I wanted to take those words back—say something eloquent or funny—but I was not good at off-the-cuff kind of stuff. I made no move to retreat.

"I would like you to stay." He swallowed hard, the Adam's apple bobbing in his throat.

"You would?" I leaned into him, drawn to him.

"Yes, I would." He released my hand and stepped to one side, motioning toward a dining room of empty tables.

"Well, okay. If it's not too much trouble." I followed him, unsure and yet certain of one thing.

Tomás led me to a table for two by the window. He stepped aside, pulling the chair away from the table, his gaze holding me hostage.

I sank into the padded leather seat, quaking—from the touch of his fingertips strategically placed on the small of my back, each one a slow-burning ember radiating heat.

"If you like seafood, I would recommend the *bacalhau*. It's one of our specialties." He stared into my eyes.

"*Bacalhau*? Is that cod?" I gripped the arms of the captain's chair, the polished wood smooth against my fingers.

"Yes, salted cod, soaked for twenty-four hours to remove the salt and then roasted," he explained, his voice animated.

"That sounds wonderful! I love seafood. Are you a chef?" I rambled, my voice squeaking. I cringed inside. I was on my left foot, and I was not sure why.

"No, I'm not a chef." His eyes flickered with amusement. "Would you like wine, Tiegan?" He carried himself with maturity beyond his years; he exuded confidence.

"Please. That would be lovely." I gazed into his handsome face. I could not imagine many women or men saying no to Tomás Ferreira.

"A red or a white?" He glanced over his shoulder. A stray forelock, a thick curl of blackstrap molasses, fell onto his forehead.

"I like red, thank you." My gaze followed him to a tall cabinet—a floor-to-ceiling rack of wine.

I studied him through the fringe of my eyelashes. A handsome guy? No, he was more than that. Angled and hard—sculptured—an Adonis, and I could be his Venus.

No. No. No. It was so not good. I should have left. I should have run and hid.

He displayed the bottle: Portuguese, Tinto da Ânfora.

With the art of a sommelier, he uncorked the bottle and poured a splash into the stemmed crystal bowl.

I could not look away. He was so not my type, but then I wondered, what was my type? I've slept with one man, well, two if you count senior prom, and I don't.

"This wine is from the Alentejo region north of Lisbon. It is full-bodied, dry with rich notes of bramble, currant, and black cherry." His gaze held my soul ransom.

"Hmm, you know your wines." I swirled the wine, inhaling a bouquet of fragrant notes.

"It is an interest of mine. Is it to your liking?" he asked in a voice more than seductive.

"It's delicious." The wine slid down my throat, a smooth caress warming my belly. "It has soul, wouldn't you say?" Tomás asked of the wine. He filled my glass to the top, leaving the bottle on the table. "You said you were visiting a friend?"

"Yes, I am. From back home. Vera Pearce? Do you know her?" I ran my tongue along my lower lip and met his heady gaze.

He nodded, but said nothing.

I wondered again, was he hitting on me?

Without invitation, he sat down in the opposite chair.

I inhaled his scent in the whoosh of displaced air. It was almost intoxicating.

"Where are you staying, Tiegan? Are you in town?" He rested his hands on the table's edge.

"I'm at the Vila Algarve, on the top floor. The view is amazing." I looked up.

"Ah, with Derek. A good choice." He studied me, his head tilted.

"Yes, and yes, it's a fabulous spot. Close to everything. I was lucky to find it." I swallowed hard, my mouth dry.

"How long are you visiting?" His gaze narrowed, a muscle in his jaw ticked.

I twisted my necklace between my fingers, attempting to still my racing heart. Racing was not the right word—it was more like an electric charge, shorting out, turning over, bouncing back and forth in my chest.

Tomás leaned in, lifting the chain from my fingers. He slid the medallion, a sixteenth-century angel coin, between his thumb and forefinger. "Where did you get this?"

"My medallion? My grandfather gave it to me a long time ago." We breathed the same air.

"Your grandfather?" His eyes turned a molten shade of gold.

"Yes, why do you ask?" I lived in that moment. His breath mingling with mine. This could be an intimate moment between lovers. A lover. Is that what I wanted?

"This is a touch piece, an amulet, meant to protect the wearer. It held great meaning to my people." His puzzled expression made me pause.

"Your people? Who are your people?" I stared into those bewitching eyes.

"I'm a Roma." He slid his thumb over the medallion once more. I had the distinct impression that he was trying to sense its magical power.

"Oh, I see. Well, I'm a Canadian." I pinned my lips together and lifted my eyebrows.

His eyes crinkled, and then he laughed.

I took back what was mine and slipped the medallion underneath my shirt, where it belonged. Tomás was staring at me when I looked up. His eyes glazed, his thoughts somewhere far away. "Is something wrong?"

He lifted his hand, brushing a strand of flyaway hair from my face. He tucked it gently behind my ear and, in that silent moment, dragged his fingertips along the curve of my jaw.

Those burning embers burst into flames. Heat swept across my skin—so much heat.

"You have the most beautiful eyes, Tiegan. You remind me of someone I once knew. Someone from long ago." He gave me a soft smile and then looked away. I wanted him back.

"Oh? Who was that?" I rested my hand over his. "Tomás?" I whispered his name in a voice not my own—a voice redolent of another time, and I didn't know where it came from. I gazed into his eyes, and the flames danced. My breasts tightened, and my nipples hardened, grazing the lace of my new brassier. An image flowed into my mind of this man, of his lips ravishing my core, of his shaft filling me. A tremor shot through my belly and into my sex—my pussy weeping. I blinked, and the world came back into focus.

He sat in that chair, his back straight, his mouth hard, whatever warmth his gaze had turned to frost.

"Miss Moss, please stay as long as you like. If you need anything at all, Catarina will look after you." He rose, leaving me to enjoy the heady bouquet of the wine alone.

I finished the first glass of wine and poured another, living in a fantasy world, dreaming of Tomás Ferreira's firm, lush lips. The server, the young girl with the pink ponytail and red stiletto fingernails, shattered the moment. She was Catarina.

"Mr. Ferreira asked me to bring this over." She planted a charcuterie plate with olives, prosciutto, apricots, and cheese in front of me, more than enough to satisfy my gnawing hunger.

I was well into my third glass of wine when Catarina reappeared with a clay platter of roasted cod swimming in olive oil, baby potatoes, and peppers, garnished with the sunny face of a hard-boiled egg.

"*Cuidado, senhorita!* The plate is hot." Catarina inclined her head toward the platter, but the first thing I did was touch the platter.

The pain diverted my attention from my raging libido and the flames licking my thighs. I couldn't focus. I couldn't think. I was in a world of my making. Somewhere between a Kalamata olive and a baby potato, I noticed Catarina was alone, the kitchen empty.

Her ponytail swung from side to side as she sang to herself, her lips moving to the rap music playing in the background.

After a few moments, Catarina reappeared. "Can I get you anything else, *o querido?*"

I smiled at the term of endearment. Back home, the server at The Blue Dog called everyone honey. "No, I'm so full. Thank you, though. The food was delicious."

"Yes, it's very good." Catarina nodded. "It's one of our specialties from Mr. Ferreira's *vovo.*"

I couldn't help but smile at her enthusiasm, but my confusion showed on my face.

"You would say…grandmother. Mr. Ferreira's grandmother, it is her recipe."

"I see. Well, my compliments to the chef." I smiled. "May I have the check, please?"

"Mr. Ferreira said it was to be on the house." Catarina nodded her smiling face.

"Oh, no, that's unnecessary."

Catarina shrugged, making no move to present the check.

"Can I at least thank Tomás, then?"

"No, Mr. Ferreira had to leave. He teaches soccer to the schoolchildren. He will be back later for the dinner rush."

"I see. Thank you."

"You're welcome, *o querido.*"

I finished my fourth glass of wine, slipping ten euros under the empty glass for Catarina. I shook my head at what had transpired. Catarina liked her boss—that said something. He volunteered as a soccer coach. He was a restaurateur who immortalized his grandmother's recipes. What was Vera talking about? What bad boy part of Tomás Ferreira was I missing?

———

A swirling gust of wind, an invisible force, lifted sand off the sidewalk. It was turbulent and angry and stung my face with sharp granular pellets. I noted the Ducati parked out front and somewhere close by the shrill soprano of shrieking children. The high crescendo of those voices led to a laneway and a twenty-foot-tall, chain-link fence. Behind the fence was a green soccer pitch —and Tomás. He no longer wore the formal black from the restaurant. Hard muscles flexed under striped athletic shorts and a plain white T-shirt—not a morsel of body fat on that man. He yelled words of encouragement, running the length of the field with two co-ed teams of boys and girls dressed in yellow and green jerseys—the green team scored. The whoop and holler of children surrounded Tomás.

I waved, catching his eye. The wine had done its job. I leaned into the fence, gripping the chain link with my fingers. "Hi, Tomás," I said in my best smiley voice.

"I don't appreciate being spied on, Miss Moss." His voice slapped me across the face. Sweat trickled down his temple, and a muscle ticked in his jaw.

"I'm not spying on you." I stepped away from the fence, dropping my arms to my sides. "I wanted to thank you for lunch. Catarina told me where to find you. The bacalhau was amazing. The wine was good, too good actually. Catarina was lovely. Oh, please don't be angry with her. I found you all by myself." I giggled, offering the palms of my hands. This was bad—I couldn't shut up. Why couldn't I shut up?

He said nothing.

"Look, I'm sorry if I've offended you. That was not my intention. I wanted to thank you. For lunch. That's all."

No response—his eyes: two storm-filled orbs, his lips a hard line.

His hostility confused me. At Casa Rosalia, he'd made me feel welcome, more than welcome. With a toss of my head, I walked away. The farther I walked, the better I felt.

———

Three months was a long time, and I couldn't eat out every single day. But I was not much of a cook—I barely functioned in the kitchen. Back home, I lived on processed food and takeout. My mother's voice rang in my head—Tiegan, sweetheart. The way to a man's heart is through his stomach. Aaron's pretty face flashed through my mind.

I strolled the supermarket aisles, making a mental list of what to buy, filling my cart with the basics: granola, orange pekoe, and yogurt. I selected a carton of eggs. There were so many ways to ruin eggs. I found coffee. I couldn't live without coffee. As I poured the beans through the grinder, I closed my eyes, breathing in the rich aroma of dark roast.

A mile-high stack of dried, salted, and cured cod, bacalhau took center stage in the seafood section. Tomás Ferreira—what a charming piece of work. I couldn't believe how taken I was at the moment. Why did I lose myself so completely? Physical attraction? Jet lag? The wine? It was the wine. I drank the entire bottle.

I waited at the front end of the store while the cashier rang me through. The entrance doors swung open, and his scent hit me like a ton of bricks. My body reacted hot and cold all at once.

"Tomás. How are you? How was practice today?" The cashier turned her attention away from my groceries. Apparently, they knew each other.

"Looking good, Mary. The kids are working well together: team players, everyone." That soft rumble set my heart on fire.

I kept my gaze fixed on Mary. Could she not focus on the task at hand?

"It's all João talks about, morning till night. *Futebol*." Her voice rang out, filled with happy pride.

I glanced over my shoulder and caught Tomás staring back. He sent me a winning grin, and his eyes flickered. With what? Happy light?

This was so fucked up. Why was this happening?

"His ball control is coming along nicely."

I couldn't look away. I was swimming—no—drowning in those dark chocolate pools. Could she not move a little faster —stop being so damn friendly?

"He's a great kid." Tomás blinked, releasing me from his spell.

I fumbled through my wallet for the right piece of plastic, tapped the device, grabbed my bags, and escaped. Or tried to make my escape—Tomás blocked the doorway.

"Do you mind, Mr. Ferreira?" There was so much more I wanted to say, but my mind screamed, shut the fuck up.

"Miss Moss, it's nice to see you again." His gaze roved freely.

Was he happy to see me? How was that even possible? I brushed past him, eyes straight ahead. Who was this man?

Outside, the weather had worsened. Stormy skies greeted me. The wind lifted my hair—whipping it into my face—blinding me. I balanced my shopping bags and stomped down the sidewalk, cringing when a car horn blasted. I squeezed my eyes shut. I didn't want to face him again, not ever. I straightened my shoulders and braced myself.

Derek, the concierge from Vila Algarve, waved me over from behind the wheel of his vintage car. He shouted into the gusting wind. "Will ye get in, lass? Is no fit for man nor beast!"

I grabbed the passenger door and climbed in. "Derek. I'm so glad to see you." He did not know how glad. "Thank you for stopping."

"Aye, the weather can be unpredictable this time of year. You'd best always have a jacket with you." The thick burl wrapped me in warmth.

"I will. Thank you so much." My heart bloomed at his concern for my well-being.

"Have you been exploring our wee town?"

"Yes, I have. It's so pretty; I can't wait to see more." I admired the car's neat as a pin interior and the windows, lots of windows.

"The streets are quiet now, but that will change come the holidays."

"Oh? Is it a busy time?" I peered out the back, searching the busy street and the sidewalks.

"Aye, the old Vila Algarve will burst at the seams." Derek's rumbling chuckle turned my head. "They come for the Christmas market."

"Do you manage the place by yourself? Do you have help?" I rested my hands on my lap, smiling at Derek.

"I hire one or two of the local ladies from time-to-time."

"There's a lot to look after."

"Keeps the mind sharp, the body fit. It does that."

"The gear shift is on the dash, Derek. That's so cool. I've never seen anything like it."

"Aye, this is the classic Renault, Vintage 1961. She's in fine fettle, sound as a bell."

"Like you, Derek." I smiled.

Flattered, Derek elaborated, telling me he owned a similar Renault R4 as a young man in Scotland. He purchased this car, the 4L, when he moved to Portugal fifteen years ago and, with tender love, restored it to tip-top shape.

As Derek rounded the corner, rain smacked the windshield, and the wind howled. He parked the Renault in front of Vila Algarve and turned off the ignition. I gathered my shopping, dashing toward the side steps, shouting my goodbyes to Derek.

The rain pummeled down hard and fast. A waterfall gushed off the roof, and the stairs became a sluiceway of rushing water. By the time I made the top step, my hair was dripping wet. My clothes clung to my body, and my toes squished in my sodden sneakers.

In the doorway, a cat—a gray-striped tabby with four white paws and one white ear—sat huddled behind the teeming wall of water.

I shifted the clay pot to retrieve my key.

The cat meowed a pitiful screech, arching its furry little body around my legs as I shoved the door open.

I dropped my bags to the floor and hurried to close the shutters. "And just who do you think you are, mister?" I inquired as I stripped down to nothing.

The cat raised his head, meowing again.

"Really?" I was intrigued by his knowing response.

The cat shook, spraying water across the floor, then leaped onto the sofa.

I wrapped myself in the last dry towel and went in search of some comfy clothes.

When I returned, the cat was curled into a fluffy gray ball, its head nestled under its tail, fast asleep. I turned on the kettle, and while I waited for the water to boil, a sensation flowed through my being—a vibration in my bones—a hum. My heart whirled with cascading emotions. How could I describe it? An awakening? A shift of self? It was more than that—I felt alive.

———

"Dearest Tiegan,
    Your father and I were right pleased to hear your plane landed safely and you're all settled in for your holiday away.

We're off on our way to visit your Uncle Bart and Aunt Carol for the weekend. The boys will be after building a new chicken coop, while Carol & I put down that last batch of apples in the back kitchen. Many hands make light work as I always say.

All the less and the none the more, it's a bright and lovely day, but right cold with a breeze settling in, so bundle up Tiegan sweetheart, and be sure to stay warm.

We miss you.

Say hello to Vera for us.

Love,

Mom

PS. Your father says not to take any wooden nickels."

*"If at first you don't succeed, fix
your ponytail and try again."*—Unknown

Tiegan

"Hey. Where've you been? I thought you were going to bail on me." She turned her head, a smile lighting up her blue eyes.

I caught Vera just in time. She was standing under the twilight glow of a streetlamp, locking the front door of her shop.

"Yeah, I fell asleep." My thoughts flashed back to the salacious dream that sent heat fluttering like wildfire through my nether regions. I woke in a hot mess—the blanket tangled in a bunch between my legs, the whisper of Tomás Ferreira's lips on mine, a line of fire racing through my veins. Luckily for me, the shower head had three levels of pulsating jets. I could still feel it, the heady rush of release.

I peered through the shop window at eye-catching prints, flowy dresses, floppy hats, and scarves, lots of scarves, and the cutest pair of suede ankle boots. I couldn't wait to check them out, maybe tomorrow. I turned my attention from the window to the street. A procession of men, women, and children followed one another, candles held aloft. From somewhere not too far away, church bells tolled—the muffled ring of a death knell—a haunting reminder that the dead would not be forgotten.

"So, how was your day?" Vera lifted her golden eyebrows.

"Well, it's not over yet." I sighed through my nose.

"No, it's not. Are you hungry?" Vera wrapped her arm around my shoulders as we walked down the sidewalk toward the ocean.

"No, but I'll buy you dinner." I patted my handbag.

"You don't have to do that."

"Yeah, I know, but I want to. I insist."

Shivers ran down my spine as a group of young boys, hiding behind blackened faces and flowing white sheets, flew by. Their voices—a howling riot of song—were spirits, ghosts of the past. Shadows whispered, urging my feet to move faster.

"So, where are we headed?" I scanned the intersecting streets, my gaze lingering on the variety of eateries Carvoeiro offered.

"Bianca's—best burgers in town. Unless you want Portuguese?" Her voice rose.

I thought for one short second, picturing us walking into Casa Rosalia. "Nope, burgers sound good."

Bianca's was not far away, but twilight succumbed to the inky darkness of night in the time it took to walk there. A gust of wind blew sideways, tossing an empty paper cup across the cobblestone square. It was eerie; there was no moon and no stars. The sound of surf crashing onto the shore was the only evidence that the ocean existed.

An outdoor patio spilled onto the square, glowing with the sparkle of white light. With its beachfront location and sports bar ambiance, Bianca's was a happening place. This evening, a soccer game played on a series of flat-screen televisions, and soccer fans, not shy to make noise, took up each bar stool. A hostess led us to a tall bistro table in the middle of the restaurant.

"So, how's Mom and Dad?" Vera's grin lit up the dining room.

Growing up, Vera and I shared both sets of parents, hers and mine, equally.

"They're fine. Hugs and kisses from everyone. My dad wants me to get my real estate license." I shifted sideways, checking out the game.

"Real estate? You'd be good at that." She nodded her head.

"Yeah, I don't know. I kind of like being a starving artist." I smoothed my hands over the shiny tabletop.

The server arrived, a boy with a black rose inked behind his studded ear, a sequence of delicate petals. He recited the long list of daily specials from memory, finishing with a broad smile—for Vera's benefit.

"I'll have the double classic burger, medium rare, and a large fry. Oh, but with blue cheese on the burger and two amber ales. Tieg, you'll have a beer, right?" She beamed at tattoo boy.

"Okay, sure. So when's the big day?" I said in a teasing voice reminiscent of our high school days. I fluttered my eyelashes and grinned.

"No date yet…maybe next year."

"Has he met Mom and Dad?"

"Gosh, no…"

"You haven't told them." I sat taller, gazing at my friend.

"No." She ducked her head, the blonde waterfall hiding her eyes.

"Why not?" I tried to understand.

"I'm waiting for the perfect moment." She scrunched her eyebrows together. "You know what my mother's like."

I giggled. Vera's mom was the ultimate event planner, and everyone in our little town knew it.

"Oh, my God! Do you see it?" I clapped my hands together, laughter bubbling in my throat.

"See what?" She looked wary.

"The puppies, the horse-drawn carriage, the cannon of rose petals—the party tent?" My eyes widened, and I grinned.

"Oh, fuck…you won't tell. Promise me, Tiegan." Her face paled.

"Hmm…okay, but you owe me," I smirked.

Tattoo boy returned, interrupting our conversation. The aroma of Vera's burger and crispy fries made my mouth water. I plucked a fry off her plate.

"So, spill it. What did you get up to today?" Vera looked down, dumping ketchup over her fries.

"Well, I went for a walk. Wandered about town. Derek is nice, from the hotel. A cat adopted me. Wait till you meet him, he's so cute. Oh, and I met that guy—Tomás Ferreira."

"What? Are you kidding?" Her head snapped up.

"Truth, I ended up at his restaurant." I downed a long mouthful of beer, throwing Vera a wink.

"Yeah? And then?" She grappled with the burger, ketchup, mustard and special sauce, running down her hands.

"Well, at first he was friendly…too friendly, really. And then…I don't know. It was strange." I bit down on my lower lip and shrugged.

"Of all the men in this town, you had to find that one? Really?" She shook her head.

"Yeah…well, I didn't mean to." I conjured up the image of that wonderful meal and Tomás, a tingle racing down my spine. I hugged myself, hiding the shiver. "But yeah, it got kind of fucked up."

"What's that mean? What happened?" She dabbed her mouth with a napkin.

I propped my chin on my palm and explained the day's events: Casa Rosalia, the soccer pitch, the grocery store. Vera's face was an open book with a story to tell. I asked the question. "So, what gives? What's his deal?"

"Hmm, I don't know." Vera was like my mother, and like my mother, she would know everything about everything and everyone. I didn't have long to wait. "Well, okay, but I don't know a lot. He arrived thirteen years ago—after his wife died. He opened Casa Rosalia, built a nice place on the ocean. He's done well for himself."

"What happened to his wife?" Thirteen years ago, I was thirteen. How old would that make Tomás? Thirty-eight, thirty-nine, maybe too old?

"She died in childbirth. Crazy, eh? In this day and age? So sad."

"What else?" I sipped my beer, processing this information. A widower and a widow. Oh my.

"I've heard things, Tieg, that's all. People talk." She nibbled a few more fries, then continued. "He's a Roma, you know. Some people won't go to his restaurant just because of that. Awful, eh?"

I thought about that—racism, discrimination—even in this pretty little town.

Vera's gaze shifted over my shoulder, her expression changing from easy to concerned. I didn't have to ask why. Somehow, I already knew.

"Tiegan, Tomás is here, behind the bar. He's coming over."

"No, no, no," I muttered, more to myself than Vera.

"I'm sorry to interrupt, but I want to speak with Miss Moss." Tomás towered over the table, his brown eyes locked on mine.

I glared at him. How dare he show up here? If I could spit fire, I would.

Vera shot a concerned glance my way.

"It's okay, Vera." I touched her arm and nodded my head. I smirked at Tomás.

"Are you sure?" Her gaze held mine.

"I'm sure." I couldn't ignore the pounding thump of my heart. Holy hell, why couldn't I breathe? He was just a man—an arrogant, obnoxious, gorgeous man that I didn't want.

"All right, but you'll call me later?" She rose, dropping her napkin onto her empty plate.

I slid from my chair, crushing Vera in my arms, taking that moment to still my racing heart, to remind myself I had this.

Tomás waved his hand, catching the boy with the rose tattoo's attention.

"Can I help you, Mr. Ferreira?" I looked at him, sitting on Vera's stool, very much at home. I slid onto my stool.

"Yes, you can." He gestured toward tattoo boy. "Adáo, clear the table, please. Put the bill on my account."

"I pay my way. Thank you very much." I reached for my bag.

The bastard ignored me.

"Yes, sir." Adáo peered sideways at me and shrugged.

I waited for tattoo boy to leave. Before I could respond, Tomás spoke.

"Tiegan, I would like to apologize. For what happened earlier today?" His gaze held mine.

"All right." I folded my arms over my chest and sat back in my chair. I stared at the unbuttoned button around his neck, at the dark scruff shadowing his jaw.

"My behavior must have seemed strange. And it was." He blinked twice, as if surprised.

"So, explain your behavior, Tomás. Where I come from,

people say thank you when others treat them well. Was that such a big deal?" I crossed my arms.

"It's not. It isn't. I overreacted, and I'm sorry." He tilted his head, enticing me with a soft glance.

"That's it?" I widened my eyes.

"How do you mean?" His shoulders relaxed, and I had the impression he truly did not understand.

"You say you're sorry and, I'm good with that. But you haven't explained anything." I rested my palm on the table.

"I would rather not…" His gaze darkened.

"Why not?" I tapped my fingers.

His eyes darkened. He didn't answer.

"How did you find me?" I leaned in.

"I was in the back meeting the staff. I saw you sitting with your friend." His brown eyes looked around the room, then returned to me.

I studied him. I waited. I leveled out my best steely gaze. "So, you were spying on me?"

"Yes, I guess I was." He pressed his lips together, but then the corners of his mouth lifted, and he smiled—a smile that reached his eyes.

"Tell me why." I smiled back.

"Why was I in the back? I own this place now." His eyes were bright.

"You do?" I loosed a breath.

"Just signed the papers." His eyes sparkled with boyish excitement, and just like that, my heart melted.

"But what about Casa Rosalia?" I blinked and sat back.

"Casa Rosalia will stay the same, authentic Portuguese cuisine. Bianca's will become something new, something different." He nodded, his voice filled with enthusiasm.

"Really? What did you have in mind?" Bianca's was already a roaring success. Why would he fix something that wasn't broken?

"A craft brewery. Of course, it will take a lot of renovations to make that happen." He looked around the roadhouse.

"A brewery? Like with fermenters and serving tanks?" My lips peeled into a smile.

"Yes, exactly. Are you familiar with the process?" His eyes gleamed.

"Yes, a bit." My breath lodged in my throat.

"Well, Miss Moss, I wanted to apologize for my behavior. It was uncalled for." He inclined his head.

We had gone back to the formality of Miss Moss, leaving me baffled once again.

"Apology accepted, Mr. Ferreira. I wanted to thank you for lunch. That was all." Who's kidding who? What I wanted was sex—mind-blowing, rock-my-world sex with him. Damn. I exhaled a slow breath, clenching down, stilling the pulsing throb between my thighs. This was not the time. Not now, not ever.

"Perhaps."

That one word—perhaps—hung in the air, a question, and a judgment.

"What do you mean by that, Mr. Ferreira?" The room fell quiet. The voices. The television. The noise disappeared.

"That's not the impression you gave me, Miss Moss. Why don't you tell me what it is you're after?" He leaned on the table, knitting his fingers together, gazing deep into my eyes.

I tamped down my disappointment. This conversation was not going the way I had hoped. What was I expecting? A Cinderella moment? I knew better—at least I should. There was no such thing as fairy tales.

"Is that what you think? You think I'm after you?" My laughter sounded hollow. He had caught me. Yes, I wanted him, but that's not what we were talking about here. "Have you forgotten, Mr. Ferreira? You came on to me."

He smiled, his teeth sparkling white—perfectly straight teeth, a perfect smile, a perfectly lovely face.

"I've met women like you before, Miss Moss." He laughed, a chuckle rising low in his throat, echoing like the rat-tat-tat of a steel drum. "I offered you hospitality. Nothing more, nothing less."

"Women like me?" A fog settled in my mind, confusion and a knot I couldn't untangle—a knot with no beginning and no end. I bit my lower lip—hard. I refused to be that little flower, not today.

"Yes, Miss Moss. Women like you." The words crackled on his tongue.

I stared at him, rage burning in the pit of my stomach.

"It would be in your best interest to stay far away from me, Miss Moss. I have nothing to offer you." He flexed his muscled arms.

I opened my mouth to speak, but I had no words. Instead, I leaned across the table, grasped his chin between my thumb and forefinger, and tilted his face to mine. Those chocolate eyes opened wide, and before I could rethink, I closed my mouth over his. With a sharp exhale of breath, his lips parted, welcoming me inside. I explored every inch of his mouth, tasting the whisper of the wind and the swell of the ocean's surf, briny and real. For a moment, I was lost, but then I broke away, severing the magnetic hold he held over me.

I smiled.

"And you have nothing I want, Mr. Ferreira."

———

This little town welcomed me with open arms. It reminded me of home: a friendly place where everyone said hello. The exception to the rule was

Tomás Ferreira. I was confused, but intrigued. I couldn't make sense of his behavior, or mine.

I dreamed of him every night. Hot, sexy dreams, the kind you couldn't tell your mother.

He roused my need, taking me to the edge of ecstasy, cupping my breasts, suckling the folds of my vagina. I awoke —my clit a swollen bundle of nerves, my pussy an aching pool of moisture. It took little to finish. I closed my eyes, pictured those burning eyes, those luscious lips, and rode the palm of my hand, crying out with each wave of heat, leaving behind a boneless, unsatisfied mess. I wanted Tomás. I wanted his hands and his lips to ravish each nerve ending I possessed.

I had other dreams of Tomás, ones I didn't understand.

Within the realm of darkness was a circle of shadows, and if I waited long enough, he would find me. We were together then. He was mine, and I was his. When I awoke, my heart was heavy, his scent all around me, my face wet with tears.

Something was so wrong with me.

4

"Life is the art of drawing
without an eraser."—Unknown

iegan

We had established a routine, the cat and I. We woke with the sun. I fed the cat high-protein, expensive cat food I picked up at the pet store—nothing but the best for my new friend. I made coffee. The world was an empty place without coffee.

The cat was eager to leave, to lurk in the shadows, to rid the streets of Carvoeiro of unwanted vermin. He would return when the sun set in time for dinner.

I checked my emails and often found one, sometimes two, from Mom. My mom, like Vera, knew everything about everything, so I read her emails with interest and caught up on the news from small-town Mabou. Mom was one of those people who couldn't sit still, speed-walking about town, playing pickleball on Thursday mornings, and golfing on Tuesday afternoons. In the winter, she snowshoes and drinks coffee with her book club friends, volunteers at the soup kitchen, and rings the bell for the Salvation Army. All year round, she played the fiddle at the many festivals of the Mabou Ceilidh.

I packed my backpack with a sketchpad, granola bars, two bottles of water, and I explored.

A winding trail descended the cliff to a promontory of rock, and it was there where I spent most days, peering under the brim of my straw hat at pods of bottlenose dolphins playing in the ocean waves. Yesterday, I spotted a blue whale breaching the surface. Sometimes, I lay flat on my back, closed my eyes, and listened to the murmuring voice of the sea.

I made friends with João, a young boy of nine.

João and his grandfather fished from these high cliffs. They arrived before sunrise, perched together on a precipice jutting out from the rock face, casting their lines into the sea. In the evening, they returned, two silhouettes framed in the glow of the setting sun.

Two hundred feet below, the ocean crashed against the face of the cliff, João bounding like a jackrabbit, from one foot to the other, hoping for a sea bass or a mackerel to take home to his family or to sell to the local restaurants. I had seen João standing upright on his pedals, weaving through traffic, the white cooler strapped over the back wheel of his bike. From behind my paper bag of groceries, I witnessed the transaction—João waving his arms in the air, negotiating a fair price for the contents of his cooler, and Tomás Ferreira, kneeling on the sidewalk, fixing the chain on João's bike.

I added the finishing touches to the pencil sketch of João and his grandfather. A portrait of the two of them standing side by side on the summit of the cliff, fishing poles in hand.

"João. I have something for you."

He looked at the drawing and smiled, showing off a toothy grin.

"Avo." João motioned to his grandfather, saying something in quick Portuguese, Avo's wizened face spreading into a huge smile. "Miss Tiegan, my *avo* says thank you. You are kind lady."

My chest tightened, and my eyes welled; Avo had never smiled at me before. I rolled the sketch into a cardboard tube so they could carry it home without damage.

"You're very welcome, João. I'm glad you like it." I smiled after the man and boy, my heart full.

———

"Tiegan? Miss Moss? Are you alright? Can you hear me?" Tomás repeated my name over and over. I was in his arms. Well, sort of—he had a tight hold on my shoulders, his thumbs pressing into my collarbone.

My knees gave out, and I slumped forward, but he caught me. I was not dreaming. This was real.

"What's going on here? Tiegan? What are you doing here? Where are your shoes?" His voice prowled beneath my skin. I knew that voice. It hung in my mind, a memory long forgotten.

"My shoes?" I looked down—at bare feet. I curled my toes into the hard dirt of the Algarve as realization dawned on me. At least I was wearing clothes, if cartoon hero pajamas counted as clothes.

The sky was a black canopy twinkling with the pinpoint glow of starlight, the moon, a welcoming face in the darkness. The night air was crisp, frosty even. But underneath my polyester pajamas, my skin burned hot—I was on fire.

"Is that where you live?" I looked past Tomás to a rambling villa, a darkened shape on the summit of an ocean cliff.

"Yes, it is. How did you get here? What's this all about?" The wind sang, lifting his melodic voice.

How did I get here? The hell if I knew, but I did know. I couldn't deny the truth. From Vila Algarve, I found my way to Tomás's villa along the crest of the cliff, a path strewn with rock. How was that even possible? I looked down at my pajamas. "Um, would you believe I'm a superhero? A defender of justice patrolling the Algarve coast in search of villains and bad guys?" I looked up, meeting his searching gaze.

"A superhero?" His eyes danced with amusement. He smiled.

"Yeah." I picked at the hem of my shirttail. "A defender of justice, you know?"

"Where's your cape?" He studied me.

"My what?" I gazed into his chocolate-colored eyes and saw my reflection. Or was it someone else, a woman with tears in her eyes?

"Your cape? Don't superheroes wear capes?"

"Only comic book heroes wear capes. That's so not done anymore—over the top, you know?" I lifted my shoulders and shrugged.

"Miss Moss, what's going on here?" His gaze held mine captive.

"Well, sometimes I sleepwalk." I was so aware of the nearness of his presence. I wanted to tell him everything.

"You walked here? In your sleep? Is that what you're saying? That's very concerning and incredibly dangerous." He tsked. He shook his head.

"Yeah, tell me about it." I nodded, sure, of only one thing. I was in trouble. Trouble with a capital T.

"Do you do this often, Miss Moss?" He rested his chin on his fist.

"Stop calling me Miss Moss." I had the impression he lost his words. Or maybe that was me.

What was I doing here? Barefoot, in my pajamas. I swept my hair behind my ears as the frosty night air breezed through the thin cotton. According to him, I had walked for miles. But that wasn't anything new. It was a problem, and no amount of alcohol or sleeping pills could stop my wandering heart. I wondered about the cat. Where was the cat? Had the cat followed me?

"Do you know how far from town you are?" He continued in that same bossy tone.

"No." I hugged myself. There was no sign of the cat.

"Exactly two miles, in the pitch black of night. Along these cliffs, a path strewn with rock." He looked down at me, his brows furrowed.

"Superpowers, remember. You're not afraid of the dark, are you Tomás?" My eyebrows lifted.

The air stirred. A playful dance. A gentle kiss. Clouds scattered across the night sky, and the moon cast her soft light all around. It was ethereal. An essence, earth after rain. It filled my heart—with longing. My bones hummed, and the distance between us disappeared. Did I make that happen? Did Tomás? A shudder of delight passed through my body as we melded together. I felt the hard angles of his cheekbones beneath my fingers, the soft skin around his eyes.

A groan rose in his throat, and he nipped my bottom lip— teasing—tantalizing. He drove his tongue inside, tasting me. He cupped my face between his hands, skimming my lips with the flat of his thumbs—parting them, parting us. He stepped back, extricating his body from mine. Yet the heat between us raged on, a static charge—a river of overzealous electrons bouncing back and forth—his yin and my yang.

"I can't do this, Tiegan. We can't do this."

———

The whirr of tires on smooth pavement and the occasional swipe of the window wipers did not drown out the pounding thump of my heart. Tomás stared straight ahead, hands on the wheel, eyes on the road.

I opened my mouth to say something, to explain. But how could I explain what I don't understand?

The milky light of dawn broke through the horizon as Tomás veered to a stop in front of Vila Algarve. It was only then he looked at me.

"I'm sorry." His gaze cut through me, and his voice was flat.

Tears stung my eyes. He didn't want me. That, I understood.

———

Tomás

What was I thinking? Two restaurants—one big headache. And they called this an office? A table jammed in the corner, shelves rising to the ceiling, bowed under the weight of too many things. Who could function like this? Nothing labeled. Nothing organized.

I shook my head and then scratched my forehead while considering the possibilities—designate a separate space for cleaning products with stronger steel shelves. Everything needed to go. A clean sweep: the buckets, the wet floor signs, the string mop soaking in a bucket, and the coat rack draped in white aprons. The only redeeming feature was a west-facing window looking into the town square. I gazed too long through the window, my thoughts drifting somewhere else—anywhere else.

"Mr. Ferreira? Sir?" A boyish voice, verging on adulthood, interrupted my thoughts.

"Yes, Adáo." I looked past the architectural drawings littering the table at the young man—one of three remaining servers—two quit last week. A muscle twitched in my jaw. An involuntary reflex? Or a premonition?

"I'll be leaving, sir." Adáo stared at his feet, shifting from foot to foot, his shoes squeaking on the polished floor.

"Leaving? Why is that?" I sighed.

"Well, sir, my girlfriend found work in Lisbon. I'm sorry, sir. I like it here, I do. But my girlfriend…" He lifted his head, meeting my gaze.

"It's all right, Adáo. I understand."

"Uh, sir, I have a friend looking for work. I'll tell him to stop by."

I rose from the table and shook Adáo's hand. "Good luck, Adáo. I mean that."

"Thank you, sir."

Eli arrives on Monday. He could manage the renovation. And Cat—she's good with people. She could hire staff and manage things here.

I massaged my temples. I would get through this—my new mantra.

Tiegan—my mind flashed to that woman. To those kaleidoscope eyes, to those lush lips. Jesus, fuck. I lost myself around that woman. I couldn't think straight. Who are you, Tiegan Moss? Where did you come from?

Sleepwalking. Who does that? She could have walked off the cliff and fallen into the sea. Did she even realize the danger? My mouth dried. The hairs on the nape of my neck lifted. What if she did it again? The sea would claim her. She could die. I would lose her like I lost Sylvie.

The papers on the table vibrated—my phone hidden somewhere underneath, chirping, buzzing. I lifted the drawings and took the call.

———

Tiegan

The mansion once belonged to a count or a duke, I wasn't sure which. It's now a wellness spa where pots of purple lavender overflowed with manic vigor and thorny red roses climbed the stucco walls, now painted pink, filling the air with a sweet honey scent.

I was sitting on a creaky wicker chair on the front porch, waiting for Vera, unable to contain my excitement. I couldn't wait to explore the grand ballroom and its sixteen-foot ceilings embedded with glass crystals.

Vera planned a full day of spa treatments—head to toe. I wanted to go rock climbing—face my inner demons and all that stuff—but persuading Vera to get dirty had been difficult.

Steve's black pickup truck swung into the circular driveway, stopping in front of the grand steps. I had a clear view of Vera and her fiancé. Their expressions were animated, and they were talking at the same time.

She met me at the top of the steps, my eyes questioning her as I held the door. She flew past without a backward glance as the truck wheeled too fast onto the one-way road.

———

Late-day rays of sunshine warmed our bared skin as we walked down the winding hill. The air was moist, hazed with humidity. It was one of those rare autumn days that surrounded you with summer.

Vera was right—a spa-day was a beautiful thing. Exfoliated, buffed, pampered, and cleansed. The usual Tiegan Moss was unpolished. No, I preferred the casual look, more haphazard than high style, complemented with traces of oil paint and cracked, dried skin—no makeup, no glamour. I inspected the tidy manicure and the slight sheen of polish on my fingernails. I liked it.

"Hey, how about dinner?" She slowed her steps.

"Isn't Steve picking you up?" I studied her.

"Yeah, later." She snorted.

I lifted my eyelashes in muted question, but Vera chose not to share.

"Okay, sure. Where do you want to go?" I was always happy to go out for food. Restaurants, diners, and chip trucks all offered appealing options.

"Bianca's." She smiled.

"And face Tomás? After my latest walk of shame? No thanks." My stomach twisted into a knot just thinking about it.

"Oh, come on. You're being silly." She chortled.

"I am not being silly. What about the Irish pub? Derek likes that one." I scratched my head.

"But the burgers at Bianca's…" her voice cajoled.

"Is that all you ever eat? Burgers?" I plunked my hands on my hips. I knew the answer to that question.

"Okay. All right. How about Tia Mia's?" She smiled.

"That's right next door to Bianca's." I hurried after her.

"Tiegan, this is a small town. You can't hide forever." She said over her shoulder.

"I'm pretty sure I can." I looked her in the eye.

"Yeah, well, I won't let you. This is a holiday. You're supposed to have fun." She huffed.

"Vera, I was right in front of his house. In my pajamas." I loosed a breath.

"Okay, but why was he wandering the Algarve cliffs in the middle of the night?" She lifted her brows.

"I don't know. I never thought to ask." I thought about that.

"There. See. He's just as crazy as you are. Nothing to worry about." She tsked.

I bit down on my lower lip. I didn't know about that.

We waited in line at Tia Mia, but lady luck was on our side. A table on the patio overlooking the ocean freed up, and we sat down within moments. The menu tantalized my tastebuds, offering select mouthwatering seafood entrees. We ordered a platter of sardinhas assadas and a bottle of Prosecco to share.

"Today was fun." Vera bit into the last lonely sardine.

"It was. I loved the massage." I finished the last of the Prosecco.

"Hmm, Ricardo has wonderful hands."

"I agree." I dropped my arms to my sides, stretching my shoulders.

"Look, Tieg." She motioned toward the sea.

The evening sun bathed the cliff face in a golden glow. On the cliff's summit, the silhouette of a man and a boy— fishing.

"That's João and his grandfather." I peered at the small shapes high above.

João bounced from foot to foot, casting his fishing line into the pounding surf.

"Oh, the two you sketched? That was nice, Tieg. They're good people. I know João's mom. She works at the grocery store." She looked away, her eyes shadowed.

"Okay, that's it. Are you going to tell me what's going on?" I drummed the tabletop.

"Nothing's going on." She met my gaze.

"Oh, really? You're not a talented liar." I lifted my eyelashes.

Vera sighed, pursing her lips together. "Let's just say I discovered some questionable photos on the saved in the clouds."

"What? What do you mean?" I shifted in the chair.

"Our cell accounts are synced. I found a few nefarious photos in Steve's favorites he refuses to explain." Her lips tightened.

"Photos? Of women? No fucking way." Aaron's face haunted me. Damn him.

And then I heard it—a piercing scream. João's grandfather, at the top of the cliff, waved his arms in the air, and halfway down—João, arms outstretched, clung to the wall of rock.

Within seconds, I was running across the square with Vera hot on my heels, weaving through the melee of beachgoers, their faces raised, their panicked voices shout at João.

"Tieg, what are you doing? You have no ropes, no harness." Vera read my mind.

But I had been climbing rock walls all my life—the granite and basalt faces of the Cape Breton Highlands—the cliffs of the North Cape. I stared up and up again at the monster wall.

"Tiegan, don't do this. You could fall. You could die." She grabbed my arm.

"I'm the only chance he's got." Did I hide in the faceless crowd? Did I wait for a miracle?

"Jesus Christ, Tiegan. This is crazy."

"Get help up there. When I yell, throw down a rope. I mean it, Vera. Go!" I stared up at little João. How long could he hang on? I couldn't leave him up there or watch him fall.

Vera turned away, pulling out her phone to dial emergency services.

I gazed upward, calculating the best path, Aaron's voice sounding in my head. "You got this, babe."

Oh my God. Did I have this?

I placed my hands on the face of the wall, digging into the first foothold, and began the climb. I heard nothing but the sound of my breath. On any other day, this would be a magical experience, climbing layers of limestone ridges. I would have a harness, ropes, chalk, and climbing shoes on a typical climb. I would be bolted in.

I dropped my knee, bringing my center-of-gravity closer to the wall. The key to a vertical climb is to keep your weight over your feet as much as possible. I straightened my leg, hooked my toe, and stretched—I had run out of leverage and swung my foot to reach the next ledge. While copper hues streaked across the sky, I rested my face against the jagged rock. "João! Can you hear me? You're going to be okay."

"Okay." His voice reached me, thin but steady.

Golf balls of rock skittered down the face, dislodged by João's feet. I squeezed my eyes shut, pressing tight into the wall. Below, the ocean roared with rage.

And then I was bathed in a circle of light, no longer a fly on the wall. A floodlight from the beach below shone on the cliff face. I lowered my heel and propelled with my toe—the beam following me. Then I made a mistake. I looked down into the sea of faces and slipped, losing my foothold. I hung on with everything I had, but my hands were tired, my knuckles burning. Shadows floated in front of my face. My stomach churned. Vera was right: I was going to fall. I was going to die. A swirling wind rose from the sea, cradling me, and Aaron's voice whispered, "You've got to earn it, babe." I dug deep, then deeper still, clawing at the peppered edge. I found a toehold and pushed off. Below, crowds of onlookers cheered.

João clung to the wall with whitened knuckles, his eyes squeezed shut. Relief flooded my mind—the ledge João perched on was wide enough for both of us.

"Hey, bud. What's happening here? Is everything good?" I held him in my gaze.

"I think so," his voice murmured.

"Good man. We're going to get you out of here in no time. Okay?"

"Okay."

"Rope!" I yelled over the roar of the ocean.

Nothing.

"Rope," I called out again.

"Miss Tiegan…my avo." His voice hitched.

"Is waiting for you at the top. You're going to see him real soon, I promise." The end of a rope landed on my head. I grabbed it and pulled—the tension felt good.

"Yay! Look at that, João. We've got a rope. Now we can get you up, up, and away. Home in time for dinner. So, listen. I'm going to tie this rope around your waist, and the people at the top will pull you up. Okay?" I convinced myself all was well.

"Okay." He closed his eyes.

I pressed into the cliff face and slipped the rope under João's belly. All around us, the wind shrieked—gusting fits of violent storm. Somehow, I felt safe.

"Okay, I'm going to tie the knot. It's going to be tight, and it might hurt. Are you ready?"

"I'm ready."

Rescue 101—the bowline knot. I could tie this knot with one hand, which was fortunate because that's all I had. My dad's voice rang in my ears. The rabbit runs out of his hole, around the tree, and back into his hole.

"Okay, now listen, this is important. Hold the rope with both hands and don't let go. Can you do that?" I snugged it up, tight.

He nodded, tightening his fingers around the rope.

I tugged hard and looked upward. "Pull!"

The crowd cheered as rescuers hauled João, inch by inch, up the cliff face to safety.

I leaned into the limestone wall and shook out my arms.

It registered in my mind just how far up the cliff face I was and how lucky João was to hold on as long as he did. I closed my eyes, careful not to lose my grip.

Minutes later, the rope landed on my head—another perfect shot. I tied myself in and climbed. Whoever was at the end of the rope was not wasting any time. Hand over fist, someone lifted me to the top. Flashbulbs burst, blinding me as helping hands lifted me over the edge.

The rope jerked, propelling me forward so much that I stumbled. I gasped as the scent of sandalwood and musk hit me.

He brushed my cheekbones with his thumbs, tracing my upper lip and cupping my face in his hand. His chocolate eyes bored into mine.

"Tomás," I whispered his name.

"You're bleeding." He lifted my hands, kissing my bloodied fingers.

There was no pain, only the rush of adrenaline.

"Where did you learn to do that?" His voice rolled over me.

"What? Climb?" My knees weakened. My blood burned.

"No." He skimmed the flat of my belly with the palm of his hand, inching toward the knotted rope. "Tie that knot." He dropped his head, dragging his lips down my face.

I sank into him, pressing my hands against hard, rippling muscles. I breathed him in, tasting rich notes of musk.

"Tiegan. There you are. Holy cliffhanger, girl. You rocked it!" Vera called out.

A parade of smiling faces followed. Flashbulbs flashed. They wanted photos of me, of João. There were so many people and so many questions.

———

*W*e *journeyed deep into the watery wilderness: through floating carpets of duckweed, past alligators basking in the sun. We explored a maze of meandering bayous, forgotten backwater lakes: our only companions, the shy egret and a flock of white pelicans. While Tomás trapped crawfish in the brackish waters, I picked oyster mushrooms from the bark of dead and decaying black willows. We cooked on open fire and camped on far-flung sandbars. We made love under star-filled velvet skies while armies of knocked-kneed cypress stood watch.*

I jolted upright in bed, too hot and so very thirsty. The moon peeked through the shutters, throwing a ladder of light across the floor. I'd had the dream before.

———

"*D*earest Tiegan,

Your father and I were right gobsmacked to learn that you rescued that wee child from the Portugal cliffs. Tiegan sweetheart, my heart was in my mouth. If we weren't watching the late-night news, and you were on the telly. Do you know you're to be a CBC hero, Tiegan? You're to win a prize. If that's not for certain, I just don't know what is. Well, then your father was after the messages this morning, and if the Cape Breton Post didn't have your picture posted right on the front page. You've made the whole island proud, sweetheart. No guff.

We hope you're having fun and the weather is fair. Are you back to painting now? It looks like a beautiful place with all those cliffs and ocean, not too different from the Cape in some ways.

Well, sweetheart, I must be off. We have a kitchen party at Marge Patterson's to attend this evening. I've made a lovely apple grunt and a blueberry buckle, and will of course bring my fiddle. Vera's Mom and Dad are coming, and I expect your Uncle John will sing some of the old tunes. It should a right fair time.

Say hello to Vera for us.

We miss you. We are so proud of you.

Love,

Mom

PS. Your father says if the pickle doesn't bounce, don't eat it."

5

*"I am currently under construction.
Thank you for your patience."*—Unknown

Tiegan
The whisper of voices, kissed by the shadows of night, stirred my mind.

Tomás held my hand, and we jumped high into the air—over a broomstick—the old way. He caught me in his arms, meeting my lips, kissing me with such tenderness, with such joy. I was his, and he was mine. A circle of rice rained down, flashbulbs bursting.

A jolt of current, a fracture of light, a thunderclap, tore me away from that place. The world blurred out of focus. My throat parched, and my face wet with tears.

A small crowd, including the mayor and other dignitaries, had gathered for a presentation to acknowledge my heroic actions.

This past week had been a whirlwind of media attention:

phone calls, interviews, and social media madness. A video of me scaling the cliff face in a circle of white light went viral, clinching the whole wide world's attention. The notoriety of being a hero and the aftershock? So not me.

Rows of fold-up chairs sat in the middle of the town square—Vera waved from the front row. Derek caught my eye and smiled. João, his avo, and his mama sat beside Derek. João was no worse for wear. He couldn't sit still. He grinned and wiggled in his seat.

The mayor of Carvoeiro spoke.

"Tiegan, what you did to save young João was an act of selfless bravery. Faced with a dire situation, you willingly placed your own life at risk to rescue another. The citizens of the Carvoeiro will be forever grateful. On behalf of everyone here, I would like to present you with this medal of honor, the key to our city, and this plaque to commemorate your extraordinary act of courage."

He placed a medal over my head and shook my hand. To the flash of cameras and the crowd's applause, I displayed the plaque—a limestone sculpture etched with a black script, a chunk of the Algarve itself.

———

Vera had returned to her shop, Derek, to the Vila Algarve. João had hurtled into my arms, and his mama had hugged us both. His avo left me with a beaming smile.

There was one other person I was aching to see. I had waited. I was tired of waiting.

I straightened my blouse, brushed my hands down my black linen capris, and walked into the foyer of Bianca's, and then I stopped—blinded by the dim light. My mouth dried, and my head spun. Maybe this wasn't such a good idea.

Tomás came into focus behind the bar, drying his hands on a white terry towel. He wore his signature black button-down, sleeves rolled halfway up his forearms. He filled those dark jeans—thick in all the right places.

"Miss Moss, to what do I owe this pleasure?" He looked up, meeting my gaze.

"I thought I might see you at the presentation," I said in a polite and friendly voice. I stared too long at the bare skin of his forearms, at the dusting of dark hair, at the heavy gold watch. His fingernails were impeccably clean. I imagined his hands and those long fingers trailing across my naked body.

He circled the bar and stopped a heartbeat away.

"I'm a busy man, Miss Moss. I have no time for fanfare." He stared down, his eyes shrouded in dark light.

"Things are working out for you then, with Bianca's?" I tore my gaze from Tomás, noting the changes: the bar top glowed with a soft luster, and the chrome sparkled.

"Why are you here, Miss Moss? Is there something you need?" His words were unhurried.

I could answer both questions but chose the first: "I wanted to thank you for your help the other day."

"You want to thank me?" His voice held disbelief.

"Yes, I do. Why is that so hard to believe?" I lifted my shoulders and gained another half-inch. He smelled so fucking good.

"You're the hero, Miss Moss, not me. What do they call you now? *A aranha?*" He chuckled, a low laugh.

"Why do you call me Miss Moss? You know my name." The spider, a nickname, thanks to one of the many photos of me scaling the cliff face. I ignored his sarcasm.

"Because I prefer to keep our relationship at arms-length." He lifted his dark eyebrows.

"Arms-length? How do you figure?" I looked down at my scabbed fingers. How could I forget? He untied the rope around my belly and touched me there. "I don't get you, Tomás. Why do you act like nothing happened between us?"

"There's nothing to get, Miss Moss. I'm a simple man with simple needs, and as I've said before, I have nothing to offer you."

I shook my head back and forth. I would not accept that. Not now. "You kissed me, Tomás. You touched me. You want me like I want you." I laid my cards on the table. I crossed my arms and waited for his answer. He didn't seem to have one. In a slow, steady voice, I said what I came to say. "Thank you for your help—with João. I couldn't have done it without you." I was rattled, but I didn't show it. I was proud of myself.

"Anyone can pull on a rope, Miss Moss." A ghost of a smile touched his lips.

I should have left—cut my losses. But I couldn't. An invisible force, one I didn't understand—one that kept me up at night, one sleepless night after another—held my feet.

"You're right, but it wasn't just anyone. It was you. And you did a lot more than pull on a rope. Or have you forgotten?" I forced Tomás to back up. I stuck my hand in his face. "Why did you kiss my fingers?"

"You want to know why?" He caught my wrist, closing the gap between us.

"I think you owe me an explanation." I stared into his eyes, dark and hooded. I was not afraid.

With a jerk, he lifted me off my feet into a solid wall of pectorals. His hands were everywhere: one branding the cheeks of my ass with white-hot fire, the other twisting into my hair. He crushed my lips with bruising force, scorching my tongue with his own.

His kiss did nothing to soothe my need.

I wanted to tangle my fingers in his hair. I wanted to deepen the kiss, but before I could, he spun me around, nestling the swelling bulge of his cock into my lower back.

He dipped his head, scraping his teeth along the nape of my neck, nibbling my earlobe. "I'm going to make you come, Miss Moss. Right here. Right now."

"Do it, Tomás. Make me come." I taunted him, arching into him.

His voice—music to my ears.

His hands slid beneath my blouse, razing my bare skin with heat. He captured each breast, kneading each heavy swell, thumbing both pebbled nubs.

My breasts tightened, and my nipples peaked—an electric charge shot from my belly to my core. My sex, a pulsating beast with a mind of its own, screamed. Wanting. Needy. Hungry.

A groan rose in his throat, a savage growl confirming his arousal. He shoved one hand under the waistband of my capris, under the silk of my panties—the delicate fabric tore, giving way to the immensity of his palm, of his fingers. He dragged his thumb over my clit, cupping my pussy, fondling the inner folds.

I sank into him, burying my head beneath his chin.

"Do I make you wet, *meu amor*?" One thick finger invaded knuckle deep, and then deeper still. "You're so fucking tight." His voice played with my mind.

The inner walls of my vagina contracted, clutching that long digit. I could not speak, my breath stolen from me. A vision floated in the peripheral space of Aaron's face, blurred and unrecognizable. I was somewhere else, lost in an erotic fog, verging on complete release. I wanted this. I needed this.

"Do you like that, *meu amor*? Is it good?" He rocked his finger, stroking the G-spot with one and then two thick fingers, all the while driving his cock in between my butt cheeks. Penetrating. Grinding. Demanding.

When the pad of his thumb circled my clit, my entire body shuddered, and one violent spasm sent me over the edge. An orgasm rolled through me—mind-blowing, aching tremors that made my pussy weep. Words, incoherent dirty words, flew out of my mouth.

He dragged his fingers, his hands, away from my trembling flesh, resting his face in my hair. His breath ragged, he murmured, "When I look at you, I see my wife. I see Sylvie—the only woman I have ever loved."

His wife?

I was a reminder of a dead woman.

That's what this was?

I wanted to run. I wanted to cry.

He whispered soft words in a language I didn't understand.

I broke away from his embrace, my knees buckling as I attempted to stand. I stumbled backward, tears streaming down my cheeks as I gazed at him. His eyes glazed, devoid of life. There was no one there.

Before he could say another word, I ran.

———

Vera and I were in a taverna where the space was cozy, and the light was dim. The place was hopping, tables jammed together, people standing elbow to elbow with drinks in hand. A woman wearing a black sheath dress and stiletto heels was onstage singing the blues—her voice haunting, her song melancholy. Two men accompanied her: one played guitar, the other a viola. I wiped my eyes with the back of my hand and swallowed the hard lump in my throat. The woman thanked the crowd and left the stage, promising to return soon.

I was relieved she had taken a break. I couldn't take any more heart-wrench.

"Tiegan, cheer up! Let's celebrate." Her voice sang.

Celebrate what? My newfound fame? I had a million new friends. People smiled when they saw me, they shook my hand, they wanted a selfie with me. I hoped they would forget, but that's not the case.

"Tomás is a fuck-up. There's plenty of fish in the sea, hon. Let's go swimming." Vera punched my forearm and giggled.

"Vera, that's not nice." I didn't know whether to laugh or cry. Another woman—where had I heard that before? I reminded him of a ghost. It couldn't get any worse.

"Forget about him. He's a lost soul." She tilted her cocktail glass, finishing what remained.

A lost soul—lost in the presence of absence. A part of my heart bled for him. How could it not? I had lost love. I had felt pain.

"I'll be right back, okay? I need the ladies' room. I'll get more drinks." Vera rose from her stool, weaving through the crowd.

I nodded, swallowing another mouthful of my new favorite cocktail, a *caipirinha*, made with *cachaça* and muddled limes—potent enough to cure the Spanish flu. I wanted to drown my sorrows—forget Tomás Ferreira and how he got me off in the foyer of Bianca's. I leaned back in my chair and enjoyed the buzz, the warm and fuzzy euphoria of strong alcohol. I crowd watched. The bar was alive with chatter and laughter.

I looked up when Vera appeared, drinks in hand and a man on her arm—the guitarist playing onstage moments before.

"Tieg, this is Paulo. Paulo, this is my best friend, Tiegan." She placed my drink in front of me.

"Ah, you are a aranha? The girl who rescued the little one?" Paulo sat beside Vear.

"Yes, I am." I grinned as Paulo kissed the top of my hand.

"It's a pleasure to meet you, Tiegan." Paulo's brown eyes twinkled.

"I didn't know you were playing at this bar, Paulo. I would have come sooner." Vera spoke to Paulo, her gaze flitting back and forth.

"Ah, Vera, my friend, I no longer sell lemons on the street. I have steady work playing guitar for the beautiful Anca." Paulo sipped a glass of ice water.

"She has a lovely voice." I nodded at Paulo.

"Ah, yes, and look, here she is now." Paulo rose from his seat. "Anca, come sit, meet my friends. This is Vera and Tiegan."

Anca's smile greeted the world. Her round, umber-colored eyes, framed by long lashes, looked back at us. "It's nice to meet you both."

"I enjoyed your show. You have a beautiful voice." I smiled at the pretty woman.

"Thanks. Paulo makes me sound good." Anca grinned at the guitarist.

"Anca, how can you say that? It is all you. Anca sings the sadness of the world." Paulo's compliment went unnoticed.

"Paulo." Anca shrugged.

"I speak only the truth. Vera, is Anca not a rising star?" Paulo looked at Vera, then at me.

"You can stop, Paulo. I will not sleep with you." Anca reached for Paulo's glass of water and slugged it back.

I laughed at Anca's openness and the chastised look on Paulo's face.

"Tiegan, you have the most beautiful eyes and that laugh. You remind me of someone I once knew." Anca leaned forward, elbows on the table.

"Will you be playing here long?" Vera looked from Paulo to Anca.

"No, we're back in Lisboa tomorrow." Anca turned and scanned the crowd.

"Will he show up this time, Anca?" Paulo lifted his eyebrows.

"I fucking well hope so," Anca sighed, threading her fingers through highlights of copper hair.

I studied her—the action so reminded me of someone. It couldn't be, could it?

"He's here. I'll be right back. Don't go away." Anca jumped from her seat.

I grinned at Anca. I liked her.

"Tiegan's visiting from Canada, Paulo," Vera nodded. "She's here for a few months."

"Canada, eh?" Paulo chuckled. "I have not been to Canada. I hear it is muito frio."

"Yes, it is cold, but not always, only in the winter," I grinned, recalling the fierce squalls I left behind.

"Ah, I will stay here where the weather is warm," Paulo's eyes smiled.

"Paulo, you would love our hometown," Vera nodded. "Open mic at the pubs, jam sessions every night—it's a friendly place."

I listened half-heartedly to Vera and Paulo chat about the music scene on Cape Breton Island. All around me, people were laughing—having fun. My drink was almost gone again. I picked up the low rumble of a voice from over my shoulder. I turned my head and choked on the last mouthful of *caipirinha*.

"Everyone, I want you to meet my big brother, Tomás." Anca's huge grin was infectious. "Tomás, you've met Paulo. Do you know Vera? And Tiegan?"

Vera laughed, and I couldn't help giggling. There was a big smile on my face, one that wasn't there before and wouldn't go away. The *cachaça* had hit me hard—this could be nothing but bad.

Tomás threw me a stony glare.

Did he give me the evil eye?

"We've met." Tomás's mouth hardened into a mouthwatering line.

"You know each other? How great is this? Tomás, sit down. I was worried you wouldn't make it. "She grabbed her brother's hand and forced him into the last remaining seat.

"Anca, I told you I would be here." Tomás raked his fingers through the thick curls on top of his head.

I wanted to rake my fingers through those heavy curls.

Anca threw her arms around him, planting kisses on both cheeks. "I'm so glad to see you, *irmáo*. Will you come to Lisboa next week?"

"Anca, I have a lot on my mind right now." Tomás stared at me, his eyes shrouded in darkness.

I stabbed him with my very best death stare. Tit for tat, as they say.

"*Não seja saudade*, Tomás, you forget to live. I will take you to a club, and we will have fun." Anca poked his chest with a red-painted fingernail.

Tomás remained silent, but Anca paid no attention. Instead, she reached for Paulo's arm. "Paulo, I've got a great idea. You will bring Vera and Tiegan to Lisboa, and we will go dancing. Vera?"

"I won't say no." Vera grinned at Paolo.

"Tiegan?" Anca lifted her chin, her eyes wide.

"Sounds like fun." I clapped my hands together.

"*Boa*! There's a new club I'm dying to check out. Tomás, doesn't Tiegan look like Sylvie?" Anca looked at her brother.

Tomás opened then closed his mouth. What was he going to say?

I stared too long at Tomás, my pulse hammering in my head. A drink? Yes, I needed another drink.

"Tomás? Look at Tiegan's eyes. Do you remember what *Vovo* used to say?" Anca's eyes lit up as if she remembered something.

A plethora of emotions flashed over his face—none I understood.

"No fucking way…Tomás? Are you and Tiegan a thing?" Anca's mind seemed to swirl, and then she blinked, a mischievous grin lighting up her face.

"Aren't you going to be late for your set?" His voice held a hint of desperation.

"Shitfuck! Goddamn. Come on, lover boy. Let's rock this pop stand." In a whirlwind, Anca flew out of her chair. She squeezed Tomás's shoulders, plunking a kiss on top of his head. "Don't go away, *irmao*. And Tiegan, I'll be looking for you. We have a lot to talk about."

"Hey, Tieg, want to do shots?" Vera looked across the table, her eyebrows lifting.

"Okay, sure." I tore my gaze away from Tomás. Oh God. Did I need more alcohol?

"Ladies, allow me." Tomás rose, escaping the table.

I rested my chin on the heel of my hand. There were people everywhere--so many people crowding together, talking all at once. I couldn't find Tomás. I wondered if I would ever see him again.

"Vera?"

I looked up—at a tall blonde-haired man standing behind Vera's chair.

"Steve. What are you doing here? I thought you were in Lisbon another few days." Vera shifted sideways, a smile peeling across her face.

"I'm back, babe," Steve leaned in close, whispering into Vera's ear.

She jumped from her chair. After a lengthy embrace with Steve, they turned toward me. "Hey, Tieg, we're heading out. You don't mind, do you?"

"No, of course not. I'll see you tomorrow." I smiled at my friend.

She blew a kiss across her fingertips, and I lifted my hand and caught it—a throwback to our childhood days.

I propped my head in my hands, mesmerized by the timbre of Anca's voice and the acoustics of Paulo's guitar: soothing, soulful notes—each one a fat drop of rain. It dawned on me. I was alone in a crowded room of people.

But then Tomás returned. He placed a corked glass bottle and a handful of shot glasses on the table.

"You came back." I looked at him, unable to hide my surprise.

"Yes, of course. Where's Vera?"

"Her fiancé arrived. She left. What's that?" I eyed the ruby-red liquid.

"This is *ginja*." He sat beside me, his leg brushing mine.

"Look, you don't have to stay if you don't want to." My face grew hot. My belly fluttered. That afternoon came back to me when I allowed him to ravish my sex and that earth-quaking orgasm he gave me.

"I would like to start over." He uncorked the bottle and filled two glasses.

"What?" I peered at him and blinked. I was not expecting that.

"Saúde!" He smiled a crooked grin, lifting his glass.

I took a tentative sip—and threw back the sweet elixir.

"Okay, Tomás, what's going on here?" I smiled back, confused by his words.

"Anca's singing. People are having fun." He didn't miss a beat. He poured the ruby liquid again. This time, we clanked glasses. I swept my tongue over my lips, savoring the sour cherry taste. This was some potent stuff.

"I can't compete with a ghost, Tomás." The words flew out of my mouth. A chill raced down my spine, and my heart stuttered.

He lifted my hand off the table and played with my fingers—such an intimate gesture.

"What are you doing? You don't get to touch me after… what you did." I yanked my hand away. I could not survive another crash and burn with this man.

"I know, and you're right. I will apologize." His hair fell over his brow.

"Well, aren't you a ray of sunshine? This is becoming a habit with you…a bad habit." My mind ricocheted into rocket mode—all cells firing—ready to blast off.

"I would like to start again." His gaze held mine, and he spoke in a low voice.

"Start what, Tomás? Failure to launch might be a better way to put it, don't you think?" My throat tightened, the walls closing in on me.

"My sister says I am *saudade*." He sighed and looked away. Then his gaze circled back to me. "Do you know what that means?"

"I'm sure you're going to tell me." I reached for the bottle and filled both shot glasses—I liked this stuff.

"It's a yearning desire to feel the love that was lost."

"Oh, poor Tomás. You think you're the only person who has ever 'lost' someone?"

"No, I didn't mean it like that."

"So I remind you of Sylvie." I spat out the words, jealous of a dead woman. I twitched. My eyes welled—I swallowed back hot tears.

"I haven't loved another woman—since Sylvie."

"Yeah…so you said. Is this a game you're playing? Because

I am so not interested. Listen up, lollipop. I'm done. You graced the inner courtyard of my vagina. It was a mind-blowing experience, but that's it. Go find someone else to fuck with." I drew first blood, my words harsh. I sat back in my chair, my eyes stinging.

"This is not a game, Tiegan. Not to me." His voice, a low resonating rumble, lingered in my mind. Calming. Soothing.

"Then what is this—this thing we are? Like Anca said." My lower lip quivered.

"This is not the time to have such a discussion."

"No? I think it's a perfect time. But what would I know?" I left my chair—on the brink of flight. "Perhaps when you have the time, Tomás, we can have that discussion."

"I feel we have known each other forever, yet I know we have never met."

A memory played in the backyard of my mind, and for some unexplainable reason, my heart sang. I plopped back down in my chair.

"Your eyes are mine, *meu amor*, since mine were blinded by you," he murmured in such a low voice I strained to catch what he said. His eyes—two pools of emotion—and I dived right in. He took my hand, twining our fingers, and I held on tight.

"My people believe in soulmates. They believe each soul will find its other half—the person you are meant to be with. And once you have—nothing will tear you apart."

I pondered that thought—the theory of soulmates—twin flames. According to the Ancient Chinese Proverb, an invisible thread connects those destined to meet, regardless of time, place, or circumstance.

"We share a magnetic attraction; do you agree?" His gaze locked with mine.

The poetry of the moment was not lost on me. I swallowed the lump in my throat. How could I deny that powerful hum, that insatiable need to be with him? The dreams that filled my nights.

"According to the prophecy, my soulmate will have eyes the color of the ocean's tide: waves of blue, greens that mingle on the crest of gray, hazel flecks of moving sand—eyes that are never at rest." His eyes were haunted.

"Eyes like mine?" The world blurred—the chatter, the laughter, the music stilled. I saw only Tomás.

"Yes." His voice lowered.

"You think I'm your soulmate? Is that what you're saying? Are you making this up? You're serious?" The need to smile urged the corners of my mouth into a grin.

"I'm deadly serious." He stroked his thumb along the soft skin of my wrist.

"Okay. Hold on, just a minute. If I'm your soulmate, the one you've been waiting for, why do you push me away?"

"To keep you safe." He lifted my fingers to his lips, pressing velvet kisses to each knuckle.

My mind zinged, bursting flashes of light exploding, and my ears popped. "Safe? Safe from what?"

"From me, Tiegan. I am a danger to you. I would rather live a life of emptiness than put yours at risk, to lose you—the way I lost Sylvie." He reached through the veil, inviting her to join.

Whoa. Holy hell! I needed to step up my game. I stood, rising too quickly—my stomach flip-flopping. Leaning forward, I gripped the table's edge, the room spinning. "You're quite the storyteller, Tomás. Soulmates? Danger! Danger! I've heard nothing like it. A flawless performance. Congrats on that. And hey, listen up, buttercup. Have a nice life." I threw twenty euros for the shooters on the table and made my way through the weaving crowd of people.

I wanted to throw up.

———

It was three a.m., and the club, a refurbished train station in the heart of Lisbon, was alive with frenetic energy. The DJ floated above the dance floor on a raft of white smoke as pink and green lasers pierced the darkness of black-light.

I downed my vodka soda and followed Anca and Vera onto the dance floor. Who needed sex when you could feel this? The chill-inducing frisson of music, the shiver and tickle of goosebumps—an orgasm of the skin. I threw my hands in the air and swayed back and forth, breathing in the flavor of perfume and sweat. The pungent aroma of happy smoke drifted into the club from an open doorway, mingling with the haze of laughter. It was too loud to talk, and I was a little drunk, but that was okay—I was with my girls, and I felt the love.

I had almost convinced myself I didn't need Tomás Ferreira.

———

Tomás

She was the whisper in the breeze. She was the sun. She consumed my every thought, and I woke each morning possessed by something magical.

Had the gods shone down? Had the fates intervened? I had watched the world from a prison of my own making—a shell of a man, dead inside. But that dead thing rose from the ashes and flickered to life, and when I gazed into her eyes—I saw the man I was meant to be. What was it, Anca said? The world is an oyster? And if that is true, I had found the pearl. I smiled and took the remaining steps two at a time. There was no turning back.

A simple plan: I would apologize, I would make things right.

Ask Tiegan for a proper date. Dinner? No, too soon. Maybe coffee? Yes, the cafe and a pastry. Then, a walk on the beach. No, lunch would be better—Oceano—a ride on the bike, the ocean, the beach. Then, sightseeing: the castle and caves. Then, if she would let me, I will take her home and make love to her—make her come again and again, properly this time. Make it everything it should be—candles, soft music, long kisses.

I sighed out loud, my heart lodged in my throat. What was the worst thing that could happen? I stared at the closed door of Vila Algarve, my hand trembling when I turned the doorknob.

"Tomás, how are you, laddie? What brings you up this way?" Derek looked up from his computer.

"Hi, Derek. I'm looking for one of your guests. Tiegan Moss. She's on the top floor, I believe?" Convincing Derek—the first step in a well-laid plan. What plan? Who was I kidding?

"Tiegan?" He lifted an eyebrow.

"Yes, I'd like to speak with her if that's possible." Heat crept under my collar. I swallowed the frog in my throat.

"Aye?" Hard-faced, Derek peered over his glasses.

"Is she here?" Sweat pooled on my temples.

"No, she's not, but I'll tell the lass you dropped by, Tomás." His gaze sliced the room with winter's frost.

"Do you know where I can find her? I want to speak with her." I squared my shoulders and studied the older man.

"She's no mentioned you're a friend of hers, Tomás." Derek tilted his head, his gaze softening.

"Yes, well…we're not exactly." I gave Derek a weak smile and scratched the itch on my forehead.

"No?" He paused, waiting for my reply.

"We've had several conversations. Some have gone, well, not well. Badly, to be honest." I flinched, recalling our last encounter.

"Is that so, laddie?" He removed his glasses, polishing the lens with a soft cloth.

"Do you know where she is, Derek? I need to speak with her." My breath failed.

"Aye. Well, I trust you'll be doing right by the young lass?" His tone questioned my motives.

"I am. I will. I assure you, Derek, I mean her no harm." I held his gaze.

"Good. And mind, you'll have me to deal with if you don't. You have my word, Tomás."

"Of course, I talk to myself.
Sometimes I need expert advice."—Unknown

Tiegan

Within walking distance of Vila Algarve, on the edge of the sea, sat a dilapidated cottage. Most would consider it nothing more than a falling-down shack, but I had fallen in love with it. The clapboard was weathered, and more than a few shingles had flown away from the low-pitched roof. A porch rambled from one side to the other, and from the rafters, an old swing hung from four rusty chains. Sporadic clumps of wildflowers grew in the sunbaked earth, uncared for, yet more beautiful than any manicured garden could ever be. The scent of wild rock rose and woody lavender lingered on the breeze, mingling with the buzz of honeybees, the warble of songbirds, and the seismic hum of the earth.

This deserted cottage belonged to Derek. It was his retirement fund. When the day came, he would sell this along with the Vila Algarve and retire to a quiet place in the mountains. He offered this cottage to use at my leisure as a place to paint.

For me, painting was an escape—a place to hide for hours, sometimes days. I had been hiding here, away from the world, away from Tomás.

On fair-weather days, the cat followed me along the well-worn path, and we spent the day together here on the Algarve cliffs. The cat hides in the long switchgrass and, with the stealth of a panther, pounced on innocent and unsuspecting lizards and sometimes little birds. His belly full, the cat stretched out in the sun until it was time for the next hunt.

Now and then, Derek would stop by with a picnic basket full of lunch: ham sandwiches, potato chips, and chocolate pudding. Derek insisted I was too skinny. "Ye need tae eat, lass, before ye fade awa' tae nothin'," he would say in that rich Scottish burr.

I had not seen Tomás since that night at the taverna. According to Catarina, Tomás had left town—date of return unknown. Casa Rosalia remained open, but Bianca's was closed for renovations.

I added the last strokes to my latest creation, a portrait of Derek standing beside his prized Renault. Bushy eyebrows and dark blue eyes stared back at me, or maybe they were my grandfather's eyes. Either way, the painting made me smile.

Outside the cozy confines of the cottage, a storm was brewing. Black clouds filled the sky, and in the distance, a streak of lightning, a thunderclap. I stripped out of my painting attire—a ragged T-shirt and yoga pants covered with years of spilled paint. Another lightning crack streaked the sky. I gulped back the last of my cold coffee and rinsed the mug, leaving it draining in the sink. The wind howled, rattling the windowpanes. I washed out my paintbrushes with soap and hot water.

I closed the door behind me and set out. In the distance, the chimney sentinels rose above Vila Algarve. The wind sped up to gale force, and I wondered if I should wait out the storm under the cover of the clapboard cottage. The wind whipped my hair into my eyes, blinding me. I lowered my head and leaned into each blasting gust. Black clouds pressed down like a wet woolen blanket, and the skies opened. Driving sheets of rain drenched the earth. There was nowhere to run and nowhere to hide. I pressed on, one step at a time, thorny brambles slashing at my ankles. I tripped, falling onto my knees.

Strong arms lifted me off the ground and onto my feet. "What are you doing out here?" Tomás shouted through a veil of raindrops. Lightning struck, shaking the ground.

"What are you doing here?" I screamed back.

He gripped my wrist and dragged me through the underbrush. He walked too fast, and I tripped, falling and stumbling again. He then gathered me into his arms, cradling my body against the force of the rain and wind and forging ahead through a swale of madness.

I squeezed my eyes shut, tucking my head into his chest. Why was he here? How did he find me? Why now?

Somehow, Tomás found the clapboard cottage. He shoved the door with his hip, striding over the threshold. The wind whistled through the rafters. Balls of hail sliced through layers of cloud, bouncing off the roof and covering the ground with the white crust of winter. Inside the cottage, the light was dim. The air was still. He shifted his weight, and the floorboards creaked.

"Tiegan, are you alright? You're shaking, *meu amor.*" He placed me on my feet and walked from one room to another until he found what he was looking for: an old blanket, thick and warm, baby blue with satin edging. He wrapped the blanket over my shoulders, drawing my body into his. "Better?"

"Yeah…much better." He was as wet as I, but heat radiated from his body, warming me.

"What is this place? All these paintings? You did these?" His hair was untidy and wet with rain.

"Yeah." I burrowed closer.

"You're an artist?" His breath warmed me.

"Sometimes." I burrowed closer, pressing my lips to the underside of his jaw.

"I didn't know that. They're amazing…beautiful." He smelled like rain and cold frost.

"Hmm." I filled my lungs with his scent and exhaled a shuddered breath.

He trailed the palms of his fingers across my chin. The last time he kissed me was fast and hard in a moment of fury. But now he enticed me, the rough burr of his jaw scraping my cheek, his mouth nipping my bottom lip, his tongue tracing mine, a moan vibrating low in his chest.

There was an ache between my legs—one I had denied for so long, a fire sparking hot through my veins. For too many nights, I had imagined sex—raw, carnal sex—with him. I dropped my hands, fumbling with the button on his jeans, but he stilled my attempt to free his shaft.

"You don't want me?" The question had haunted me for weeks—I was a reminder of a ghost, but I didn't care. I didn't care who or what she was.

"I want you." He swept his hands through my hair.

Shivers coursed through my body, tingling sensations from my head to my toes—flames licked my inner thighs.

He twined his fingers with mine, and in one quick motion, I was on the floor, the blanket under my back with Tomás leaning over me, his hands on either side of my shoulders, caging me within his heat.

"I wanted you the moment we met." His lips grazed my forehead. He skimmed the underside of my blouse, slipping each button loose, baring my breasts to cool air. He circled his tongue around each aching nub, taking the hardened pearls into his mouth, one at a time. "I've wanted to taste you."

Arrows of heat shot straight to my core—my mouth watered, yet I could hardly swallow. I lifted my hand, brushing that loose curl away from his forehead.

No man had ever looked at me that way, ever.

My pussy quaked, flooding my panties with wet heat. I had never been so wet, so aroused. My heart staggered, an erratic beat—my mind lost in indecision. Was this what I wanted? Was this what I needed? "Wait. I don't. I can't. Do you have any condoms?"

"I want to look after you, *meu amor*." He turned his head, kissing my fingers, taking each one into his mouth, his eyes blazing.

He wanted to make me come? My pleasure, not his? My voice caught in my throat. "Okay."

He tugged my leggings, sliding them and my panties away.

The air inside the cottage was cool, but my skin flushed hot. I was completely exposed, but he was not.

"So pretty, *meu amor*." He teased, drawing soft circles on my belly with the backs of his knuckles. He trailed his fingertips across my outer lips, separating the swollen cleft.

I curled my hands into the soft blanket, arching my hips, bucking into the scorching caress of his tongue, tremors pulsing through the inner walls of my vagina. My thighs trembled.

"Slow down, *meu amor*. We have all day, don't we?" Leaning close, he slipped the tip of his tongue between the sensitive folds, tantalizing my sex with soft pulls and wet kisses.

I wet my lower lip with the tip of my tongue and gazed into his chocolate eyes. Sweet Jesus. What had I done? "Tomás? Why are you here? How did you find me?"

He sent me a smoldering look and a wicked smile. Dropping his chin, he sealed his lips around my clit and sucked the hard bud. The scruff under his chin scraped my swollen cleft, increasing the stimulation. His lips tightened, his cheeks hollowed.

With each rhythmic suck, my clit swelled. I cried out, my voice an unrecognizable whimper. I plowed my fingers through his silky curls, pressing my lower back to the floor, arching my hips upward, giving Tomás full access to my core. I wanted him to touch me as he did before.

He did not disappoint.

Easing through heated folds, he slipped two digits inside my hot channel. While his greedy mouth worked my swollen clit, his fingers scissored, gliding in and out, thrusting deeper, stroking and curling, massaging the G-spot with unbearable pressure.

My mind went to that nowhere place, my hips jerking, my legs shaking—an orgasm ratcheting through me, waves upon waves of release. My eyes drifted open and shut, my screams echoing high in the rafters.

"So, good. Tomás. Oh, God. Yes. Again...do it again." I twisted my fingers into silken curls and whispered his name.

His lips skated across mine––his breath cool and calming. He kissed me again, and again, and again as his fingers played havoc with my senses.

God, what would his cock feel like—filling me, pumping into me?

We stayed spooned together in that nest of blankets for what seemed an endless eternity. I had lost all sense of time and reality. I was sure of only one thing: more would never be enough.

When I thought he was done, I was mistaken. Tomás excited my desire with his hands, with his tongue—each surge of orgasm leaving me undone—sated.

We hid from the storm, safe within the walls of this little cottage, but when I looked out the window, the skies were at peace. Sunlight broke through the clouds, raining light on frozen ground. An expanse of sparkle, as far as the eye can see: each branch, each leaf of grass, each delicate petal, a glistening work of art, a million miniature suns, mother nature's masterpiece.

"You're beautiful, so beautiful." A smile lifted the corners of his lips. He sat with his legs stretched out, leaning against the shiplap wall.

"Tomás." I didn't know what to say other than I was game all day, every day, for more of the same.

"Tiegan, there are things you must know…about me." His careful words hinted at a serious conversation. He drew his fingers through my hair over and over again.

"Okay, like what?" I curled into him, fireflies dancing over my skin, a relentless hum of need.

"I went to your apartment. Derek told me about this place." There was a hint of desperation in his voice.

I pulled myself up, breaking away from his touch, and looked at him. "Tomás? What is it? What's wrong?"

"I've tried to stay away. I want to be with you. I want to make you happy." He angled his mouth over mine and kissed me, his lush lips and swirling tongue stirring my desire.

"I want to be with you, too." I straddled his hips and kissed him back, sliding my tongue deep into his mouth. I slipped my hands under his waistband. I was naked, yet he was not. What was wrong with that picture?

"We can't." He twined his fingers with mine, stilling my seduction.

"But I want to make you come." I squeezed his fingers, fisting our hands together. I wanted to see his cock, feel the soft satin blanketing that stiff shaft. I wanted to wrap my lips around the velvet knob and taste his release.

"No." His grip tightened.

"Not fair, Tomás. I showed you mine. You show me yours." I did the next best thing and rocked my pussy over his straining erection, a thin layer of denim standing between the pleasure I sought. I closed my eyes, biting down on my lower lip, sensations rolling through my sex. Needing him. Wanting him.

"Tiegan, I've done things I'm not proud of." His eyes shadowed.

"I don't care," I whispered into his throat, then bit him.

"You don't understand." He rose from our nest, and I fell onto the floor in an ungracious heap. Walking toward the front door, he picked up a backpack I hadn't noticed before, unzipped the bag, and returned with a photograph.

Fingers of silver moss hung from the gnarled branches of an ancient oak tree, providing a lustrous backdrop to the couple's portrait just married. Tomás smiled into the camera. The hard angles of his face were soft and less defined. But it was the woman I stared at. White satin hugged a tiny waist. Black hair spilled onto her shoulders. Her face was fine-boned and ashen. I dropped the photo onto my lap and met his gaze. "This is Sylvie?" I already knew the answer.

"Yes." He paced back and forth, his shoulders

"She looks an awful lot like me, Tomás." He told me I reminded him of his wife. He failed to mention Sylvie could be mistaken for my identical twin.

"Do you remember our conversation at the taverna?" He watched me dress.

"I ran out on you." Snippets came back to me: soulmates, danger. I scoffed it off at the time, believing it to be a tall tale meant to let me down easily.

"I let you leave." He turned away, facing his demons on his terms.

"You said I was your soulmate." I pulled my shirt over my head and glanced back over my shoulder.

"I should not have allowed this to happen." He raked his hand through his hair, sending me a furtive glance.

"What are you talking about?" I retrieved my underwear and slipped into them.

"I should have stayed away. I should not be here." His voice haunted the room.

"What? Why not? What's wrong?" The hairs on the back of my neck lifted.

"I am cursed. My life is cursed." He sighed through his nose and handed me my leggings.

"Cursed?" I pulled them on, one leg at a time.

"Sylvie died because of me and the little one. Rosalia told me Sylvie was not the one, but I didn't believe her. I ignored her warning. Sylvie. The baby. Their deaths lie on my shoulders. Mine alone." Tomás crossed his arms over his chest.

"You think they died because of a curse? Is that what you're saying? Who is Rosalia?" I was aghast to see his eyes were moist.

"Rosalia is my grandmother." He followed me into the hallway.

"Your grandmother?" I swept my hair into a messy bun, looping the hairband once and then twice.

"She is a *chovihani*."

"A chovihani? What's a *chovihani*?"

"Some would say a witch. I prefer to think of her as a healer."

My mind spun. A witch? A curse? I stared at Tomás.

"From the time I was a child, Rosalia told me a woman would come: frail of bone, black hair, fair skin—so like Sylvie, but not Sylvie."

"Sylvie died giving birth, didn't she? Were there complications? Was the baby too early?"

"I am cursed, Tiegan. My seed is cursed. Don't you see? If I choose wrong again, that woman will die, as will the child."

"Tomás, no. How can you believe that? This is crazy." My heartbeat stilled, and at that moment, I understood.

"No, *meu amor*. This is real. It's all true. Listen to me now. No good can come from this. I am poison to you. I am death. That's what I was trying to tell you." He ran his hands through his hair.

In his eyes, I saw pain and anguish. I saw fear. I shook my head back and forth. I wanted to roll my eyes, but I didn't. I couldn't. He believed this, and he was so damn serious.

"Tomás, what you said about finding your soulmate—your invisible thread. Do you believe I'm that person?" I willed him to answer me. I cupped his face in my hands and gazed into his soul. I saw everything.

"Yes…I do, but—"

I cut off his words and kissed his beautiful face, the corners of his mouth, and his lips. What he was asking was more than I was ready to give, and yet I could not comprehend another day without him in it.

"When one door closes, another opens.
Or you can open the closed door.
That's how doors work."—Unknown

iegan

I lay flat on my back on a promontory of limestone overlooking the sea, staring into the forming clouds, the blue sky, thoughts of Tomás and our time together playing in my mind, an endless loop of mouthwatering, orgasmic pleasure.

Tomás traveled through Spain, touring craft breweries, leaving me in Carvoeiro alone—with time on my hands. Time to consider the secrets he shared, a prophecy, and a curse. I didn't know what to think. But when I closed my eyes, the air stirred, and I wanted him again.

My cell pinged. I stared at the text message—from Tomás.

—Where are you?—

Every night for the last seven, my cell has pinged, burning up with happy face emojis and adorable text messages—from Tomás. And every morning, a delivery arrived at the Vila

Algarve with my name on it: a rainbow of rosebuds over-flowing with the pale ivory of baby's breath, white lilies interspersed with fragrant sprays of cobalt lavender, a fish-bowl terrarium with a real live turtle in it—although I don't know how long the turtle will survive with the cat—a teasing display of tropical crimson ginger and an evocative bird of paradise and today, a trio of cacti; Tomás had a sense of humor. My attic apartment looked like a Mediterranean flower shop. Even Derek was impressed.

And now Tomás was back, and we had a date—our first date. I was not ready to jump into another relationship. Was I?

—I'm at the cliffs. Should I meet you?—

He responded with no hesitation.

—I know where you are. I'll be there soon.—

The struggle in my head was real. Yes. No. Maybe. Was I doing the right thing? Was this what I wanted? My phone beeped, my heart skipped a beat, but this time it wasn't Tomás. It was Vera.

—Hey, girl. How about lunch?—

—I'm waiting for Tomás.—

I packed my backpack, stuffing my water bottle, my sketchpad inside.

—Oh, yah, right? No worries.—

—I'm nervous.—

I wiggled my toes and chewed the inside of my mouth. Why was I nervous? Where did my confidence go?

—What? Why?—

—I don't know. Is it too soon?—

I searched the horizon—nothing but gulls, screeching gulls. I wondered if they were trying to tell me something.

—Noooo. Your vagina needs this. Do you have a condom or two or three?—

—Yeah.—

I chuckled. I thought about that. Was I prepared?

—Good. You go, girl. Fuck his brains out. Make it golden.

—

Footsteps and the rumble of a deep voice interrupted my texts with Vera.

Tomás looked great in his faded denim jeans, a simple white T-shirt, and a black leather jacket. He wrapped his arms around me, and his scent—a captivating mix of rich leather and earthy musk—surrounded me.

He cupped the back of my head, threading his fingers through my hair, and tilted my face to greet his mouth. He nipped and licked—his tongue playing with mine, a teasing game of cat and mouse, and then he rested his hands on my shoulders and gazed into my eyes. "Hello."

"Tomás, maybe this isn't such a good idea." I curled my fingers around the open zipper, thumbing the soft leather, a ball of lust spinning out of control.

"Is something wrong? Have I done something?" His gaze held mine.

"No. It's not you. It's me." I placed my hands on his chest and tore my gaze away from Tomás. I stared at my feet, my mind riddled with doubt.

"Tiegan, give me today. You won't regret it, I promise." He cupped my shoulders, catching my lips one more time.

Tingling sensations danced across my flesh, my nipples protruding shamelessly. Whatever this was? This fire burning in my veins? I wanted more.

"You look beautiful. Is this new?" His lips curved into a smile, his eyes sparking with golden light.

"It is. Do you like it?" I twirled, showing off the open-backed floral midi-dress, Chantilly lace floating on a sheath of white silk—held up by skinny spaghetti straps. Vera insisted I dress for the occasion; I said no to the high heels—strappy sandals worked just fine for me.

Tomás took my hand, and we walked side-by-side. He veered off the trail to another, one so narrow we walked single file. Still his fingers were twined with mine. The path led to a dirt road where the Ducati waited. I broke into a cold sweat. I had a thing about excessive speed and crashing metal. Aaron's face flashed into my mind.

"Tomás…I don't know." I gazed at the bike, fear licking my spine.

"Do you trust me?" He lowered the helmet over my head and snapped the clip.

"It's just that…I'm afraid." I raised my eyebrows.

"I won't hurt you, sweet Tiegan."

Did he mean that literally, or was I courting disaster? Would I end up smashed and broken with no one to blame but myself?

I climbed onto the bike, the cramped position leaving my legs scrunched and my knees tucked tight to Tomás's hips. I clung to him, my breasts flush to his back. The hum of the engine and the proximity of Tomás's powerful body ignited a fire I could not extinguish. I thought I was in for a wild, screaming ride, but I was wrong—Tomás cruised along the coastal highway at a slow pace—a lazy, sensual ride.

We left the smooth pavement, turning onto a dirt track filled with potholes. Every bump in the road caused my pussy to explode, my inner thighs to tingle.

Our ride ended at an out-of-the-way restaurant on the beach. The parking lot was so busy, I wondered if we would find a seat in the restaurant.

Tomás parked the Ducati under the canopy of a sprawling umbrella pine and climbed off the bike. He extended his hand, steadying my escape from the monster bike.

"What is this place?" I unsnapped the helmet, handing it to him.

"I thought you might be hungry." His smirk sent a line of fire straight to my core.

"I am." I grazed the white cotton of his T-shirt with my fingertips. Lifting my face, I caught his lips.

His mouth welcomed me—he deepened the kiss—but then stepped away, leaving me breathless. "Miss Moss, we will eat. I will not take advantage of you again." With his hand resting on the small of my back, he leaned close and kissed my nose.

I thought it was the other way around. That day of pleasure was all mine.

We followed a path beyond wild cactus and long grasses to a wooden ramp, climbing out of the sand and leading to an open-air restaurant. It was more than charming: it was fun and relaxed, a beachfront oasis of glittering sand, sparkling waters, and bright sunshine. A series of cables held down sheets of canvas sail, nautical stripes billowing with each gust of wind, protection from the sun's shining rays. On the beach, banners of white chintz fluttered from a wooden arbor.

"*Boa tarde e bem vindo ao Oceano.*" A baby-faced teenage boy greeted us at the top of the wooden ramp.

"*Boa tarde.* We have a reservation—for two." Tomás slipped a Euro note into the boy's hand.

We arrived at the tail end of a wedding—the reason for the packed parking lot. The attendees sat at a banquet of linen-covered tables adorned with vases of green leaf and yellow rosebuds, a backdrop of turquoise sea framing the bride and groom. The happy couple posed for candid photos before joining their guests.

"Ah yes, *Senhor* Ferreira, we have been expecting you." The boy led us to a marble-topped table for two at the far side of the canopy, far enough away from the joyous celebration.

I sat and enjoyed the view of rolling sand and blue ocean —and Tomás, my artist's mind framing the picture.

The server's arrival, a young woman wearing navy blue capris and a white tank top interrupted us. Her name was Amalia, and she spoke fluent Portuguese.

"What would you like to drink, *meu amor*?" A smile lifted his lips.

"A *caipirinha*, with lots of ice. Please." I grinned at Tomás, at the sunlight glinting off his dark hair. Oh God, and his lips. How could a man have such kissable lips? I did a double take as Tomás reached into his pocket for a pair of glasses. The thick plastic frames made him even more delectable.

The server left us alone.

I picked up the menu and happily noticed that it was in English.

"Do you know what you want?" He glanced over the edge of his glasses.

I knew what I wanted. Did I dare voice my desires here and now? My face heated.

"Everything looks wonderful." I scanned the menu.

"The grilled octopus is one of their specialties."

"Hmm, that sounds good to me." I set the menu aside.

Amalia returned with our drinks, my *caipirinha*, and a beer for Tomás.

He returned the tortoiseshell frames to his shirt pocket and met the server's gaze. I watched her scribbling on a notepad, recognizing the odd word—mexilhão, camarão.

"Your glasses. They suit you." I touched his hand.

"To our future…" He lifted his beer glass and smiled—a picture worthy of a frame.

"Really?" I clinked my glass against his.

"Yes…" He sipped his beer, watching me with those chocolate eyes.

"And what do you have in mind for our future?" I tried to hide my grin.

"I thought, a walk on the beach." He trailed his fingers across mine.

My core throbbed—I imagined his tongue, that thick muscle, tracing a wet path across my naked body.

"And then?" I purred, sidling to the edge of my seat.

"Perhaps I will show you the castle." He looked toward the ocean and nodded.

"The castle?"

"Yes, In Silves. The castle is impressive, and the town is picturesque. It's a pleasant drive, about an hour from here."

"Hmm, I'm sure it is." Sightseeing. I couldn't hide my disappointment. "So, how was Spain?"

"Good. I have one more brewery I would like to visit in France." His smile brought him back to me.

"Oooh. Should I book a flight?" Paris: the Louvre, the Champs-Élysées, and, of course, the Eiffel Tower. I couldn't wait.

"Would you come with me?" He lifted his eyebrows.

"Yes, I'd love to." My heart hummed.

"I will take you to Paris. But we will drive." A muscle twitched in his jaw.

"Drive? Why?" I cocked my head, searching his eyes.

"Planes and I don't exactly get along."

"You don't fly?" My eyes widened.

"I prefer keeping my feet firmly on the ground." He supped his beer.

"But you ride the Ducati like the wind." I leaned on my elbows, inching closer.

"It's the thought of being trapped in a tin can thousands of miles in the air." His face paled. He drew a long swig of beer into his mouth.

"You know there are meds you can take for that kind of thing." I studied him. I smirked.

"Perhaps so, but I don't like drugs."

"You've been nowhere?"

"My feet have never left this continent and probably never will."

"But it's such an enormous world. Don't you want to see it?"

"Everything I need is right here." He traced his index finger along my forearm, sending shivers of delight coursing through me.

Amalia arrived with an open bottle of rosé and the boy with a large platter overflowing with buttery steamed clams, tiger prawns, and toast fanned with avocado, drizzled with feta and red pepper flakes.

"Thank you," I said as she filled my wine glass. She ignored me. Her attention focused solely on Tomás. I couldn't blame her.

I didn't know what to try first, so I helped myself to everything. When I looked up, Tomás seemed preoccupied with his phone. His fingers tapped; his brow furrowed.

"Is everything okay?"

"Yes, no worries. A delivery delay." Tomás placed the phone face-up on the table. "How is it?"

"Wonderful." I snuck a glance—my smiling face, the screensaver.

"I'm happy you're here, that we can spend this time together." He lifted a napkin, dabbing the corner of my mouth, his eyes softening as he stared too long.

"Me too." I couldn't lie; it was true.

The main course was a platter for two: grilled octopus sprawled atop a fragrant array of broccoli rabe, roasted peppers, and jacket potatoes—doused with olive oil. My mouth watered, and my stomach growled—reminding me I had missed breakfast.

A solo guitarist played love songs in the background: glasses tinkled, a toast to the bride and groom.

"Tomás? Tell me about Sylvie." I sat back in my chair.

"What would you like to know?" He placed his fork on the table, meeting my gaze.

"Everything…how did you meet?" I saw warring thoughts. I saw pain.

"Sylvie was an international student from the US. We met in our last year at university. We dated for about two years, and then Sylvie became pregnant. We got married. We would have anyway, but the baby hurried things along. Sylvie died giving birth. The child passed two days after Sylvie." He relived those moments and shared them with me.

"I'm sorry, Tomás. That must have been very painful." I could imagine what he had lost. I placed my hand over his.

"I would see Sylvie's face everywhere: around every corner, in every crowd. I was not myself for a long time." He brushed my hand with his thumb.

I let the conversation falter, giving him a moment with his thoughts. He has had many years to process this, even so, there was sadness.

"You named the restaurant Casa Rosalia for your grand-mother?" I remembered Catarina's conversation and the details she shared.

"Yes, that is the deal we struck. In exchange for the family recipes, I named the restaurant after her. My grandmother is very fierce—a good negotiator." His eyes glimmered with amusement, and at that moment, I saw another side of Tomás Ferreira, a boy who was once happy-go-lucky and quick to laugh. "I hired a friend—David. He's a chef, but my grandmother taught him the rest."

"What's it like to be a Roma?" I blurted it out, immediately regretting my words. It sounded slanderous.

"What's it like to be Canadian?" He tilted his head and smirked.

"Eh?" I laughed. "Okay, you've got me there." I wanted to wrap my arms around him and kiss the corners of his mouth.

"The Roma migrated from the north of India during the middle ages. Some say we are the chosen ones. More say we are cursed, meant to wander the earth forever—a people with no homeland, an invisible nation. For centuries, persecution, enslavement, expulsion, and murder plagued the Roma. I'm the President of the Unión Romaní here in Portugal," His matter-of-fact voice caught me off guard.

"You are? What's that?"

"In a nutshell, the Unión Romaní is an organization whose mission is to defend the Roma community. We aim to achieve equality with society and react to events directly related to the Roma population here in Portugal."

"I did not know." A political activist, a champion of the people. To say I was surprised would put it mildly.

"You thought I was just another pretty face?" He leaned back in his chair, threading his hands behind his head.

"Yes, I did. A very pretty one." I laughed and met his grin.

"How about that walk?" He escorted me off the patio, away from the crowded restaurant.

We walked together through pillows of soft sand, and I wished I were wearing flip-flops or, better yet, bare feet. We walked farther to the water's edge, where the surf rolled in and out, a cresting eddy of foamy bubbles where the sand was wet and hard. I looked at the restaurant: at the festoon of banners flapping in the wind, the roofed shed housing the kitchen, and the alfresco dining platform raised high above the beach on weathered piles. It was rustic—quaint and perfect in every way. I studied the wall of sandbags piled around the perimeter and wondered if it was enough to protect this little place from the rage of the wild seas or whether it could all just wash away.

Tomás wrapped his arms around my waist, his breath mingling with mine.

I sank into his chest, lifting my face and brushing my lips across his. My senses scattered—just a taste, that's all I wanted.

His tongue swirled with mine. He deepened the kiss, his hunger tugging at the knot in my belly, unraveling the threads holding my world together.

I was on another plane of existence—I wanted everything and everyone to disappear. But a gale of laughter carried on the breeze, reminding me we were not alone. I broke away from our kiss. It was almost painful not to touch him. "I don't want to be a tourist, Tomás. I don't want to see the castle. I want to be with you."

8

"Frogs have it easy,
they can eat what bugs them."—Unknown

Tiegan

Our ride ended at Tomás's home: an ocean side villa, a low-slung rambling affair painted pale yellow—the one I had glimpsed on my previous nighttime walk-about. I swung my leg off the bike, waited while Tomás engaged the kickstand, and climbed off.

He removed his helmet, turning to me, lifting the helmet from my head. With a gentle touch, he brushed my cheekbone with his thumb.

My lips parted, my mouth watered, and I followed him inside, answering the unasked question. I barely noticed the home's interior. It was architecturally pleasing, masculine, and sparsely furnished. It was spotless and smelled like lemons. But I was not interested—I was under the spell of desire.

An expanse of marble led to a grand bedroom with a wall of glass overlooking the Atlantic Ocean. A king-size bed dressed in white linens and one tall dresser adorned the otherwise vacant space.

Tomás swept his hands through my hair, drawing his thumbs along my cheekbones. He kissed my lips—a soft press, a delectable lick, a teasing bite.

I traced the lines of his face with my fingers, holding him away ever so slightly, keeping a whisper of distance because if I didn't, I would lose myself. I savored the moment, and then, to my utter surprise—my throat closed, and tears ran down my face.

"Tiegan, what is it? Have I done something? Have I hurt you?" He cupped my shoulders.

"No. No." I curled my fingers into his shirt and tried to regain some composure but couldn't. I couldn't swallow. I couldn't breathe.

"Come with me. Let's go outside." Tomás guided me to an expanse of terraced stones and an open-air pergola—a massive post and beam structure.

Grapevines, heavy with shiny balls of fruit, clambered with amorous abandon over thick timbers, offering a shady place to hide from the blazing sun. Dapples of sunlight peeked through the greenery. A breeze played underfoot.

"Should I take you home?" Tomás folded himself onto the plush cushions of a chaise lounge.

"This is so stupid. I'm sorry." I strained to get up, but he held me in his arms.

"I know why, and it's okay." His breath mingled with mine.

"What do you mean, you know why?" I buried my face in his chest, breathing in all that sunshine.

"Your friend told me about your husband. She told me to stay away. To leave you alone." He ran his fingers through my hair.

"What?" My breath left me.

"You told Vera about the flowers?" He pressed his lips to the side of my face.

"I'm sorry, Tomás. I don't know why Vera did that," I whispered into the warmth of his neck.

He was silent but then shifted his head, peering into my tear-stained face. "I'm not who people think I am. I won't hurt you. I want you to know that."

I leaned into his embrace, my mind muddled—with the past and this moment. What was I afraid of? Tomás? No. Myself? Bingo. I closed my eyes and leaped. I opened up and told Tomás everything. I shared how Aaron betrayed me and how he died, all those in-between moments.

"I'm sorry, *meu amor*." His whisper echoed sorrow.

"For what, Tomás? It is what it is." I could hear the bitterness in my voice.

"If I were your husband, I would trust you with everything I am and everything I'm not. The man was a fool." He caught my lips in a soft kiss.

I turned, facing him, taking ownership of the lust coursing through me. I ran my hands through his hair and tasted him back. "I want to be with you, Tomás."

"Are you sure?"

"Yes, I'm sure."

He rose from the lounge, carried me into the bedroom, and set me on my feet. He rested his hands on my shoulders, his eyes filled with shadow. "Tiegan, before we go any further, I must know something."

I gazed into his eyes, lost to the emotions hiding there.

"Is there anyone standing in the way? Of us?"

"What do you mean?"

"I won't share you, Tiegan."

I wouldn't share him either—I was not good at sharing. "You want to be exclusive? Is that what you want?"

"That's exactly what I want." His voice rolled over me and

around me. It was primal and dangerous, and I wanted to taste it. How could I deny my need to be possessed by this man and my desire to possess him?

"There's no one," I answered with a half-truth—only the past and the ghosts that lived in the space between us. I wondered if they counted.

———

Tomás tapped a keypad, filling the room with soft music—a mashup of erotic lullabies flirted with my mind: a slow, sexy vibe, instrumental, sensual vocals—an endless aphrodisiac.

"Dance with me?" He trailed his hand over strands of my hair, gazing into my eyes, his eyes smoldering.

"You want to dance?" I bit the corner of my lip, my face heating. I was not a confident dancer. I had two left feet and walked like a duck. I tilted my chin.

"Yes, I want you to dance with me." He wrapped me in his arms, one hand pressed to the small of my back, his rigid cock resting against my belly, confirming his arousal.

I melted into his arms, and we swayed to the music, lost in a euphoric haze—a state of nothingness. There was only Tomás and me.

He kissed my forehead and the nape of my neck, his fingers walking each vertebra of my back to my shoulders. He slid the spaghetti straps over my arms, and my dress fell to the floor.

I was naked except for my bra and panties. My lips were tender, swollen from the crush of our last kiss. I knew what I wanted, and I wanted it now.

Tomás pulled his T-shirt over his head, loosened his belt buckle, and stepped from his denim jeans. He was all male, lovely and delicious, with defined grooves I wanted to explore.

I knelt in front of him, grazing the taut muscles of his buttocks as I slid his boxers to the floor. His shaft greeted me: large and thick, beautifully veined, nested in a patch of soft brown curls. I skimmed my fingertips across the heavy crown, a bead of pre-cum glistening on the tip. He surprised me when he backed away.

"Take off your bra." His voice was heavy with need.

I rose from the floor and stood before him, unable to ignore the flush of heat spreading through my extremities. I had always been self-conscious of my body: too small in all the wrong places, and since losing weight, my breasts were almost non-existent. I unclasped my bra.

"So beautiful, *meu amor*." He reached out, caressing each soft swell with his thumbs. Dipping his head, he flicked his tongue, scraping each nub between his teeth, then closed his mouth over the arrowed peaks and suckled hard. He was not gentle, and I liked it.

My heart coiled in my chest, my core hard-wired to the tugging bite of his lips. How could I describe what I was feeling? Desired. Adored. He made me feel all of that and so much more. I plunged my fingers into his hair, moaning with a breathy exhale. Heat surged through my sex—a flood of liquid fire.

"I'm going to make you come over and over. Your pleasure will be mine." He dragged his lips down my face and backed me into the glass wall. With an easy nudge, his knee parted my legs, and he lifted me off my feet, settling my core onto the hard muscles of his thigh.

"Yes...all yours." My emotions swirled. I dug my fingers into muscular arms and enjoyed the ride, the pulsating tremor building inside me, the flaring heat.

His hand tangled in my hair, cupping the back of my head, drawing my mouth into the swirling strokes of his tongue.

Mine. He was mine. I was close, at the edge of my undoing.

With his other hand pressed strategically against the small of my back, he rocked my hips, dragging my swollen clit into him—each heady motion grazing the thick shaft standing proud against those defined abs.

I lost myself to hunger, crying out as flames licked my thighs and my pussy quivered, soaking my panties with liquid heat.

"Tomás." I clung to him, my legs around his waist. His cock, that thick column, rested between my outer lips, tantalizing my heated entrance.

"I will make you come over and over again, sweet Tiegan." He carried me across the room to the bed, leaving my legs hanging over the edge, his eyes glimmering with varying shades of chocolate. He hooked his fingertips under the lace of my panties, sliding the slip of wet silk away, then gripped my knees, spreading them wide, exposing my core to his mercy. "I want to look at you. I want to taste you."

"Tomás, I want you. I need you." I cried out, my voice a mewling whimper.

He parted the outer folds with the pads of his thumbs, trailing the tip of his tongue across the swollen cleft. He was turning me upside down and inside out.

My pussy tingled, engorged, and raw from the heated friction only moments before, yet my need raged—for him. I cupped my breasts, squeezing the pebbled nubs.

"Do you like that?" He sent a sizzling gaze my way. With slow kisses, he circled my clitoris, grazing the hood with a gentle scrape of his teeth.

"More, don't stop." My hips rocked, my arousal burgeoning. Never had a man worshipped my sex like this.

"So delicious. Like honeydew." He left my pussy, trailing his tongue across my belly, circling my navel, drawing a wet path to the hollow of my neck, nibbling my earlobes, kissing my temples, my eyelids, catching my lower lip.

Tendrils of heat snaked my burning flesh, desire ratcheting higher—ever higher—vibrating thunder.

He separated my needy folds with one long finger, circling the entrance of my heated channel, taking me to the brink of madness.

"Please, Tomás, I need to come," I moaned, biting down on my lower lip, verging on delirium—white light dancing in my eyes. I pressed the back of my head into the mattress, my breath ragged, my pulse hammering in my head.

He dipped his head, his breath skittering across my skin. He suckled my clit, working the beaded swell with teasing licks—hard, then soft.

A moan slipped from my throat. The walls pressed in on me then, the darkness threatening to swallow me whole. I was neither here nor there. I screamed his name, combing my fingers through his hair—my hips rolling in a rhythmic dance.

"Come for me, Tiegan." One and then two fingers delved deeply into me.

My legs spasmed. I tingled all over—I was on fire.

———

I heard drawers open and close and water running from a tap. I opened my eyes. "Tomás?"

"You are lovely, *meu amor.* A tender morsel, falling on the palate in plump juicy layers, a delightful whisper of apple blossom, delicate notes of honey. A standout finish."

"Really?" I giggled. A fine wine, a gourmet meal? I had never heard that before. I leaned on my elbows, gazing at him.

His face was damp, his hair curly at the ends from a quick wash. He was everything glorious, from his thick trapezius to his perfectly contoured pecs. And his ass, hard globes I wanted to dig my fingers into.

I dropped my gaze and let it linger. I wanted to slide my mouth along that hard column of steel.

He ripped open a condom, sliding it over the purple head and down the thick shaft.

"Tomás, you don't need that. I'm protected."

We talked—about safety. He was clean—I was clean.

"A precaution...I will keep you safe, *meu amor*." He returned, hovering on all fours over my naked body, the heavy bulb of his cock resting on my clit, an exquisite pressure.

More than anything, I wanted to feel his muscles quiver beneath my fingertips, but he had captured my hands, entwined his fingers with mine, and stymied my ability to touch him. I could move my hips, though, and with a greedy thrust, I took the head of his cock; my core tightening all around him, clutching the wide rim. It was good, but not good enough. "I want you, Tomás. I need to feel you."

A moan grumbled in his throat as he eased halfway into me, my pulsating sex drawing him inward.

I lifted my knees, digging my heels into the mattress, thrusting into him, taking him deeper. my inner muscles contracting, clutching the velvet-encased rod—a sigh of pleasure escaped my lips.

"You're too small. So fucking tight. I don't want to hurt you." His voice rumbled over me.

"More." The voice was not my own. Confusion crashed

down on me, my mind lost in layers of haze. I swallowed hot tears and clawed my way back.

"Gods." He withdrew halfway and then, with one long sweep, reached the end of me. He stilled, his hands resting on my hips, trembling.

"Again, Tomás. I need this. I need you." I urged him, bucking my hips. I writhed beneath him, greeting each thrust, each heavy slap of his testicles with ragged breath. I cried out, riding the edge of another orgasm.

But then he stopped. He gathered me into his arms and leaned against the upholstered headboard. With his legs stretched out long, his cock pressed like a hot poker between my thighs, leaving me empty inside.

"You need this." I whimpered into the pulse of his throat. I cupped his shoulders and repositioned, lowering my wet pussy onto his shaft.

"Tiegan…no. I don't want to hurt you. We should stop." His voice strained. His eyes squeezed shut, his cockhead throbbing inside me.

I threw my head back, rocking over him in slow circles. "Touch me, Tomás. I want you to feel me."

His eyes glazed over, his lips half parted. His hands plumped my breasts, kneading the heavy swells.

I leaned into his outstretched palms, my body lax, my arms loose. He filled me completely.

I rode him. With each pass, his cock reached the end of me. I clenched down, finding that mindless place, crying out with every tissue burst, every explosion. I sank into him, sated and replete.

He swept my hair away and kissed my forehead.

"Tomás…you haven't come." I lifted my face and held his sloe-eyed gaze.

"No…" His lips parted, his breath heavy.

"Why not?" I kissed the corner of his mouth.

"I promised I would never hurt you. I keep my promises."

"You're wearing a condom. I have an IUD. I don't understand." I swirled my tongue over his lower lip.

"I can't. I won't…"

The curse—the prophecy—this whole soulmate thing; he believed it. The immensity of our situation bore down on me. I realized then in one of those lightbulb moments. "Tomás, when was the last time you had sex with a woman?"

His eyes closed.

"Tomás?" I clenched my pussy muscles.

"Not since Sylvie."

For a moment, I couldn't breathe. Tomás had lived the last thirteen years of his life in fear—of this curse. My heart ached for him and for what he had lost. "Tomás, no. How could you? Why?"

"I've been waiting for you."

A sensation flowed through my being, a whisper echoing in my mind: he was mine, and I was his, and I couldn't—I wouldn't leave him like that. I lifted away from him and slid between his legs, slipping the condom away and fisting my hand around the base of his shaft.

"Tiegan…no. What are you doing?" He clawed at the sheets, his hips sinking into the mattress.

I ignored his attempted escape. "What does it look like?" I swirled my tongue around the velvety crown of his cock, tasting a salty bead of pre-cum. "You're going to come for me, Tomás. Remember the rule? Each one will be mine."

I wrapped my lips around the supple head, sliding my hand along the length of his shaft. His male scent filled my nostrils, enticing my pussy to clench. Working his shaft with one hand and cradling his testicles with the other—I drew on those round spheres—his ball sac tightening. Lapping the tip of his cock, I pumped him harder, faster. "Come for me, Tomás." My voice was a low rasp.

A guttural moan rose from somewhere deep inside his chest, and he peered at me, his eyes blazing with heat, his breathing labored. His cock jerked, filling my throat and mouth with an endless bounty of seed.

My hand drifted to my clitoris. I pinched the hard bead, taking myself over the edge with Tomás.

"Tiegan…"

"Tomás?" I looked up from my task, lazily licking my lips. I loved the taste of him, salty-sweet with a hint of garlic.

"You don't play fair, do you?" His lips curved into a crooked grin.

"No, never…want to do it again?"

"Yes. Every day."

"Is that a promise?"

He lifted me into his arms and carried me into the bathroom, submerging our bodies in a pool of warm, delicious water infused with essential oils, sweet lavender, and lemongrass. Candles burned, dripping rivers of wax onto driftwood slabs—soft music played. A sense of peace washed over me as I floated in his arms, limp and weightless. He caressed me with his hands and lips with close kisses, whispering soft words in Portuguese.

My eyes drifted shut to the echo of his heartbeat.

———

Confusion pressed down, and my thoughts scattered. I drifted away, lost in the shadowland.

The skies raged, the winds shrieked, and I knew it for what it was—the keening song of the banshee, a harbinger of death, and I was her prisoner, caught in the cries of her rhythmic chant. I could find no way out—there was no way out—I was on the other side, weighed down by a blanket of darkness. In a sliver of hallowed light, a woman wearing a blood-red gown of shimmering satin stared back at me, her eyes a kaleidoscope of color.

I woke, covered with a light cotton sheet, alone in Tomás's bed. The wall of windows dwarfed the bed opening to the terrace where Tomás and I sat earlier, where I shared my most intimate secrets. My heart fluttered as I played the conversation back in my mind. It was not like me to open up and bare my soul—to anyone.

My clothes were folded neatly on one corner of the bed—Tomás must have done that. The thought of him tending to my delicates made me smile.

I walked into the bathroom, shocked by my reflection in the mirror. Glazed eyes stared back at me. My skin flushed a rosy hue I was not used to seeing. My typical look—pale ghost, and my hair, lanky straggles of black, did nothing to contradict. Snooping through the drawers, I found a brush and tamed the tousled mess.

From somewhere inside the house, Tomás's voice droned low. In sock feet, with cat-like stealth, I glided across the marble floors, following the course of blood-like veining—a treasure map to Tomás. I found him sitting on a black leather couch, his arm slung over the back.

A stranger sat on the opposite matching couch.

Long, shaggy layers of sun-bleached hair hung to his shoulders, and a rough-edged goatee hid his chin. He wore a Hawaiian shirt, faded blue jeans, and white sneakers. His hands motioned every word he spoke, but when he saw me, they dropped to his sides, and his face paled. He rose from the couch, staring with the intensity of a man possessed.

Tomás reacted to the man's sudden change in position. Those beautiful chocolate eyes locked with mine, and I was again swimming into the abyss. He greeted me with a possessive display of affection, circling his arms around my waist and resting his lips on my forehead. He dipped his face, closing his lips over mine, his tongue teasing me. "How are you? How do you feel?"

"You shouldn't have let me sleep for so long, Tomás." How do I feel? My pussy throbbed, my thighs quivered, and I wanted him. My face heated, my mouth filling with cotton balls.

"Tiegan, I would like you to meet a friend of mine, Eli—Eli, this is Tiegan."

Eli extended his hand in greeting, and I offered mine in return. The flavor of the sea, a tidal current with undertones of coconut oil and beeswax, drifted from his being.

"It's an honor to meet you, Miss Tiegan." Eli's voice was soft, slumberous, with a slow Southern drawl. His eyes, a shade of golden amber, were wide open. He did not hide his curiosity, yet Tomás seemed oblivious.

"Eli is the new brewmaster at Bianca's."

"It's a pleasure, Eli. Congratulations." I wanted to know why Eli stared at me.

"I have a proposition for you as well."

"Oh? And what might that be?" I giggled, wondering what Tomás had in mind.

"I would like you to paint the artwork for the new Bianca's."

"You want to commission me to paint? For you?"

"Yes, I found your website. I've seen your work. I like what you do."

My maritime pieces: rugged shore, fishing boats, ocean, and big sky well known, at least back home.

"I don't do seascapes anymore." At least, I hadn't since Aaron died. I didn't finish the sentence.

"Whatever you decide, I know it will be perfect. The subject, I leave up to you."

I considered the possibilities—free artistic reign. It could be fun, or it could become a nightmare of nightmares.

"I will need ten large pieces before the eighteenth of December."

"I don't work cheap, Tomás. And a commission of that many pieces, in such a short time frame..." I'm not sure Tomás realized what he was asking.

"I'm not concerned with the cost. Can you do it?"

"Yes, of course."

"Good." He cupped my face and kissed my mouth, sealing the bargain.

"Eli, we'll meet again tomorrow to discuss the layout. It would also be a good idea for you to meet with the contractors."

"Yeah, man, I'm down." Eli dropped his chin, acknowledging me. "It's a pleasure to meet you, Miss Tiegan."

"Eli, I'll walk with you." Tomás placed his hand on Eli's shoulder, leaving me to stare after them.

They stood side-by-side in the driveway: Eli waving his hands in the air and Tomás nodding. Something was quite similar about the two of them besides their herculean size. After more than a moment, Eli climbed into his vehicle, a mud-splattered four-by-four tricked out with big knobby tires and wheeled out of the driveway.

―――

Tomás

"Jesus, man. You could have warned me." Eli came to a sudden stop in the cobbled path.

"What?" I shielded my eyes from the blazing sun, a smile lifting my lips.

"That chick...fuck me, man. Where did you find her?"

"Eli…Tiegan is not Sylvie." I ignored the accusation in his voice. I knew where this was going.

"You sure about that, man? You could have fooled me." He shoved his hair away from his face, his fingers twitching.

"Relax, bro."

"You don't see it? Those eyes? That face?" The space between his eyebrows narrowed, and he glared at me. "I don't like it, man. There's some bad mojo going on. I feel it." He threw a darting glance toward the villa. He paced back and forth.

"Eli, don't go off on me." I should have warned him—the likeness between Tiegan and Sylvie was uncanny. I knew what it did to me the first time I saw her.

"Those eyes—stare right through your fucking soul. Scary, man. Fucking scary. Where did you find her?"

"She found me. Walked into Casa Rosalia two weeks ago. Thirteen years to the day Sylvie passed." Knowing Tiegan waited inside my home filled my heart with happiness. I was struck by the obvious—the time waiting had not been wasted.

"No way in hell." He stared at me, his sun-kissed face turning crimson.

"Yeah, thought I saw a ghost," I recalled her face, similar to Sylvie's. My mouth dried at the memory of her taste on my lips.

"It's a bad sign, Tomás. I'm telling you." He paced back and forth.

"Eli…she's a nice girl. That's all." Clamping Eli's elbow, and in more than a hurry, I walked with him toward his truck.

"A nice girl? She's more than that, Tomás. Mark my words." Eli stared toward the villa, his face pale.

"I'll see you tomorrow, okay? Bright and early." I closed

the door firmly behind him and, without a backward glance, went searching for what I so desperately needed.

————

"Dearest Tiegan,
How are you, sweetheart?
Your father and I miss you, and we wish you were home, but don't worry about us, dear. We're doing just fine and hope you're having a fair time over there in Europe.

Sweetheart, I'm after some awful news to share. John Appleby, God rest his soul, passed away last week. Do you remember him? He was your grade two teacher back in elementary school? He drove that big black car, the one with the noisy muffler, to church every Sunday? Well, John was dating the widow-woman, Marjorie Jones. A wonderful woman. Let me tell you, the hours she puts in at the soup kitchen, she is a saint, God bless her. Well, the poor man, just last Thursday, he was just after supper, he stood on Marjorie Jones' doorstep, and Marjorie all dressed up right beautiful. They were on their way to the Ceilidh at the community center. Marjorie was good to sing, and she with the voice of an angel. Well, the poor man, his heart gave out, right there and then, and nothing could be done to save him. By gosh, though, the funeral was so well attended, and when the church choir sang "Amazing Grace" there wasn't a dry eye in the place. The ladies club put out a wonderful banquet with cold cuts and finger sandwiches, and your Aunt Joan made her famous butter tarts. Well, your father says there was not enough raisins in the butter tarts. Upon my word and honor. I told your father to button his lip. Never mind, Marjorie was pleased and that's all that matters. It was a lovely do. And you'll never guess. Well, John Appleby's nephew arrived from Toronto and what a wonderful young man he was. He stayed with Marjorie and was such a help to her. I'm sorry you weren't here to meet him. I told him all about you, dear. What a handsome young man, and a Bay Street lawyer to boot. Imagine that.

Oh, for pity's sake, Tiegan sweetheart, I have to go. Your father can't find the leftovers, and they're just there in the icebox, fair in front of his face. I will talk at you later.

Love,
Mom"

9

"Let each day be your masterpiece."—Unknown

Tiegan

Seven days had passed since I agreed to this exclusive arrangement. We had not spoken again of the curse, but it was omnipresent. It breathed a fire of its own making. I awaited each day with eager anticipation.

"Are you awake?" I rolled onto my side and stared into his beautiful face, studying his moist lips, and his eyes flickering with golden light. I loved watching him wake up. I loved the smell of him. I loved those happy to see you, sleepy eyes.

"Come closer, *meu amor*," his sleepy voice murmured.

The mere sound of him filled my core with heat: my breasts tightened and flames licked my thighs. I was in a constant state of arousal, and I wondered if something was wrong with me. It was more than good sex. It was an insatiable hunger I couldn't satisfy.

"Tomás, I have to start the paintings." Ten paintings for Bianca's grand opening, and I didn't even know what to paint. I was running out of time.

He tormented me with a teasing grin while sliding his forefinger knuckle deep into my sex, brushing the roof of my vagina with sweeping strokes.

"I need supplies: brushes, canvases, an easel." I ground into each stroke, my words breathless.

While his finger seduced me, he made love to my mouth, sucking my tongue, nibbling my lower lip—swirling deep within.

My pussy pulsated, sending a line of fire to every pleasure point. I doubled down, rubbing my clit into the hard bone of his forearm, the heel of his hand, crying out as the crescendo rose. "Tomás, I need you inside me."

In one motion, he lifted me off the mattress, impaling my pussy with his hard shaft.

My inner muscles contracted, sheathing him in wet heat, tightening all around him—I rested one hand on hard pecs and braced myself, rocking over him, enjoying the ride. My fingers drifted to my clit, providing just the right amount of pressure to that needy bundle of nerves. I was verging on the cusp of orgasm.

"No, not yet." Tomás rose from the bed, his hands clasping my bottom cheeks.

"Where are we going?" I clung to him, my legs wrapped around his waist, my hands tangled in those lustrous curls: licking, sucking, kissing, biting—tasting him. I couldn't get enough.

"You'll see. Be patient." With each stride, his cock slid deep. He walked barefoot through the sliding door into a black sky shot with gray, stopping at the edge of the terrace where the wild coastline began.

Hidden among the twisted branches of woody rock roses, birds twittered a welcoming song. Far below, the ocean thundered.

The next villa was a dark shape on the barren landscape.

Tomás eased out of my pussy and repositioned, leaving me standing in the cold, my back flush to his chest. "Spread your legs, *meu amor*. Hold the railing."

"What are we doing?" I giggled, curling my fingers over the metal bar. It was cold and wet, sending shivers down my elbows. I held on tight and widened my stance, bowing into him, aching for him. "Why are we here? It's cold out."

He stood a heartbeat away, his breath hot on my nape. His hands caressed my shoulders, his fingers brushing the taut nubs and heated swells. His whispers poured over me.

"You'll see." His hands pressed into my hips, a growl rising in his throat as the velvet head of his cock found entrance. He filled my pussy again and again.

"Hmm." I arch against him. The wind whispers, playing havoc with my senses. My body quivered. My blood hummed. Breathy moans rose and fell—my own.

"Look." Tomás cupped my breasts, tweaking the pebbled nubs between his fingertips.

I opened my eyes to a theater of color. Shafts of light burst through the veil of twilight, and the skies erupted— pure fiery orange hues of saffron. Aurora, the goddess of dawn, flew across a painted sky, announcing a new day. Clouds scattered, catching the first light and bathing in her golden glow.

"it's beautiful." I gazed into her face, into blades of mythic light—my spirit, so long buried, stirred with awakening. I breathed in the sweet, heady perfume, the earthy scents, the morning dew.

"You're beautiful, *meu amor*. You're everything I want. Everything I need." He kissed the corner of my mouth, the soft skin under my jaw, serenading my flesh, trailing his fingertips on either side of my swollen clit.

The stubble on his cheek set my senses on fire, stealing

away my last defense and throwing me over the edge. Heat rippled through me, so much heat.

———

Tomás

"Will you throw your hat in the ring, Tomás? Elections are just around the corner."

"No, Merko, I don't think so. Union duties keep me busy enough. And I have a lot on the go right now with the restaurants." I filled Merko's empty glass with water.

"Ah, but you are what we need, young man. You have what it takes to turn things upside down, to shake things up. It is what the Roma needs. A change in direction." The older man peered at me with a sharp glance, his eyes scanning the faces in the room.

"I'm not sure everyone would agree with you, Merko. Some support the old guard would vehemently oppose a change in leadership." I leaned back in the schoolhouse chair as the room emptied. Only a few remained.

"Tsh…old men stuck in old ways. And what do they know? We need a voice our young people will follow. I will nominate you when the time comes if you are not opposed." He leaned closer, his voice a graveled whisper.

"Let me think about it, Merko." I glanced at my watch.

"Good man. We will talk more about this, and I will speak quietly with the others. Now, off with you. I cannot help but notice the spring in your step and the glint in your eye. I am an old man, but I remember well what it was like to be a young man." A smile broadened his face. His eyes crinkled.

"Merko…you read too much into little things. I am meeting my sister and a friend. Yes." A smile played on my lips. I placed my hand on the older man's shoulder.

"Good. It is as I thought. You have been alone too long, Tomás. It is not wise for a man to be alone. Hurry on with you. Go! It is never good to keep a lady friend waiting. We will speak again soon."

———

iegan
T Lisbon, the city of seven hills, was a mix of medieval, modern, and bohemian. It was compact and hilly. It was also an open-air art gallery known for its street art, now welcomed by the city council, bringing life back to the inner city. Walls and sidewalks doubled as a canvas for street artists, showcasing their work to an admiring public. I wandered the labyrinth of narrow streets, rediscovering my passion for paint. The work was surreal and imaginative, and each one evoked an emotion, a fleeting pleasure—here today and then gone—replaced by another enthralling statement.

"Can I help you?" The man looked up from behind a pair of thick-glassed black spectacles.

"Do you deliver to Carvoeiro?" I unloaded my loot onto the counter: paints, brushes, palettes, knives, mineral spirits, beeswax.

"Every Wednesday." He smiled.

"Wonderful…I need ten gallery canvases, five feet by five feet, two seventy-two-inch basswood easels, and all of this."

———

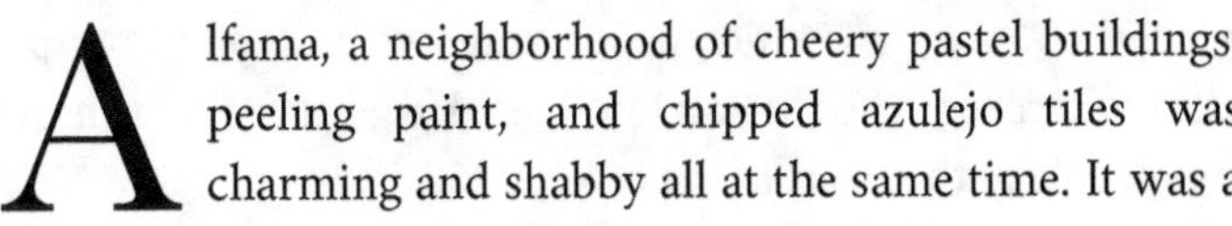

A lfama, a neighborhood of cheery pastel buildings, peeling paint, and chipped azulejo tiles was charming and shabby all at the same time. It was a blue-collar work of art, a part of town everyday folks called home—the telltale clue—the climbing trellis of laundry draping the wrought-iron balconies of every apartment. Cats slept in doorways. Birdcages hang from every nook.

I had found a cafe and stood in line waiting to buy a coffee and maybe a tart.

"Try the *bifana*." A soft lilt, an Irish cadence, enveloped me in warmth.

I shifted sideways and into the face of a man with an easy-going smile and brilliant blue eyes.

"I hope you don't mind. You were looking at the menu." He sported a swag of ginger curls—the unruly man-bun conflicting with the gray suit and the crisp white shirt.

"I thought I might get a tart."

"Na, for *pastel de natas*, you must go across the street. Worth the wait, I promise. Some would say they're to die for." His grin was infectious.

"Thanks for the tip." I followed his gaze to a shop: a bakery, with a line-up out the door. "What's a *bifana*?"

"To put it simply: pork in a bun. It's grand." The ginger-haired man studied me.

"Well, I guess I'll have to trust you." I was now at the front of the line.

"Two *bifanas* and two red ale, please." He spoke to the cashier, flashing her a brilliant smile.

I lifted my eyebrows and opened my mouth to say—something—but what could I say?

"Please allow me." He tilted his head, his eyes sparkling.

"Okay, thanks," I pressed my lips together and nodded.

"I'm Sam, by the way." He picked up the tray—two sandwiches wrapped in white paper and two red plastic cups filled with beer. "Would you join me?" He gestured to a shiny metal table at the front of the cafe.

"Okay, sure." I studied him. He seemed nice—a friendly smile, a kind voice.

"Where are you from? Your accent is almost Canadian." He glanced sideways, his gaze steady.

"Cape Breton, the Maritimes." I chuckled and sat in the molded plastic chair, leaving my bag at my feet.

"Well, Miss Cape Breton, welcome to Portugal." He unloaded the tray, handing me a wrapped sandwich.

"Thanks, Sam, but please call me Tiegan." I lifted the plastic cup and sniffed its contents.

"Hey, I know you. You rescued that kid. You're the spider." He laid his palms on the table, his eyebrows arching.

"Yes, that's me." I pursed my lips. My fame followed me everywhere. There was no escape.

"That was deadly—the way you scaled that wall. Why did you do it?" He studied me, wide-eyed wonder written all over his rugged features.

"I guess because I could." I shrugged, taking another swig of the beer—I had decided I liked beer. It was a refreshing choice, suiting the climate.

"Takes a special person to risk their life like that." Sam nodded his head, his voice suddenly serious. He tapped his red cup on mine. "To courage!"

"To courage." I pondered his salute—I didn't consider myself brave. I was afraid of most things—including spiders.

"What brings you to Portugal, Tiegan?" The chair legs scraped the floor when he shifted his weight.

"I'm visiting a friend. She lives here." I unwrapped the sandwich.

"In Lisboa?" He looked up.

"No, Carvoeiro." I nodded.

"A friend in the Algarve? Lucky, lass." Sam squirted a drizzle of mustard over the open face of his sandwich.

"Oh my God, this is amazing." I bit down on mine. Thin slices of pork melted in my mouth, and the sauce, a blend of garlic and chilies, dripped down my fingers.

Sam chuckled and handed me a napkin. "Do you have plans this afternoon, little spider? I could offer you a tour of this fine city—I know it well."

"I'm sorry. I appreciate the offer, but I'm meeting someone—soon. What are you doing in Lisbon, Sam?" I wiped my chin and dabbed the corners of my mouth.

"I'm here on business—tomorrow I'll be in Greece, then Turkey."

"What kind of business? I'm sorry, I'm being nosy."

"No, not at all. My family operates a scrap metal facility. We recycle and export to several international clients."

"I'm guessing you're from Ireland?" I dabbed my chin with a napkin.

"I am. Dublin-way, born and bred…four brothers, four sisters…two sets of twins."

"Wow, that's a big family. Must be amazing." I enjoyed the last sip of my drink.

"Yes, it's grand." His eyes shone.

"My Dad's from Ireland. He took me once when I was a little girl. I remember green hills and lots of sheep."

"Ah, it's the land of faeries, my emerald isle, and a thousand welcomes. If you visit again, you tell my people that Sam Dunne sent you." He gathered up his empty wrappers and rose from his seat. He extended his hand. "I wish you a peaceful farewell, Tiegan. In the language of my people—*An munia tober!*"

"Thanks for lunch, Sam. It was nice meeting you."

———

The screech of the yellow tram forced me flat against the nearest wall. The tram stopped, made a hairpin turn, and then rumbled on its way. I followed the track to the cobblestones of the next plaza. Before me stood the Se, with its famous rose window. Massive walls topped with crenellations flanked imposing bell towers. It was a dark place, this cathedral.

In the year 1383—Bishop Dom Martinho Annes, accused of plotting against the people, was thrown to his death from the north tower by an angry, hostile mob.

All Saints Day, 1755, the day of the great earthquake—hundreds died when the cathedral's ceiling collapsed on their heads.

As I walked through the center aisle of the nave, I heard the hushed echo of voices—whispers of the dead lingering in the shadowed alcoves, chapels, and tombs. I left, happy to leave this place.

Outside, the air was fresh and filled with sunshine. Pigeons cooed as they waddled among the tourists. Horns honked, brakes screeched, trams rattled—strains of Fada spilled from the open doorways of the many bars and restaurants.

Tomás's voice echoed in my mind: Meet me at the castle —be careful.

The Castelo de Sao Jorge was at the top of a winding, steep staircase. The great earthquake almost destroyed the castle and was resurrected to its former glory in the 1940s. Now, the battlements and watchtowers stood guard over the city of Lisbon.

I hurried through the crowd of jostling people and up the endless stairs.

"Lady, necklace for you—pearls from the sea." A young girl with a pretty face and long black hair shoved a string of iridescent beads before me.

"No, thanks." I smiled and stepped sideways. I had no intention of being waylaid.

"Handmade, lady, so pretty." She cajoled, her eyes flashing with guile. She shifted her thin frame, blocking my way.

"I'm sorry, but no." I side-stepped once more and hurried up the remaining steps.

The castle gate was open, and a line of people filed through the security check. Tomás had not yet arrived. I turned back around and studied the girl with the necklace. Her schtick was the same each time. She had little success, and I wondered why she had persisted. But then I saw a boy, not much older than little João, sidling up behind the next unsuspecting mark.

"Tiegan, there you are. I've been looking all over." Tomás snuck up from behind, wrapping his arms around my waist.

"Tomás, did you see that girl? The one selling the necklace?" I looked again. The boy and the girl were gone. "I think they stole a man's wallet."

"Oh, probably." Tomás was not perturbed.

"But, Tomás, what about the man? Should we try to find him? Shouldn't we do something?"

"What can we do, *meu amor*?" He scanned the sea of so many heads, his gaze returning to me. "They're gone?"

"I don't see them." I scanned the crowd, unable to find the dark-haired girl or the little boy.

"It's a petty crime, and the police won't get involved."

"But the boy, Tomás, he was so little."

"Tomás! Tiegan!" Anca arrived and, without hesitation, slipped her hand around my elbow, pulling me away from Tomás and to her side.

She was a feminine version of Tomás—dark eyes with the same golden flickers, fringed with the same long lashes, but her hair was the color of fire, cropped short, accentuating fine features, and a delicate nose. She was not tall—she was vertically challenged, like me.

"Tomás, you have so lucked out!" Her eyes twinkled, and her laughter filled the air. "Tiegan, please promise me you will put up with my brother. I'm warning you, he can be such a bore. You'll come to Lisboa every time Tomás has one of his stupid meetings, okay? We're going to have such fun together."

Anca led me through the gateway, past the statue of the renowned King Alfonso I, and into the courtyard of the dilapidated Royal Palace. Shaded by cork oaks, chestnuts, and umbrella pines, little remained except for the few curved walls of the ancient Romantic Garden.

Beneath the gnarled branches of an umbrella pine, a woman cloaked in indigo velvet sat on a bench, reaching her hand in and out of a brown paper bag. She scattered a handful of scratch onto the dirt for the famous Castelo de Sao Jorge peacocks.

I wanted to see the flamboyant birds. As I neared, the woman lifted her grayed head. Eyes like black coal met mine. Her lips curled up, revealing rotted protrusions that were once teeth. Her fingers reached out to touch mine but didn't quite connect. I stared, unblinking, into a realm of darkness.

"Tiegan?" Tomás clasped my shoulder. "Where are you going?"

"I hate these fucking birds. Can we go?" Anca turned to leave.

What did I see? Did I imagine the whole thing? My thoughts spun, and my mouth dried. I reached for my medallion and held the coin tight between my fingers. The medallion burned hot against my skin.

"Anca, tell Tiegan who the castle's named after." Tomás nudged my elbow, his grin reaching his eyes.

"Saint George, the patron saint of England... The man is a

hero, Tiegan. He saved a virgin girl from a fire-breathing dragon." Her words hung in the air, and then she laughed.

"Really?" My eyes widened.

"Absolutely…can you believe it? Why can't I meet a guy like that? Right? Can we speed up this castle thing? I'm starving." She reached into her blouse to adjust her bra strap.

Tomás lifted his eyes to the heavens and smirked.

10

*"I know I'm a handful but that's
why you got two hands."*—Unknown

Tiegan
I had reorganized the entire rack of boho skirts, facing all the hangers in the same direction. I picked one—a sparkly red number with intricate black embroidery and a fishtail hem. I flounced in front of the mirror. "Vera, I love him."

"Tiegan, come on—that's not even possible. You've known him for how long? Three weeks?"

"Hey, I know what I like." I put the skirt back on the rack.

"Look. Why can't you just enjoy him? Sleep with him, fuck his brains out."

I thought about that for a moment: a fuck-buddy. I admired another skirt—one with layers of raw, white silk. I liked the red one better.

Vera sighed and walked toward a vibrant display of color on the far wall of the shop. She handed me a silky black tank and the red skirt.

I grinned and slipped behind an emerald curtain draping the floor.

Was I making a bad life choice? I got where Vera was coming from—and only a genuine friend would tell you when you've got salad stuck in your teeth.

"Steve's in town tomorrow. Want to do dinner at Fiori's?"

"Sure, can I bring Tomás?" I sashayed across the shop floor, twirling the hem of my new red skirt.

"Tiegan, you look like a Gypsy princess."

"Okay, I'm sold." I retreated to the changing room, slipping out of the silky tank and bejeweled skirt.

"What are you doing today?"

"Tomás said something about a castle."

"Hmm, in Silves? Sounds like fun. There's a great burger place there. You should check it out."

"Yep." I tapped my credit card on the machine while Vera created magic with tissue paper and curly ribbon. At the same time, the door opened, and two gray-haired ladies entered the shop.

"Stay out of trouble, eh?" Vera handed me the tote.

"Yeah, yeah. You're no fun. No fun at all." I lifted my eyebrows and grinned.

Vera turned her attention toward the browsing customers.

The door closed behind me, chasing me out of the shop. I was running out of time. I needed to drop off my latest purchase and change my clothes. Tomás was picking me up in less than half an hour. Tomás said something about horse-back riding—this was what I thought while waiting for the traffic to pass. I stepped off the curb and onto the road.

Like a rocket, I was catapulted sideways, cradled within the grip of two big, brawny arms. The hurtling force of the man's body knocked the wind from my chest, but I was unhurt. He had absorbed the brunt of the cobblestone sidewalk. The messenger of my intended death—a whoosh of wind and a flash of black metal left the scent of burning exhaust in its wake. Those same arms lifted me off the sidewalk and onto my feet.

"Miss Tiegan?" A soft drawl engulfed my senses.

My knees wobbled as I rocked back on my heels and stared into the warmth of Eli's amber eyes.

"Eli?" My heart fluttered, but I told myself not to panic. I allowed my gaze to wander. Before Eli could answer, mayhem arrived.

"Tiegan! Oh, my God!" Vera shrieked as she exited her shop and hovered in front of my face. "That car drove right for you. Are you okay?"

"I'm fine." My voice shook. Vera waited for some sort of explanation, but I didn't know what to say, so I blurted out the only thing that popped into my mind. "Vera, this is Eli."

A mantle of fog quieted my mind, slowing my thoughts. Tomás was calling me, sprinting across the square, almost upon us.

Eli handed me over—a silver box with a bow on top.

Tomás pulled me into his arms, whispering kisses into my hair. I thought I would cry.

"I didn't see the car." I leaned into him, mumbling into his collarbone. "Eli, that car could have killed Eli."

"Don't worry about me, Miss Tiegan."

"Eli, thank you." I found the wherewithal to voice my appreciation to Eli for his heroic actions.

Tomás tightened his grip, half-lifting, half-carrying me away from Eli and Vera to a narrow alley behind Bianca's where the white SUV waited.

"Where are we going?" His need to steal me away confused me.

"Your apartment?" He braced his hand on my shoulder.

"Okay." I turned my head as we exited the alley. Vera and

Eli were engaged in vivid conversation: Vera's hands were on her hips, and Eli's finger painted the wind.

Within moments, we arrived at Vila Algarve. Tomás threw the SUV into park, but before I could even shift in my seat, the passenger door swung open. He lifted me into his arms and carried me up the winding steps. When we reached the landing, his gaze searched mine.

"Under the clay pot—the key's there." I shared the only secret I had left.

He unlocked the bolt, and then we were inside.

"If I were to lose you…I don't know what I would do." He swept his hands through my hair, resting his forehead on mine.

"I'm okay, Tomás. I'm fine."

"I'm sorry, *meu amor*, I'm so sorry."

"For what? I didn't see the car. I didn't see Eli. Where did he come from?"

"Are you sure you're okay?" He pulled me into the wall of his chest.

"It had to be nothing. A drug deal gone bad, maybe?" I rested my face beneath his chin.

"Perhaps."

"Well, what else could it be? Who else would drive that fast?" I gazed into his worried face. "Should we call the police? File a report or something? Eli or Vera could describe the car."

"I will have Eli report the incident. He was directly involved." His voice, that low rumble, calmed me.

"Okay."

"Tiegan." He dipped his face, catching my lips between his. His scent was intoxicating.

I melded into him, driving my hips into his swelling erection, my need unfathomable. Clasping his hands, I dragged him through the strand of dangling beads, all the while loosening the button on his fly and yanking the zipper. His cock sprung free, ramrod stiff. I shoved him onto the bed and straddled his hips.

"Tiegan, wait." He reached for me, his hands trailing through my hair.

I closed my mouth over his, ending the conversation. My skirt hugged my waist, but I didn't care—I wanted him, needed him. With a hiss and a slight shift of satin and lace, I lowered onto his cock, my pussy clutching the wide knob, and for a moment I hovered, savoring the pulsing sensations. My sex trembled as I slid down the hard mast, riding him—hard and fast. With each downward thrust, a moan slipped from my lips. The way the head of his cock caressed the roof of my vagina…

I came apart, rocked by an explosive surge of quivers. Relishing the last wave, I swayed back and forth, my fingers and my thumbs branding his pecs, my hair falling into his face.

"You know, it's bad luck to be superstitious." I traced his tongue, licked his teeth, and flicked his mouth's roof. I kissed him the way he liked to kiss me.

He answered me with a crooked, pained smile.

"Come for me, Tomás." I clenched down, rocking over him, unwilling to admit defeat.

"No. Stop," he groaned, his voice a husky murmur.

His ball sack lay heavy between his legs. My hand drifted, tormenting him, drawing slow, lazy circles. Those globes tightened to my touch, but still, he was unswayed. The curse haunted him—the one that would be the death of me.

I lifted myself and straddled his knees, running the tip of my tongue down his length. I licked his testicles, suckling each round sphere, all the while pumping and twerking the root of him.

A shudder trembled through his body, and his shaft

jerked, spurting hot seed over his belly. His gaze leveled with mine, brimming with dark lust and something else—an emotion I couldn't put into words.

I whispered his name and climbed over his beautiful body, our mouths colliding as we searched for something we needed.

I struggled with a storm of thoughts. That age-old question—what was love? Was it a simple mathematical equation? Free energy combined with a chemical reaction? A spontaneous attraction—a big bang?

I accepted that whatever we had was unlike anything I had experienced before. If it was love, it was a love of mythic proportion laced with prophecy and a curse—a not-so-little curse leading to my ultimate demise, the stuff nightmares were made of.

———

"*Boa noite, Senhorita.* Welcome to Fiori's. My name is Antonio, and I will be your server this evening. Can I offer you a beverage to start?"

Antonio, a slight man in a black suit, introduced himself. The only thing distracting from his distinguished face and slicked-back, thinning dark hair was perhaps the sparkle of his leather shoes.

"Just water for now, please. I'm waiting for a friend."

"Of course, *Senhorita,*" Antonio replied in an attentive voice.

While I waited for Vera and her fiancé, Steve, I admired the restaurant's unique decor. I was in a cavern where sculpted stone statues depicted the life of ancient Rome. If I could pinpoint my location, I would be in the villa of Sperlonga on the Italian seashore, a guest to the great emperor Tiberius, in the company of Apollo and the vanquished race of orb-eyed Cyclops. The grotto overlooked an open kitchen where the Chef tossed pizza dough high into the air. I inhaled the tang of roasted garlic, oil, and hot cheese. What more needed to be said?

At seven p.m., Vera entered the foyer. She was the image of a love story dressed in a floral blouse of ruched silk, popping with pink roses, cropped jeans, and black canvas sneakers. The hostess led Vera through the archway and into the cavern.

"Hey, nice skirt." Vera slid into the chair next to mine.

"Yeah, I know this great little shop." I giggled, pleased with the ensemble: the black tank hugged all the right places, complementing the flashy skirt. I spent too much time with the bathroom mirror—hair up—hair down. I chose up and heavy gold hoop earrings.

"So, where's Tomás?" She looked up.

"Held up…might get here for dessert, though." I lifted my shoulders, unable to hide my disappointment.

"Hi, Antonio. We're waiting for one more. I'm expecting him any moment." Vera glanced at her phone.

"Of course. Perhaps a cocktail to start?" Antonio dipped his head.

"The house chardonnay for me." Vera smiled.

"And for you, *Senhorita*?" Antonio tilted his face in my direction.

"I'll have the sangria, please." I had dreamed of sangria since I booked my airline ticket—fruity and spicy and so very Mediterranean.

"Would you like the red or the white?" Antonio said.

"The red is nice, Tieg. You know what, Antonio? I've changed my mind. I'll have sangria as well. Want to share a pitcher?" Her gaze returned to me.

"Absolutely." I nodded.

Antonio left us.

Vera's gaze drifted around the room. Her smile had vanished.

"Hey? Are you all right?" I asked because I knew my friend. She was the person with a bright, sunny smile.

Vera's phone chirped, and she made a frustrated noise.

Antonio arrived with a crystal jug of blood-red sangria, blueberries, and citrus slices floating on top. He poured the sangria into two fishbowl-size glasses.

"Wow. Thank you." My taste buds popped in keening anticipation.

With a nod, Antonio left the pitcher in the middle of the table.

"That was Steve. He won't be here. He's in Lisbon another few days."

"Oh, that's too bad. How come?"

"He's a busy guy. What can I say?" Vera tapped the table-top, the designed mosaic of blue and white tiles, her voice clipped.

"Okay, what's going on?" Questions danced on the tip of my tongue, but before I could voice them, the deep rumble of Tomás's voice reverberated off the domed ceiling, and he was not alone—Eli followed a close second.

I bounced from my seat, meeting Tomás halfway down the aisle. He looked terrific: dark jeans and a white button-down shirt.

He caught me in his arms, lifted me off my feet, and kissed me on the forehead.

"You made it. I'm so glad." I closed my eyes, breathing in the fragrant aroma of sawdust and wood chips. The renovation at Bianca's was still in the reconstruction stage. I loved how he was not embarrassed to show affection.

"Have we missed dinner?" His voice, a heavy bass, invited a taste.

"No, we just ordered drinks." I couldn't look away. My mouth watered—for him.

"And what kind of trouble have you been getting into?" He held me inches away, his gaze undressing me.

"I've been a perfectly good girl." I batted my eyes and pouted my lips. Lifting my hand, I removed a sliver of pine from his hair.

"You look beautiful, *meu amor*. Is this new?" He lifted my hand into the air, spinning me in a half-circle.

"Thank you, kind sir." I pecked his cheek with a quick kiss.

Resting his hand on the small of my back, he led me toward the table.

"Hello, again." Eli slid into the chair next to Vera.

I was surprised when Vera blushed.

"It seems I wasn't on the list." Eli chuckled, tilting his head. "Do you mind if I join?"

"The more, the merrier. Right, Tieg?" Vera nodded, cascades of blonde hair swirling over her shoulder.

"Yes, of course."

"Ladies, you are both looking especially lovely this evening," Eli's soft drawl was enchanting. A shock of golden hair fell across his forehead.

"Hi, Eli."

"Miss Tiegan, how are you feeling?" I knew he was referring to my recent dash with death.

"I'm fine, thanks to you."

Tomás placed his hand over mine, and my heart skipped a beat.

"Vera, you were right. The sangria's amazing." My gaze drifted between Vera and Eli.

"Do you like sangria, Tiegan?" Tomás tilted his chin.

"Yes, it's good, not too sweet. Try some." I offered the fishbowl glass to Tomás.

"Hmm, perhaps we should have this on tap. Eli, what do you think?"

"This color suits you." Eli plucked the baby pink rose budding on the curve of Vera's shoulder.

The velvety murmur of Eli's voice confirmed my suspicions as their conversation continued in hushed tones.

I shifted in my chair, giving Tomás my full attention.

"What are you going to order?" I already knew what I wanted, but it wasn't on the menu.

"How about a pizza? We can share."

"Okay, but lots of cheese, okay? And no anchovies."

"Welcome, everyone, to Fiori's. My name is Antonio, and I will be your server this evening. Chef Giorgio has added several delicacies to our menu for this evening's selection."

I listened while Antonio described the ingredients and spices used to create four mouth-watering entrees, astounded at the ease and enthusiasm with which he could reiterate the qualities of each dish.

"Can I offer the wine list this evening?" Antonio concluded his eloquent speech.

Antonio waited with his hands clasped while Vera and Eli, their heads bent together, studied the wines.

"If you're looking for an elegant white, the Mirabilis Grande Reserva Branco 2017 pairs well with our Pistachio Kale and Zucchini Tagliatelle and truly brings out the pistachio." Antonio finished with a slight bow of his dark head.

"A bottle for the table, Antonio. And a red, the Barca Vella Douro, 1999, will do." Tomás lifted his eyebrows.

"A good choice." Antonio nodded.

"We will start with a Calzone pizza and a Caprese salad," Tomás looked at me.

Antonio looked at Vera, who was now engrossed in a conversation with Eli. They discussed the concentration levels of heartworm disease affecting dogs in the Mississippi

River Delta's mosquito-infested bayous in southern Louisiana—a strain of said worms proving resistant to the medication currently available to pet owners.

"Vera!" I nudged her elbow.

"Oh, sorry. I'll have the White Truffle Gnocchi Verde, please." Her face turned pink.

"And for you, *se Senhor?*" Antonio's chin shifted toward Eli.

"I'll go with your recommendation, the Pistachio Kale Pesto with Zucchini Tagliatelle."

Antonio nodded his head.

"Would you like to share an appetizer?" Eli asked Vera. "The Bruschetta sounds amazing."

"How's the renovation coming?" I asked Tomás. The immensity of the Bianca project had swallowed him up, but I was doing my part. I'd put my creative flair to work, developing a new online presence with a new logo for Bianca's Brew Pub.

"Very well. The interior finishes are almost complete. The menu boards and tables should arrive next week." He held my hand.

"The canopies look great, Tomás." Vera nodded, her smile touching her eyes.

"Thanks. That was Tiegan's idea, the sandbox and the blackboard for the kids." He drew his thumb over my knuckles.

Antonio returned, pouring a tasting of red wine for Tomás and white wine for Vera. I leaned back in my chair, listening to voices chatter in the background as Antonio filled our wine glasses.

We were interrupted by the appearance of a stranger. I looked twice—Sam Dunne, the ginger-haired man who bought me lunch in Alfama. Today, he was someone else. He wore an army-green tank, cargo pants, and black boots.

Black ink: intricate symbols and Celtic knots sleeved two brawny arms, flowing artfully onto his chest.

"Sam. How are you?" I grinned, looking sideways at Tomás.

His posture had shifted. His jaw was tight, and his fingers flexed against the table's edge.

"Ms. Cape Breton, you're looking well." Sam's smile did not reach his eyes.

I realized then that something was wrong. This was not the friendly traveler I remembered.

"Dunne. Why are you here?" Tomás rose from his seat, reminding me how imposing he could be. He leaned forward with both hands flat on the white tablecloth.

"I heard a rumor. I see it's true." The soft Irish lilt I remembered so fondly was gone. Sam's tone was a bare-knuckle punch to the gut.

"A rumor?" Tomás murmured.

"Hmm, yes. The great Tomás Ferreira has found the woman he waits for, who will make him whole. I wasn't expecting the little spider." He slid his gaze back to me, lifting the corners of his mouth into a smile. "Those eyes: so beautiful, so hypnotic—I felt it myself the other day. A friend in Carvoeiro—"

I gaped at Sam. I didn't know what to think—I didn't know what to say. I sucked in a long breath and cringed as Sam extended his hand toward me.

Eli slammed his hand down, shaking the crystal and spilling the wine.

"Now, boys, no need to lose your shite. It was not my intention to spoil such a fine evening." Sam stepped just far enough away. He shrugged, lifting his hands into the air.

"Is there something you want, Dunne?" Tomás's voice lowered to a snarl.

Sam chuckled, low in his throat—a muscle feathering in his jaw.

"Such a pretty girl and a nice one, too—a lot of bad things can happen to nice girls, but you know all about that, don't you, Ferreira?" He shifted his gaze toward me and curled his lips into a smile. "Stay safe, little spider. Take care you don't get stepped on."

A shroud of silence descended over the table, and I stared, open-mouthed, as Tomás reached out and wrapped his right hand tight around Sam's throat, lifting him off his feet high enough that the toes of his leather boots skimmed the marble floor. Sam's eyes bulged, and his lips lifted, but no words came out, only the rasping sound of strangulation.

"Is that a threat, Dunne?" Tomás dug his fingers into the blood vessels on either side of Sam's windpipe.

I wondered how long it would be before he lost consciousness. I had witnessed hatred before, but this was different—this hatred had a flavor, a taste all its own. It burned my throat and stung my eyes.

Tomás loosened his fingers, releasing Sam.

Sam inhaled a gasping breath and staggered once. He said nothing—but he smiled and nodded—at me. Then he walked away, leaving the cavern without a backward glance.

"Well, that was exciting," Vera murmured.

"What? What was that?" I stared at Tomás, my heart pounding in my chest. I expected to see an enraged man.

"Some people don't much like me, as hard as that might be to believe. I'm afraid Dunne is one of them." Tomás shrugged.

"I met Sam in Lisbon. We had lunch together." I bit my lower lip and studied him.

"Don't worry, *meu amor*. I will keep you safe from the likes of Sam Dunne, I promise." He lifted my hand and kissed my fingertips.

Under the shadow of moonlight, I lay naked on Tomás's bed. The sliding doors were wide open, and the night air flowed into the bedroom with a deliberate force. Closing my eyes, I listened to the roar of crashing surf while wisp-like fronds ghosted my bare flesh with winter's icy touch. My nipples peaked. My skin burned hot.

"Jesus, why is the door open? Aren't you cold?" Tomás was damp from his shower, steam particles floating around him in a heavenly aura. He crossed the bedroom, standing just beyond my outstretched fingers.

"Tomás, come to bed." I swept my tongue across my lower lip, yearning for him. I reached out, clawing the distance between us with stretched fingers, but I was too late.

"Yeah…be right there, almost done. Did you floss your teeth?" Tomás closed the heavy slider, stilling the ocean's song.

"Are you going to tell me what happened tonight with Sam?"

"There's nothing to tell."

"You assaulted him in the restaurant?"

"He got what he deserved."

"What was he talking about?"

"It was nothing, I promise."

"It was not nothing, Tomás. Why are you avoiding this conversation?"

"Why? Because I have a beautiful woman lying naked on my bed. Why would I want to talk about Dunne?"

"Am I just a beautiful woman, Tomás?" I shifted onto my side and studied his profile, the chiseled lines of his face, the stacked muscles, and his resting cock.

"Hmm? We have history, that's all."

"You and Sam? What kind of history?" I listened to the splash of water in the sink and the buzz of his electric toothbrush. I listened to Tomás spit.

"What would you like for breakfast tomorrow? How about pancakes? I have blueberries."

"Okay." I turned onto my stomach, flexing my inner thighs, curling my toes, basking in the feeling of sensual nakedness. "Why did Sam say those things? Why did he say I should be careful?"

"To get under my skin because he's an *encrenquero*—a troublemaker."

"Not an explanation." I closed my eyes, savoring the sound of Tomás, his breath, how his body moved, his heavy step.

"Okay…fine. He's a Traveler: an Irish, of a different origin than the Roma, although the lifestyle is the same. Sam is the son of Brady Dunne, who proclaimed himself to be the King of the Gypsies. That gives him the right to interfere with Roma business—with my business." He showed no sign of emotion—good or bad. In three strides, he reached the end of the bed.

"I still don't get it. What made you so angry?" I bent my elbows and wrapped both hands around his swelling arousal, taking the bulbous head between my lips. Forgetting my question, forgetting Sam Dunne, I swirled my tongue around the velvet tip, grazing the delicate ridge and lapping the sensitive frenulum.

"Fuck, do you know what you do to me?" Tomás flinched and played with my hair. "You're going to make me come."

I made an unrecognizable sound, filling my mouth with half his length. I flattened my tongue and hollowed my cheeks, sliding my lips over his shaft, again and again. Squeezing the globes of his ass, I took his full length into my wet mouth, his scent, his taste, heightening my desire. Heat flared between my thighs, my pussy flooding with moist arousal.

He groaned a low exhale, closing his hands on either side of my head, tilting my face, aligning my throat with his shaft, driving his cock past my tonsils—one, two, three driving thrusts and his cock jerked, releasing pearls of hot seed.

I wrapped my lips tight around his girth and swallowed every last drop—an appetizer, a tasty treat. All I could think was how achy and needy my entire being was.

"Tiegan, let me look after you." He ran his fingertips over my shoulders, caressing the nape of my scalp. "Roll over, *meu amor*, onto your back." He lifted me, shifting my limp body and joining me on the bed. With his knees bent and his shaft tight against his belly, he drizzled oils, releasing the intoxicating scent of lavender and rosemary over my breasts and down to my navel. With smooth, heated strokes, he kneaded my flesh, skimming each swell, circling furled nubs, teasing my sex with trailing fingertips, slipping in and out of my heated channel. A slow dance, one I had become accustomed to.

———

"Dearest Tiegan,

How are you, sweetheart?

Your father and I are keeping well and busy with our doings. What with the Friday soup kitchen, the festivals going on, and the kettle starting up next week, sets my mind amuck just to think on it.

I have to tell you, Tiegan. I was after watching my stories on the telly, and if your father doesn't barge right in set to steal the clicker. Well, if that wasn't enough to put a bee in my bonnet, there he was right bowled over with the gas. If I've told him once I've told him a thousand times he can't have ice cream after eating fish. Lord love a duck. It's a darn good thing he's got gold in his heart. Well, enough said on that.

Well, I must be off. Finn's barking like all get out. Must be someone in the dooryard. Be good, and I will mail you later.

Love, Mom

PS. Your father wanted me to tell you not to be running around barefoot on those cliffs or you'll get worms."

11

____

"We were given:
Two hands to hold. Two legs to walk.
Two eyes to see. Two ears to listen.
But why only one heart? Because the
other was given to someone else.
For us to find."—Unknown

T*iegan*

—Hey, where are you?—

I gazed at the message from Tomás, a smile lifting my lips. I threw my paintbrushes into the sink and wiped my hands on my sweats.

—Painting. Why? Do you miss me?—

Tapping my response, I walked into the sunshine and peered across the stretching sea. Seagulls flocked to the edge of the cliff, and I wondered why.

—Do you miss me?—

He answered my question with a question. I giggled to myself and returned to the dim light of the studio, pulling the door shut behind me.

—Come find out.—

—I can't.—

I stretched out on the only piece of furniture, a worn sofa covered with the blue fleece blanket.

—Tiegan?—

—Tomás?—

I wiggled out of the sweatpants and threw my leg over the back of the sofa.

—What are you doing?—

—Touching myself.—

I played with my outer lips, drawing my fingers back and forth, enticing my flesh.

—No.—

—Yes, so wet…come see.—

Pressing my teeth into my lower lip, I rubbed the hooded bead from side to side.

—I can't.—

My breath raged—my arousal rising.

—Tiegan? What are you doing?—

With one finger on the button of my phone's camera, I stretched my labia wide open and clicked send.

—Jesus…do you know what you're doing to me?—

—Show me.—

Clasping my pussy, I closed my eyes and imagined Tomás.

———

*T*omás

I found Eli in the back alley behind Bianca's, lying flat on his back underneath his four-by-four, his legs hanging over the end of a creeper, his knees bent, his feet planted in the dirt. The surfboards strapped to the roof, a telltale sign of his destination.

"Eli? I need a favor." I crossed my arms and waited for a reply.

"Hand me that wrench, will you?" His voice was muffled.

"I won't get there till late. Can you keep an eye out?" I crouched down, twisting my arm under the vehicle.

"Surf's up, man. You don't know what you're missing, but I'm on it."

"Are you sure you can do it? I don't want to impose on your fun." I inspected the brand-new roof racks glinting in the sun—an improvement I helped Eli install—and gave the tie-downs a hard pull.

"Got you covered, man. Tiegan will be fine." He rolled out from underneath, his hands smeared with grease.

"Not with Dunne in town. I don't like it." My blood boiled at the thought of it.

"You think it was him?" He leaned over the hood, reaching into the engine bay. A quick twist removed the cap and dirty filter.

"Who else? Jesus, I don't know." I exhaled sharply, my mind racing through one hypothetical catastrophe after another.

"It's not his style, man. He's all mouth." Eli stuck his index finger into the fresh jug of oil and seated the O-ring.

"Maybe." I handed him the new filter.

"Look, I've been tailing her for days. It was shit bad luck, that's all it was." He spun the filter to the bottom, hand tightening the last quarter turn.

"I can't take that chance. If something else happens. Fuck, I don't know what to think." I pictured Dunne's cunning eyes bulging out of his face. I could have ended it there.

Grunting, Eli lowered himself onto the creeper, slid between the wheels, and torqued the drain plug.

"Ready?" I shifted sideways and unscrewed the filler cap.

"Yeah, fill it up." He called out.

"Thanks, man. I owe you a solid." I reached for the funnel and poured the jug, filling the engine with fresh oil.

"Hey, you smell that?" Eli rolled out, dragging the dirty oil pan with him.

"Gas." Scrunching my nose, I inhaled the somewhat floral scent.

"Yeah, you were right. The pistons are leaking."

———

*T*iegan

The hike down the jagged cliff was worth the reward: an expanse of wide beach, rock formations, undercuts, and horizontal breaks known as furnas caused by erosion and the elements of time.

Vera and I spent the day there, hidden away in a quiet corner of the Algarve—bouldering. Convincing Vera to goof off for the day—like pushing a three-story house up a hill. But when I reminded her, she promised to take me rock climbing in the Algarve. How could she say no?

We traversed horizontally from one end of the *furnas* to the other: no ropes or harnesses required, just a bag of chalk clipped to a loop on our shorts and a pair of climbing shoes. It was an easy fall into pillows of sand when we failed or simply gave up. When we needed to cool off, we laid flat on our backs on the hard sand at the ocean's edge, squealing like giddy schoolgirls with each bone-chilling wave, and when the backwash sucked the sand beneath us away, we waited for the next surge and shrieked all over again. Vera packed lunch—we feasted on potato chips and cheese puffs, bricks of sponge toffee, sesame snaps, chocolate kisses, and cream soda.

Beyond the rolling dunes lies a peninsula, a scrubland of eucalyptus wood, a headland, a rocky spur, a point break, where the land juts out to sea. It was there that the ocean swells were of avalanche size. Mega waves—a king tide—caused by the moon's gravitational force and the sun coming together. And the surfers were out in full force, riding the waves in full-body neoprene wetsuits.

"Hurry, Tieg. We're going to be late."

"We won't be late. You can't be late for a bonfire."

"I don't want to miss the moon."

"We won't miss the moon."

I sighed, but was happy to hurry. This was an "Anca" event—a bonfire on the beach and a celebration to witness the November full moon's rise, a rare Supermoon. Tomás would be there. Anca and Vera's friend, Paulo, would be there.

We slogged through shifting valleys of sand and tufts of marram grass. Blowing winds whipped up the sea, tossing salt spray and beach sand sideways.

We hid under floppy-brimmed sun hats, shielding our eyes from the biting gusts as tendrils of wood smoke welcomed us to the party.

We were not the first to arrive. People mingled. Some scoured the shoreline, gathering driftwood for the bonfire. Others pitched tents in the backlands, a safe distance from the surging tides.

Paulo greeted us with a wave of his arm. Paulo wore a black suit and a skinny leather tie at the taverna. Tonight he wore a faded sweatshirt and board shorts with sandals on his feet.

"Paulo." Vera reached for his arm, sending him a smile.

"Ah, Vera, it is so very good to see you." Paulo kissed Vera's cheeks.

"Hi, Paulo." I smiled and waved.

"Where did you come from?" Paulo looked over Vera's

shoulder to the far side of the limestone cliffs. "Did you come from the sea?"

"Yes, Paulo, we are mermaids from the deep." Vera lifted her arms over her head, swaying her hips in a circular motion.

"And I hear your siren song, beautiful Vera." Paulo chuckled, extending his arm outward to the sea.

I had to laugh; Vera and I were covered in sweat and sand, sticky with ocean salt, not the beautiful sea creatures one would like to imagine.

"I hope you're hungry, meus amigos. Anca has prepared a feast. Espetada and papas, enough for everyone." Paulo flipped the lid of a cooler open, displaying trays of skewered swordfish interspersed with wedges of lime and red peppers.

Already simmering on the fire was a massive cauldron bubbling with the sweet aroma of cornmeal porridge.

"Wow, Paulo, that looks amazing. Did Anca make that?" My stomach growled.

"Ah, yes, our Anca is muito talentosa. You must be very thirsty. We have many beer." Paulo dug into another cooler and handed out two tallboys, one for me and one for Vera.

"Thanks." I popped the tab, guzzling the cold lager—it went down far too quickly. Around the blazing bonfire, I saw faces. Some I recognized from the dance club in Lisboa. "Where is she?"

"Anca is in the sea." I followed Paulo's gaze and spotted Anca, her copper hair a beacon in the setting sun, paddling a surfboard into the rolling crest. I watched, mesmerized, as Anca popped up and onto her board, made a hard turn into the face of the wave, and then skimmed across the vertical wall of water. I held my breath as the lip of the wave feathered over the top of Anca's head. It seemed like the ride would never end, but then Anca and her board pitched out of the eye and into the foaming whitewater.

"Miss Tiegan."

"Eli. I didn't know you'd be here." I turned at the sound of a familiar voice, taking in the full-body wet suit, amber eyes, and wavy golden hair.

"Epic waves, a bonfire, a full moon…"

"I didn't know you were a surfer."

"Do you surf, Miss Tiegan?"

"No, but it looks like fun. Those are some scary-looking waves, though." I gazed into the crashing wake.

"Yeah, they're totally going off."

"Tiegan." Anca arrived onshore, her board under one arm. She welcomed me with a wet hug.

"Yo, Eli! You were shredding it up out there." Anca met Eli's palm with a high-five.

"Hey, you too. Those were some definite badass curls." Eli's grin set the world on fire.

"Anca, come sit and be warm." Paulo motioned to the vacant space between him and Vera—a circle of timbers surrounding a fire pit dug into the sand.

"Jesus, that man. What will I do with him?" Anca smirked, rolling her eyes, heading toward the bonfire, but then she circled. "Tiegan, come with?"

"I will. I'll be there soon." I nodded, signaling for them to leave without me. I didn't want to join the party. An urgent sense of longing filled my heart. I was, however, acutely aware of Eli's presence, of his shadow looming in the sand.

"Are you going out again, Eli?" I gestured toward the wild surf.

"Um, no." Eli rubbed the rough edge of his chin, glancing up and down the beach, but then his gaze returned to me. "I've had enough ocean for today."

I nodded. I had the impression Eli was waiting for something.

"Can I get you anything, Miss Tiegan? Another drink? Are you hungry?"

"No, thanks. I'm fine." I followed Eli's gaze toward the crackling bonfire.

"Would you like to join Anca and Vera?"

I shook my head. I looked away to the east, where the moon would soon rise. "Eli, if you don't mind, I think I'll go for a walk."

"Of course, Miss Tiegan."

Still, Eli stayed by my side. His presence was almost over-bearing. "Eli, what's going on?"

"What? Why would you think something's going on?"

"Well, maybe because you're hovering." I raised my eyebrows, crossing my arms over my chest.

Eli whispered slow words. "I promised I would watch over you."

"What? Why?" I gazed into the burning light of Eli's eyes and deciphered his meaning. Tomás was worried about me— about my safety? What did that mean?

"If anything were to happen, Miss Tiegan, he'd never forgive me."

"And what could happen?" I placed my hands on my hips and tilted my face. I saw the indecision in Eli's eyes. How could I reassure him? As much as I enjoyed Eli's company, I didn't need or want a chaperone. "Eli, I don't need a babysitter."

"All right, Miss Tiegan, but you'll be careful?" Eli gave in, but he seemed worried.

"You're a good friend, Eli. Thank you." I threw my arms around him. He tensed but then hugged me with one arm.

"You're so like my sister. I keep reminding myself you're not." He stepped backward, his eyes shining too bright.

"Your sister?" I looked at him.

"Yeah. Sylvie always had something up her sleeve. You're

the same. I see it in your eyes." Eli shook his head, his expression sad and happy at the same time.

"Sylvie, was your sister? Tomás's Sylvie?" My mouth dropped open, and my breath left me.

"You didn't know, Miss Tiegan?" He studied me, his eyes worried.

"No, he didn't tell me. Why didn't he tell me?" I lost my breath.

"He's like that...bottles things up. I wouldn't worry about it, Miss Tiegan." Eli shrugged, his hands flying about.

I stood beneath the fading sky, watching Eli walk away. I didn't know what to think. Sylvie's brother—Tomás's brother-in-law—why the big secret?

Eli joined the others at the bonfire, sitting beside Vera. She looked up and smiled at him. I caught Vera's eye and waved. Leaving the ripple of laughter behind, I followed the sand as far as it would take me—to the rocky headland where the waves tripped over themselves and crashed onto the shore. It was there. I sat and waited for what would happen next. Warmth tingled my skin, and my mind slowed. I was blissfully unaware of everything around me. The moon cut the horizon, beginning her ascent into the sky. It was bigger and brighter than any moon I had ever seen.

This Mourning Moon touched me in a private place. I opened my heart and rose to greet her. I heard her voice—jump, burst forth, rise. I lifted my face to the crystal of soft light and waded through the foamy surf into the darker shallows. The ebb and flow of the tide, the earth's blood, raced through my veins while the hand of sadness brushed my heart with everything and with nothing.

Tears fell from my eyes—salty tears the ocean accepted as hers. My heart bled, and I let the dead go.

12

<hr>

"Every rose has its thorn."—Unknown

Tiegan

The cafe hummed with the voices of tourists and locals alike. I broke the fast with a strong coffee, a croissant, and a fruit plate, then dove into a Pastel de Nata, Portugal's famous cream tart, warm from the oven. I crunched through the flaky crust and closed my eyes, savoring the zesty flavors of an egg custard doused with sugar and cinnamon.

"Would you like sugar in your coffee, *meu amor?*" He looked up from the stream of sugar flowing into his coffee mug.

"All that sugar isn't good for you...not to mention the carbs." I considered the sudden spike in blood sugar and the rise in insulin levels. I wondered if he had a family history of diabetes, high blood pressure, or heart disease. I was neurotic about some things. Okay, most things. I chewed the corner of my mouth—a habit I couldn't seem to break.

"Has the bloom fallen off the rose? Are we no different

from an old married couple?" He chuckled as I sipped my naked coffee. He lifted a spoon off the table, stirred, and then added more sugar.

I kicked his foot under the table and smiled. That's what he did—he made me smile. I could sit there all day and look at him. I wanted him, needed him too much. I was falling too hard.

"Tomás, you know everything about me, but I know nothing about you." I have shared everything. Yet Tomás has not, and I wanted to know why.

"What do you mean? I've told you everything."

"You haven't told me about your life." I pressed my lips together and raised my eyebrows.

"There's nothing much to tell." He sipped his coffee.

"Yes, there is. What's your favorite color? Where did you grow up? Do you like baseball? Hockey? Do you believe in Santa Claus, the Tooth Fairy?" I wanted to know everything.

"Red. Yes. Yes. Yes. Yes. Okay?" He slathered white toast with raspberry jam.

"Where did you and Anca grow up?" I ran through his answers. He missed one.

"Do we have to talk about my childhood? It's not something I like to dwell on." He dunked his toast into the coffee.

"I'm sorry, I didn't realize." I sipped my coffee, finding comfort in the dark roast.

"It's fine. You want to know?" He finished his last toast and brushed his hands with the napkin.

"Yes, of course I do." I placed my hand over his, drawing circles with my thumb.

"My mother and father were travelers, part of a caravan." He paused and looked out the window at the street, at the passing traffic.

I thought he would stop—right there.

"What was it like? Traveling?" I framed a notion in my

mind: a dark green vardo, ticked with yellow, with spoked wheels and shuttered windows, sloping sides, and a barrel roof—tambourines tinkled, and voices laughed. I saw Tomás: a sturdy little boy, dirty-faced and happy.

"We traveled throughout Eastern Europe, following the festival circuit from town to town. My father would play music on his gadulka, and Rory would dance." His face softened, his thoughts traveling somewhere else.

"Rory? Who's that?"

"Rory was our bear. We always had a bear. My father was good with animals."

"That's so cool."

"My father would perform at festivals with Rory; people would give us money. My mother read the tarot cards for extra cash. And then it was over."

"Why? What happened?"

"We left the caravan. We traveled to Rosalia's Mountain. My father took the bear, and he left." He stacked his coffee cup on his plate and waved to the server.

"Oh, Tomás. I'm so sorry."

"It doesn't matter, not anymore." He shrugged, but his face told a different story. His lips were tight, drawn in a straight line.

"I have another question." I clasped his hands and squeezed, willing him to come back. I wanted to change the subject. I wanted his smile.

"Okay?"

"I'm curious about this whole soulmate thing. What do you know about that? What does it mean? Do you think we are two parts of a whole? A reincarnation of oneself, meant to find each other with every lifetime? Do you feel a burning desire to be with me? Is that what it means to find your soulmate?"

"That's a lot to consider. I know one thing for sure. That

burning desire you speak of? I feel it every moment of every day."

I grinned—I was a bubble about to pop.

"Anything else today, folks?" The server only had eyes for Tomás, and I couldn't say I blamed her. I suffered from the same affliction.

Tomás looked at me, and I shook my head. Breakfast with Tomás was a full five-course extravaganza, carbs and more carbs. I lost my mind just thinking about it.

"Just the check, please."

The server nodded, leaving us.

"You know she's flirting with you?"

"No, I can't say I noticed."

"It's not fair, you know."

"What's not fair?"

"How, as the male species age, they maintain that distinguished look."

"Are you calling me old?"

"Well, not old…not if you're a tree." I drew my forefinger down the front of his shirt, widened my eyes, and smiled. I found him gazing at me.

"Have I not proven myself to be a satisfying lover, my sweet Tiegan?" He pinched my chin, tilting my face to his.

"I think, Tomás Ferreira, I need a reminder." Me, and the voices in my head, clamored for his attention.

He guided me onto the sidewalk, his hand cupping my elbow. He smiled that sexy half-smile and swept me against his body, closing his mouth over mine.

"Where are we going? My place? Your place? The hotel down the street? They have an hourly rate." I pressed into him, my heart racing, my flesh tingling, my panties pooling with moisture. Jesus, did I say that?

"I can't. I wish I could, but—" He smirked, closing his

hands on either side of my face. "I have to meet Eli, but I'll catch up with you later, okay?"

I pressed my lips together and tried not to show disappointment. Unlike me, Tomás was not on holiday. He had two restaurants to manage, one a complete restart. Bianca's renovation was nearing completion. All that remained was installing the equipment required to run a microbrewery, the kick-off to coincide with the Carvoeiro Christmas market.

I learned a lot from Tomás about microbrewery operation. A few craft specialties meant a longer brew length, larger fermenters, and serving vessels. I did not doubt Bianca's would produce an award-winning product, and the droves of noisy soccer fans would be back.

"It shouldn't take long. Would you like to go to the beach later?"

"Okay." I smiled. I liked the beach.

We walked, hands intertwined, through the empty street. I stayed on the lookout for runaway black cars.

Eli, wearing his signature Hawaiian shirt, leaned against Bianca's entrance doors, his arms crossed over his chest, waiting for Tomás.

"Miss Tiegan." That soft drawl and a slow smile welcomed me. He nodded his head, peering at me and then at Tomás.

"Hi, Eli. It's nice to see you today." I acknowledged his smile and turned toward Tomás. Standing on my tiptoes, I kissed his cheek. We held hands until we couldn't, and then our fingers drifted apart.

I left Tomás behind and climbed the hill to Vila Algarve. I found things to do—menial things needing attention, like laundry. I changed the bedsheets, and refreshed the towels. I carried the basket back and forth to the shared facilities on the main floor behind Derek's office. I chatted with Derek.

Derek was pleased that Vila Algarve was fully booked for the upcoming holiday season.

I mopped the tile floor, watered the flowers in the window boxes, and swept the forty-five steps to my attic apartment.

I answered the email from Mom & Dad. They told me it was snowing back home. I chuckled—glad I was here and not there. I played with the cat. I was very fond of the cat and thought about what to do with it when I went home. And then my mind swirled—how could I go home? How could I leave Tomás? I didn't want to say goodbye—ever.

Somehow, time passed, and before I knew it, there was a knock at my door. I rushed to open it and found Tomás filling the doorframe.

"Whoa!" As I leaped into his arms, he laughed, a deep, rolling chuckle. Much to my chagrin, he set me on the floor and walked past me.

The cat wound himself between Tomás's legs, meowing and purring. Tomás squatted on his heels and rubbed the cat behind his ears.

I stood with my arms crossed, observing this developing bromance.

"Are you ready, *meu amor*?" He looked up, meeting my gaze.

"I have to shower. I'm all sweaty." I plucked at the hem of my clingy tank.

Tomás strode with graceful stealth across the room with the cat cuddled in his arms.

"Would you like to come with?" I asked in my most seductive voice. I walked toward the bathroom, slipping out of my shorts, lifting my tank top over my head, and dropping my bra on the floor, but Tomás was oblivious to the invite. He was lounging on the couch, whispering sweet nothings to the cat.

———

There was no wind; the ocean was tame. My kayak, a yellow sliver of plastic, glided across the water. I stared through the looking glass at Mother Nature's underwater garden. The seabed was alive with purple fans, sea whips, and coral fingers—exquisite pastel shades. I saw a jellyfish, a lobster and a whole lot of nudibranchs—teacup dragons fluttering along the ocean floor—my favorite with their striking colors of cobalt and bright orange. I spied an octopus and stared, open-mouthed, as the eight-legged sea monster propelled through the deep.

"Tiegan, over here. Come this way." His voice carried across the water, finding me. He leaned back in his seat, his bare feet hanging over the sides of his kayak—a sexy smile on his beautiful face.

I threw my back into it and dropped the paddle into the water. Aspray of ice-cold water splashed me. I tried again. I reached for my toes, lowered the blade, and pulled. I paddled hard in search of Tomás. Rounding the headland, I discovered the entrance to a cave—a vertical crevice in the rock face, a breathtaking oasis where layered rings of sand and shell formed a ceiling where sunlight peeked through a wide eyeball, filling the cavern with soft light. Littered with remnants of charred driftwood, a narrow strip of sand—we were not the first to discover this romantic hideaway.

Tomás was out of his kayak, waiting. He dragged the bow of my boat onto shore.

"What is this place?" I gazed upward into the eye. I stared, mesmerized.

"Well, I'd like to tell you it's my little secret, but I can't. It's a popular spot for tourists. But at this time of year, we should have no interruptions..." Tomás pressed a kiss to my forehead.

I kicked off my sandals and wiggled my toes. I followed the water's edge to the cavern wall—hardened sand and fossilized shell. It would be a fun climb—caving—I had always wanted to try it. I resisted the urge and returned to Tomás.

"What's this? You brought a picnic?"

"For you, my sweet Tiegan." He spread a large blanket—the kind that sand doesn't cling to—onto the widest stretch of sand. Packed into another compartment of Tomás's kayak was a basket containing a bottle of red wine, two stemless glasses, a container filled with strawberries, and slabs of dark chocolate. They screamed eat me.

I sat cross-legged on the red blanket.

"Are you having fun?" Tomás popped the cork, filling each glass.

"I am. Can't you tell?" I savored the wine and nibbled on a piece of chocolate.

"I'm sorry I had to leave you this morning. I wanted to make it up to you." He stretched beside me.

"You have." I grinned and dived into a strawberry.

"You're beautiful, *meu amor*. Do you know that?" Tomás touched the side of my face, dragging his fingertips along the curve of my jaw.

My face heated the same scarlet shade as the strawberry.

"I have something for you." He rose to a sitting position and dug into his pocket.

"Really? You do? What?" I grinned. I loved presents.

Extending his hand, he presented a ring—a marble of ocean-blue sea glass set in twisted threads of white gold.

"Tomás, it's beautiful." My voice caught, and my heart thumped. I couldn't hide my surprise.

"I like to tinker a bit with gold, sometimes silver." He held my hand and slipped the ring onto my pinky finger.

"You made this?" I gazed at the ring—it had an organic

feel. It breathed life. I swallowed a rising ball of emotion. It's too soon for a ring.

"It's the color of your eyes when you wake in the morning." He leaned in, pressing his lips to the edge of my mouth.

Moaning into his breath, I edged closer. I slipped my hand into his shorts, wrapping my fingers around his thickening cock.

"Wait." His hand drifted across my collarbone, skimming the underside of my jaw.

"What do you mean, wait? Wait for what?" I widened my eyes, flitting my lashes.

"You're overdressed, don't you think?" He slid the back of his knuckles across my breasts, grazing each rising nub.

"I guess I am. What are you going to do about it?" Spandex layers protected me from the sun's ultraviolet rays —a swim shrug, a half-zip swim-shirt, and matching baby-shark stretchy tights.

"We'll start here." He peppered my jaw with close kisses and slid the clingy swim shrug over my shoulders, tugging each sleeve one at a time. "You taste so good, *meu amor.*"

"Tomás, hurry." I lifted my arms high over my head.

"You're always in a rush." He dragged the half-zip as far as it would go, plucking the stretchy fabric with his fingers, relieving me of the cling fit, and exposing my breasts to moist, cool air. He nibbled, pulling my lower lip into his mouth. Running his palm across my belly, he untied the drawstring. "How's that? Better?"

"You're making me crazy." I leaned on my hands, squirming my hips—I couldn't sit still. I couldn't wait. I wiggled out of my pants, tossing them into the sand. I cried out when his face landed between my thighs.

"Look how wet you are." His tongue speared a hot path to my pussy, separating the swollen cleft.

"Tomás, I want you." I bit down on my bottom lip, curling my fingers into the blanket.

"And I want you. I want to make you happy. I want to give you everything. If one day, you'll have me." He had waited so long to share his life with someone. Why now?

"Are you sure, Tomás? About all of this? You hardly know me." I played with the ring, twisting it on my finger.

"Let me show you, *meu amor*, how sure I am." He repositioned sideways, pulling me onto the blanket with him, slipping his arm in the crook of my other knee, exposing my sex to his lapping tongue. He suckled the outer folds, tapped the hooded bead, and stroked my inner walls with a curled and fluttering tongue.

I closed my eyes and savored the sensations coursing over me—more than lust, more than need. They had become the same. I stole a glance at Tomás, and my heart filled with happiness. I had been sleepwalking my entire life—I knew that now.

"Tomás?"

He looked up, a wet grin on his face.

"You're squishing my arm."

I stroked his shaft from base to tip, caressing his ball sac with a teasing touch. I ran my tongue along the delectable ridge, pumping the broad crown onto the flat of my tongue —a soft, spongy place for his cock to land—his pleasure mine.

Together, we moved our hips, undulating to the rhythm of the ocean's tide. In this vaulted cathedral of rock, gentle waves lapped the sand—a lover's kiss, a soft caress. Is that what I wanted? Is that all I needed? Something that simple? A love like that?

———

The sun hung low in the sky, yet within the cavern, hues of golden light washed the sand. Tomás had packed the blanket and the remnants of our picnic into the compartments of his kayak.

Perched in the cockpit of the yellow sliver, with my knees bent and feet braced, I dropped the skeg and balanced my paddle. Tomás bent low, propelling my kayak through the basin of calm water toward a cleft of shining light. Slipping through the stone fissure, I glided into the open sea. I paused, marveling at the reflection of clouds: a spider web of wispy bands sprawling across a canvas of ocean. Then, I rediscovered my equilibrium, squinted past the sun's glare, and dipped my paddle, gliding across the water toward a cluster of rock stacks. An excellent swimmer could make it from there to the beach to the horseshoe of white sand lying in the sun's path.

I was one with this hollow piece of plastic.

I paid no attention to the wail of the high-powered engine skimming across the glassy surface. I did not sense the displacement of the atmosphere or the impending surge of the tide. But when I heard Tomás screaming my name, my heart staggered. I twisted my head into the sun's glare—it was too late for words.

The speed demon was flying straight toward us—toward me. On a hairpin, the powerboat turned. The ocean reacted with rage, and I was its innocent victim. The kayak dropped down the backside of a waterfall and flipped over. Like the egg timer in my mother's kitchen, I was upside down, submerged in the swirling cauldron of a tumultuous wake.

My nose filled with the sting of salty brine—my throat burned—my heartbeat a thundering echo inside my head. I kicked my feet, clawing for a surface I couldn't find. On top of the water, the sky was a brilliant light, awash with pink rainbows. A bird circled over me—a peregrine falcon riding the waves on feathered wings.

I drifted at one with that endless moment. And then that endless moment faded into peace.

———

"Dearest Tiegan,

Sweetheart, we haven't heard from you lately. Is everything all right over there in Portugal? Your father's fair worried.

We're after another snowstorm over here. A bad spill of whiteouts yesterday and again today. The roads into town are shut down tight. Folks were stranded on the Ceilidh Trail and was after being rescued with the snowmobiles. What a time it was, and all those poor folks right freezing in their boots.

Well, I have to say, young Angus McLeod was good to run the plow. That boy's Vera's mother's cousin, on her father's side. I'm sure you remember. It goes to show you can't always judge a book by its cover. Always so sullen and withdrawn. Well, now, that boy turned out right fine. All that time dancing between the lines, as your father says. Well, he's a happy camper now, coming out and all, embracing his true self. His partner, such a fine man from over Halifax way, and a big wedding planned this Valentine's Eve. How romantic is that? Will you be home then, sweetheart? You're sure to get an invite.

Your father will run by your house once the roads are handy. I hope it's soon. We're running out of just about everything and could sure use a few bun of bread from the dairy.

We miss you.

Love,
Mom"

13

"A bend in the road is not the
end of the road...unless you fail
to make the turn."—Unknown

iegan

My mind stirred. Wisps of vapor filled my lungs, and I coughed. Tomás whispered over me, and my body tingled with awakening. I was in a bed, the old-fashioned kind with an iron headboard, the mattress feathery soft, the sheets cool. I ran my hands down the soft flannel of a nightgown, the kind my mother wore. I fought to raise my eyelids. My throat was dry and scratchy, and my chest hurt.

"Tomás?" I tried to sit up, but his hands forced me back down.

"Don't move, *meu amor.*" He sat beside the bed on a small wooden chair, his body massive compared to the floor space and the raftered ceiling's angled slope. A table lamp lit the little room, casting a soft glow against the yellowed boards.

"Where are we?"

"We're in the mountains. How do you feel?"

"The mountains?" I struggled again to sit up. "Why?"

"Because it's a safe place." He lifted me into a sitting position, fluffed the pillows, and pushed me back down. "Don't move. I'll be right back."

"What does that mean—a safe place?" I rubbed my eyes, my arms heavy bricks of mortar.

Tomás returned, balancing a silver tray containing a pot-bellied teapot, a red mug, and a bottle of what looked like cough syrup.

"How do you feel?" He searched my face with worried eyes.

"Fine, I think."

"Drink this." He held the mug to my lips.

"What's this?" I took a tentative sip, the liquid lukewarm and tasting like green grass and dandelions. I smiled at his attempt to mother me and swallowed another mouthful. I tried not to gag.

"Tea. Open." He took the mug away and poured a dollop of thick syrup onto a spoon.

"What's that?" I had never tasted such a flavor, the earthy undertone biting my tongue. The syrup was almost as bad as the tea, but not quite.

"Elderberry. Homemade." He returned the spoon to the tray.

My eyebrows rose, but he did not expand on the recipe.

"How long have we been here?"

"A few days."

"A few days." I sank into the pillows, exhaustion weighing heavily, struggling for the right words. "I saw a bird, a falcon…did you see the bird?" I grasped his hand. His was warm. Mine was cold.

"When did you see a bird?" His voice was gentle.

"When I died." I moistened my lips. They were dry and cracked and tasted like elderberry syrup.

"You didn't die. And no, I did not see a bird. I was pulling you out of the ocean." He rubbed my hand within both of his.

"I didn't see the boat—I should have seen the boat." Memories of those last few moments flashed through my mind: the swale of water, the scream of the high-powered engine—Tomás screaming. My eyes burned as tears ravaged my face—an unstoppable river. "You must hate me."

"What? No. How can you think that?"

I stared into my lap at the ball of sea glass on my finger. I remembered how we made love in the shelter of the cavern, how our sighs echoed off the limestone walls. Tomás made this beautiful work of art for me—a ring and with it, a world of promises.

"This is not your fault." He lifted me from the small bed, wooly blanket and all, and carried me into a cozy living room raftered with timbers and lined with boards of rough-sawn pine. River rock climbed the gable wall on both sides of the fireplace, and logs crackled in the stone hearth. He sank into a sofa draped with crocheted throws of multi-colored granny squares.

"This is twice someone's had to save me." I blinked away a rush of hot tears.

"If anyone is to blame, it is me. You almost died because of me."

"What are you talking about? You saved me." My thoughts scattered. I couldn't make sense of his words. I held my medallion between my thumb and my forefinger, rubbing it gently.

"Tell me about your medallion." Tomás exhaled a long breath, nestling me into his arms and tucking my head under his chin.

"My grandfather gave it to me. He said it would help—with the nightmares." I lifted my eyelids and stared into the fire. A log exploded, bursting into a thousand golden embers.

"What nightmares?"

I played with the coin, tracing the age-old ridges with the pad of my thumb—I had memorized each one. "I haven't had one nightmare since I met you." I smiled, hoping to end the interrogation.

"And the medallion helps?"

"I don't know, Tomás. Maybe." I wanted to blurt out a quick no. I didn't believe in superstition or myth. I walk under ladders. I spill the salt. I put my shoes on the table. But then again, maybe I would have had more nightmares if I hadn't worn the medallion.

"What are these nightmares about?"

I didn't want to talk about my nightmares. I had never shared those dreams with anyone, not even my mother. Why? Because that would make them real, and I didn't know how to handle real. I sucked in a big breath, held it, and then let it go, answering him with a whisper, "There's blood, lots of blood and bright lights—my heart…my heart is stopping." I paused and then spat out the rest of it. "When I wake up, I'm not in my bed. I'm always somewhere else."

"When did these nightmares start?" Tomás tightened his arm around me—chasing away the demons, chasing away the night.

"I was thirteen. My mom, dad, and grandfather were camping in the highlands—Cape Meat—overlooking the ocean. It's beautiful there." I closed my eyes, pressing my teeth to my bottom lip. Logs crackled. Tendrils of wood smoke curled into the sky. Leaves rustled underfoot. "I'd gone to sleep but wasn't in my tent when I woke up. I was on the edge of the cliff staring over the sea."

I remember that night like yesterday. The sky would have been black but for the burned hue of a blood moon. It was a time when the moon passed through the earth's shadow, a time of shifting forces—when the veil between worlds thins.

I often wondered if I had stepped through the nightmare to the other side and how long I had stayed.

"My stomach churned, and I couldn't see straight. The blood was everywhere: on my hands, on my blouse, streaming down my legs." I giggled, a hysterical high-pitched sound.

Tomás gasped, a choked breath, but I continued.

"My first menstrual cycle. That's when the nightmares began. We never went back to the mountain."

"Tiegan, this amulet has great meaning to the Roma. It holds powerful energy. I think your grandfather placed a protection spell on this coin."

"A spell?" My heart skipped a beat. "What do you mean?"

"Did you ever see your grandfather do any kind of magic?"

I raised my eyebrows. Magic? I wanted to say no, but then, for a moment, a fleeting memory found me. "Sometimes, he would hold my head and whisper words. I don't know what they were. I had to lie still and take deep breaths. The nightmares would stop for a while."

"Tell me about your grandfather."

"He lived with us when I was little. I used to walk home from school—for lunch. He used to make the best soup. He always called me by my other name, my secret name. I was never Tiegan." I recall my grandfather through a cloud of darkness—I see him. It pains my heart but made me smile.

"What? What did you say?" Tomás peered at me, his forehead furrowed into three distinct lines.

"Hmm? My real name is Kavan. My grandfather picked it when I was born. It means brave one."

"What was your grandfather's name?"

"Maloney Lock, but everyone called him Paddy." I chuckled, but Tomás did not.

"Lock?"

"Yeah, don't you get it? Paddylock?"

"Tiegan, those names. They're Romani names. Lock is an alias for Boswell—a well-respected Romani clan. Did you know that?" A change came over him—his body stiffened, and his eyes flashed with an excitement I had never witnessed before.

"No, my grandfather never talked about his past. Not that I can remember, anyway. He was one hundred when he died. He used to tell me that only people who were ninety-nine years old wanted to be one hundred."

"He was your mother's father? That's why your name is Moss," Tomás murmured, his voice filled with wonder.

"Yes, my dad's Irish. Why?" I sipped the dandelion tea. The taste was growing on me.

"Tiegan, I believe you're a Roma. A Roma from a long line of kings."

"I'm a Roma?"

"Yes, you are."

"Tomás, I have to throw up." I pitched forward, but Tomás had me by the waist, and I was staring into a large stainless-steel bowl, gagging on a rush of green tea and elderberry syrup with tears running down my cheeks.

"It's okay. You're going to be okay." He pulled my hair out of my face. He dabbed my face with a hot washcloth. He combed his fingers through my hair. "We need to get you back to bed, *meu amor*. You need sleep." Tomás carried me into the bedroom, laid me on the bed, adjusted the pillows, and tucked the blanket under my chin. Almost immediately, sleep found me. My eyes fell shut, and my mind drifted.

I woke to find the bedroom glimmering with moonbeams. Forest whispers comforted me: the hoot of an owl, the bark of a squirrel, and from somewhere far away, the wailing call of a wildcat. Another more human sound was the rasping see-saw of Tomás snoring in the other room. With my hands outstretched, I swung my legs to the floor and found my way through the darkened living room.

"Tiegan? Are you all right?"

"I'm okay," I called out from the bathroom. I washed my hands at a stone sink. It was rustic and made of the earth, and it agreed with this cabin in the woods.

My reflection in the oval mirror scared me. My hair was a rat's nest of disarray. I ran my tongue across my teeth and grimaced.

Beside the sink was a basket filled with stuff from my apartment: my hairbrush, my toothbrush, my multivitamin, and even my shampoo and conditioner. I stood in the shower, waiting for the water to warm.

When I returned, Tomás was asleep, sitting upright on the couch, breathing long, even breaths. I curled beside him, our last conversation dancing in my head—a Roma from a long line of kings. What should I do with that?

———

It's been two weeks since I almost drowned. We stayed in the little cabin, hidden from the world, for the first of those weeks. With each day, I grew stronger.

We spent our days exploring forgotten footpaths and wandering deep into a savanna of cork oak and sweet chestnut. We gathered buckets of spiny burs, the fallen fruit of those noble trees. Tomás split each one with the heel of his boot, and in the evenings, we roasted the *castanhas* on the hot coals of the dying fire.

The winds rustled through stands of maritime pine, branches creaked, and voices whispered. With Tomás by my side, I learned to wake the spirits, acquiring a taste for *Medronho*—the firewater—the moonshine of the Algarve.

The process of collecting berries, fermentation, and distillation, Tomás shared with pride—his secret recipe.

When it was time to leave, we returned to Carvoeiro—to my apartment. When Tomás was not at Bianca's supervising the renovation, he stayed with me. I had grown used to his ways and missed him with all my heart when we were not together.

It was easy to pick out the throaty grumble of the Ducati as it tore through the night and the stamp of his leather boots as they climbed the winding staircase to my apartment. He had a key, but I swung the green door open anyway, and then he was mine, and I was his. I was in a constant state of desire —a hunger I couldn't satisfy—a thirst I could never quench. We had no secrets.

We slept in my little bed. I was unsure of Derek's opinion of our arrangement, but I believed all was well. I had seen Tomás peering under the front-hinged hood of Derek's Renault just the other day. Snippets of conversation drifted through the iron rails of my balcony—something about carburetors and a close-circuit cooling system.

Tomás hinted I should stay at his place, that even the cat would be welcome.

———

Tomás

I scanned the dining hall of Bianca's Brew Pub, its windows covered in brown paper to conceal the renovations inside. Soon, the doors would open, and the tables would fill with paying customers. I glanced at my watch for the third time. At this hour, Tiegan would be asleep. The balcony doors would be open, the ocean breeze drifting through the apartment. My heart raced at the thought of her, alone and unprotected. I tapped the app on my phone's screen, checking the security camera I had installed at Derek's building. I flipped through the screens, looking and looking again for signs of intruders.

Eli leaned over the pool cue, took the shot, and sank the eight ball, finishing the game in record time. He shot me an amused gaze. "Another game?"

"Sure." I searched the lower cabinets and found what I was looking for—Irish Whiskey, aged twenty-one years, in a bourbon cask. As an afterthought, I hit the remote. Six television screens dropped from the ceiling. The sound system engaged, blasting the *futebol* game throughout the dining hall.

"I will not roll the dice with Tiegan's life. I won't do it." I sighed through my nose, filling two lowball tumblers with liquid gold and a toss of ice. I handed one to Eli.

"The dice have already been tossed, my friend. Can you not see it? I knew the moment I saw her." He sniffed the contents of his glass, nodding approvingly.

"No. You thought Tiegan was the devil incarnate of Sylvie." My gaze settled on the *futebol* game. I whistled as the player dove headfirst across the grass, scoring a goal on the opposing net.

"Yeah…well, it's fucked up, man. Same hellfire in her veins. Same look in her eyes." He rubbed the stubble on his chin, his gaze pensive.

I glanced at my brother-in-law. Some days, I almost forgot he was Sylvie's brother. Where Eli was lanky and blonde, Sylvie was petite and dark-haired. But something in his smile reminded me of her.

"You're not helping. When was the last time you showered?" I lifted my eyebrows. Eli camped out in the back room, what used to be my office.

"Want to break?" He racked the balls in an offset pattern of stripes and solids, the black ball placed strategically in the center.

"You go ahead." I stared at the television screens, each in sync except for one—I made a mental note.

"Look, man. It is your destiny to lead the kumpania. You can't deny that." He handed me his pool cue.

"All of it, the ramblings of an old woman." My grandmother's dark eyes flickered in my memory—a prophecy, a curse, and a new line of Gypsy Kings. "I will not put Tiegan's life in jeopardy. Twice, she's almost died because of me."

"Do you think both events were related?" Resting his palm on the felt, he took the shot. The cue ball smacked the apex full in the face, scattering every other ball across the table, sinking a solid.

"Don't you?" I held his gaze.

"No. I think it was bad luck. Wrong place, wrong time." He walked around the table. "Come on, man…no one would hurt her, not on purpose."

"You're naïve, Eli. You believe what you want to believe." I sipped the Irish, comforted by its warm, honeyed sweetness and burned oak tones.

"You think it was Dunne?" He lifted an eyebrow.

"I told you before. Dunne can keep his crown. I don't want it." I pushed off the bar, my pulse hammering.

"You've waited years. It's time. Take what's rightfully yours." He made his argument just as he had since he first saw Tiegan standing in my living room—his sister reincarnated.

"Too many people think like you, Eli. You believe the words of a witch." I balanced the heavy glass in my hand and studied the clarity of the yellow-gold colors. "What if there's a next time, Eli? And what if I'm not there?"

"Jesus, I've never seen you this messed up." He shook his head, refusing to accept the truth.

"Yeah, well, you're seeing it now. I won't ruin her life for my sake. I have to let her go." I lost a breath, angry with myself, Dunne, and the situation I created alone.

"You're fucking in love with her, man…you're not letting her go anywhere." A smile ghosted his lips.

"What other choice do I have?" I hung my head, unable to deny his claim. The thought of her sent a thrill coursing through me. "I've thought it through. There's no other way."

"Okay, so when are you going to do this?" He asked with a low laugh.

"Soon." I envisioned Tiegan slipping the silver band onto her finger, the light in her eyes reflecting the setting sun.

I turned away from Eli, my hands shaking.

I relived those moments—diving to the ocean floor, pulling her into my arms, and sealing my mouth over hers. Her hair floated wildly, framing her face in shadows. Her eyes, those sea-green eyes, unseeing. I dragged her through the wash, lifting her into my arms, screaming and screaming her name. Her lips were blue, and her skin—cold to the touch.

She had died on my watch, just like Sylvie.

"Do me a favor, will you? Check on the house. Stay awhile." I tossed him the keys to the villa and walked out the door.

———

"Dearest Tiegan,

How are you, sweetheart?

Your father wants you to drink flat ginger ale and eat soda crackers, the salted ones. That will help settle your stomach. He also mentioned something about sleeping with your socks on and rubbing Vicks on the bottom of your feet. What a tough puck to get so sick when you're after a holiday.

Love,

Mom

PS. Your father and I went out for dinner last night at the Crazy Horse, that's the new restaurant on Front Street. My goodness it was busy. We were right lucky to find a table for the early bird. They do serve a lovely chowder. Your father was as happy as a clam."

14

*"I am presently experiencing life at a rate
of several WTFs per hour."*—Unknown

Tiegan

"Ah, but then we will spend the whole day in this bedroom, in this bed—not that I would not enjoy that." Tomás crossed his arms over his chest, gazing at me—one eyebrow lifted.

"We have all day, don't we? That's what you said." I grinned, stretching my arms over my head, flexing my thighs, and curling my toes.

"Aren't you sore? I'm a little tender down there." He lifted his semi-hard erection, pulling it from side to side, inspecting the flaccid member. His eyes filled with worry.

"Let me kiss it better, Tomás. Come back to bed. I know just what to do." I pinned my lower lip under my two front teeth and grinned.

"We can't. I have a big day planned. Get out of bed." His brows furrowed as he studied me.

"That's all you got, big boy?" I arched my back and sighed.

"Yes. Now. Hurry. Let's go." He clapped his hands three times.

"You're always in such a rush, Tomás." I peeked through my eyelashes, throwing a sly grin his way.

"Do I have to drag you out of this bed?" He placed his hands on his hips.

"Well, aren't you a bossy boo…all right, all right. Geez." He reminded me of someone else I knew—my mother.

"I do, and besides, there's someone I want you to meet."

His tone was casual, too casual. I had a good idea about who he was referring to. I backed into the headboard, hugged my knees, and stared. "Who?" I sound like an owl.

"I want you to meet my grandmother."

"What for? Do you think that's a good idea?" Jumping up, I wrapped my arms around him. It was normal to meet family, but our relationship was far from normal. If I didn't get his grandmother's blessing, whatever Tomás and I shared would be over.

"Tiegan, Rosalia can help. I'm sure of it." A muscle ticked in his jaw, yet his gaze held mine.

"What about sightseeing? I want to see the castle." I met his lips, driving my tongue into his mouth, heat flooding my core—my hunger—insatiable.

"I know what you're doing." He pulled away, the smile on his lips setting my heart on fire..

"What? You kissed me." I tilted my head, feigning innocence.

He dragged me through the dangling beads into the living room, leaving me no other option.

———

I had to admit, it was a beautiful day for a drive. The stark cliffs and red clay of the Algarve gave way to an estuary where herons swooped low in all their prehistoric splendor. A string of hydro poles walked across wide mudflats, and I marveled at stork nests dangling like a ballerina's crinoline atop each one. Crossing the Arade River, lowlands transformed into rolling green hills, starred with farmhouses painted white. In the distance, a mountain range: blueberry cupcakes crowned with clouds of white icing. We continued our upward ascent as the road tunneled through forests of cork oak and carob, narrowing as we arrived at the sleepy village of Monchique, rows of canvas tents festooned with zigzags of white and blue streamers lining the town square.

"Look…a festival. Let's stop." Baubles of color caught my eye: a tent tiered with shelves with buckets overflowing with tulips, hydrangeas, and painted daisies.

"What for?" He loosed a breath. He seemed far away, his eyes on the road, his mouth hard.

"I want to buy flowers for your grandmother." I pointed toward the fair.

"You don't have to do that." Tomás slowed the Land Rover to a snail's pace.

"I know, but I want her to like me." I smiled—happy—I had delayed the inevitable meeting with Rosalia a while longer.

Tomás found a parking spot on a one-way street angled between two vehicles. We held hands and followed the cobbled road back to the market square.

"Are you hungry?" I gawked at the impressive multitude of food carts, my stomach growling.

"Only for you." Tomás swept his arm around my waist, pulling me off my feet.

I returned his proposition with a peck on the side of his

mouth and stirred once again. I could never get enough—of Tomás.

"You know Rosalia is expecting us." He pressed his lips to my forehead.

I widened my eyes and gave him my best smile.

"All right, how about a churro?"

"Okay." I followed Tomás to the churro cart. We were at the back of a long line.

"Back home, we have beavertails." I gazed into his eyes.

"Beavertails?" He looked at me with confusion on his face.

"It's like your churro but made in the shape of a beaver tail—doused in sugar and cinnamon. It's iconic." I grinned.

We were now at the front of the line. Tomás ordered a heaping platter of star-shaped ropes and two steaming cups of hot chocolate. We found an empty table in the center of the square beneath a giant chestnut tree.

"Did you know churros arrived in Portugal from the Orient by Portuguese sailors?" He lifted his chin, leaving his churro untouched.

"No, I didn't know that." I dunked my churro into the hot chocolate, biting into the crispy goodness. "What?" I gazed into his eyes, my upper lip covered with sugar crystals.

"I love you. No matter what happens, I want you to know that." He cupped my face, his words soulful, almost reverent.

Red and gold leaves fell from the branches, landing all around us.

"Really?" I just couldn't say it. A part of me refused to utter those simple words and acknowledge that I loved him, too.

Spiny burrs—chestnuts—hit the tabletop and bounced onto the bench seat. One bounced off my head.

"Ow." I lifted my hand, sweeping my fingers through my hair.

"Eat your churro, *meu amor.*" The corners of his mouth twitched, and he smiled.

I couldn't wipe the grin from my face. I sighed happily and squeezed Tomás's hand, my heart a big red balloon.

The market was a medley of aromas, but the most alluring was the scent of lavender. I left Tomás and stepped into a space packed with everything purple—shabby metal buckets overflowed with dried bouquets, silk sachets, and balls of bath balm. I held a rough-edged slab of soap to my nose, inhaling the sharp scent that reminded me of my walks along the Algarve cliffs and the wild lavender growing there.

A woman sat behind the counter, weaving tendrils of lavender stalk into a wreathed circlet.

"May I help you?" She placed her creation on a basket of lavender boughs and then stood, heavy with the weight of pregnancy, one hand resting on her round belly.

"Yes, I'd like to buy these." I stared for a moment too long, painting a picture of this young mother-to-be glowing with profound strength and anticipation, bursting with brand-new life. I could not ignore the pang in my heart that had never been present before.

"Can I offer you a sample of our essential oil? A drop or two on your pillow will do wonders for a good sleep," she answered with a smile, wrapping folds of white paper around the purple slabs and packing them in a paper bag.

"Yes, please. That would be amazing." I handed over the correct euros.

After leaving the tent, I searched for Tomás and found him sitting on a bench, his head bent and his fingers tapping the keys of his smartphone.

"For Vera and me." I held the paper bag open to his face, distracting him from his conversation.

"I thought we were looking for flowers." He scrunched his nose, cringing when the floral scent hugged his face.

Two stalls beyond the lavender lady—a farmer's tent with wooden crates overflowed with giant stalks of asparagus, monster-sized tomatoes, and enormous lettuce leaves—I snapped a photo.

"Tiegan, what about the flowers?"

I needed to kiss him, so I did. I stopped dead on the walkway, wrapped my arms around his waist, and tasted him. Tomás answered my need but was quick to break away.

I loved shopping and browsing. The obvious was hard to miss: Tomás was not having fun. He trailed behind me, moving in and out of tents and nodding with disinterest.

The flower vendor was not far away, just beyond the man with the silk scarves. I found a lovely indigo blue with a paisley print, which would look amazing with my white blouse. Then, there was a woman who made cheese. She was offering samples. The rich, creamy zip of aged goat cheese tantalized my taste buds and complimented the gluten-free flax seed cracker.

We were now in front of the flower stall—an extravaganza of pastel and primary colors. Tulips, roses, and various potted plants lined the tiered shelves. With the kiss of lavender on my lips, selecting a bushy plant in a red clay pot was a no-brainer.

"What do you think?" The mass of purple buds awaited Tomás's scrutiny.

Somewhere between there, then, here, and now, I had lost Tomás. I followed his gaze past the string of tents, my mouth dropping open.

A brown Carpathian bear stood on its hind legs, a gold bell hanging around its thick neck. A man wearing a black felt hat, a green vest, and a flowing white shirt accompanied the bear, waving his hat high in the air and attracting the crowd's attention.

The man bowed, drew the bow of a gadulka, and

peppered the strings. The bear tapped its clawed feet, dancing to the ethereal and shimmering strains of its master's song.

The crowd clapped, and I stepped closer, wanting to see the man and the bear, but Tomás gripped my elbow.

"Let's go see the bear." I lunged toward the clapping crowd.

"No, let's not," he answered, his voice cold.

"Why not?" I stared at the man in the felt hat, walking in a figure eight around the dancing bear.

"Tiegan, we've dilly-dallied long enough. Rosalia is expecting us." His grip on my elbow tightened.

"Is something wrong?"

"No. Nothing. Now let's go." Tomás shifted sideways, weaving through the crowd, holding my arm tight.

"Tomás, stop. What's going on? You're hurting me." I jerked away from his hold.

He turned as if seeing me for the first time, his face red, his eyes shining too bright.

"I'm sorry, Tiegan, but we have to go. Right away." He twined his fingers with mine, lengthening his stride, leaving the music, the man, and the bear far behind.

The truck was exactly where we had left it, uncomfortably wedged between two massive vehicles.

I squeezed myself and the little lavender plant sideways into the passenger seat.

With a sideways glance, he checked that my seatbelt was engaged. The engine roared, and the truck zoomed way too fast down the one-way street. Within moments, we had left the quaint village of Monchique far behind.

———

The SUV continued its ascent along the mountain road. The view was spectacular: a green patchwork quilt. Tomás hadn't said a word since we left the village of Monchique. What caused his demeanor to change without warning? Why the rush to leave?

"Are you going to talk to me, or what?" I shifted in my seat and studied him—eyes straight ahead, his knuckles white on the steering wheel. "Tomás? What was that? At the market?"

"I saw someone from long ago."

"Who did you see?"

"My father."

"Your father?"

"The man with the bear."

"That man was your father?"

"Yes, that was my father." He exhaled through his nose and swerved to the left, passing the slow-moving vehicle in front of us.

"But you didn't talk to him."

"No.

"Why not?"

"I have no use for a man who runs out on his family."

"Oh."

His emotions, his feelings; this was unchartered territory. Was I flirting with disaster? I bit my bottom lip and stared out the window.

"That must have been very difficult. Seeing your father."

"I'd rather not talk about it."

"Um, all right. If you say so."

"Look, I know you're trying to help, but don't. Okay?"

I glanced at Tomás, but he was somewhere else. He had shut me out.

We left the asphalt safety, marked yellow lines, and followed a fire route—a one-lane, graveled trail skirting the mountain's edge, the grinding tires gripping each switch-back. I shifted to the edge of my seat, my hands fisted—my ears popping. What would happen if we came face to face with another vehicle?

I exhaled with relief when Tomás nosed off the track and into a cut in the mountain's slope. There was barely room for his vehicle. I climbed out and planted my feet in the dirt.

A stocky man, his skin weathered rough like the mountain we traversed, walked through the trees, leading two horses: a black stallion and a white mare. A talisman hung from each horse's martingale: brass symbols of the sun, the moon, and the stars. The black horse fought the lead, kicking up skiffs of dust, but the man did not seem perturbed.

"Tiegan, this is Jack. Jack works with Rosalia." Tomás beamed at the older man.

"It's nice to meet you, Miss." Jack welcomed me with an easy-going smile. "Have you ridden before?"

"Yes, once, a long time ago." When I was ten, at a birthday party or a trail ride in a meadow—I had a horse who wanted back in the barn.

"You'll have nothing to worry about, Miss. Our Luna is a good girl. She'll look after you." Jack dipped his head.

Tomás walked away with the black horse, leading him to the edge of the tree line. He whispered words I couldn't hear as the horse nuzzled his head into Tomás's chest.

I gazed past Tomás into a wooded thicket. As my eyes adjusted, I saw a structure: a drive shed and a trail winding deep into the mountain.

"Don't worry, Miss. Tomás can handle our Romulus." Jack patted Luna's neck, grinning at me. "Tomás raised that horse from a foal. He's the only one Romulus will allow on his back."

It made perfect sense. Tomás was good with the cat and the high-spirited horse. He was good with animals, like his father. I hoped the big horse did not possess the same diabolical personality as its namesake.

I smiled at Jack and swallowed my trepidation, extending my palm, flat side up, to meet Luna. Luna showed little interest in meeting me. Instead, she nuzzled the lavender plant, her pink nostrils flaring against the purple tendrils.

"Hi, Luna," I whispered into the glassy depths of her soft brown eyes, her white ears twitching in my direction. I patted Luna's neck, breathing in the pungent, horsey smell.

"Miss, I'll give you a leg up," Jack motioned toward the horse's left side. "Put your hands on the saddle horn, Miss. That's it. Now, your left foot in my hands." Jack twined his fingers together, ready and waiting.

I followed his directions as he lifted me into the sky. I lurched forward, hovering a moment too long, and swung my other leg over Luna's broad back. I settled into the saddle, my knuckles white.

"There you go. Let your legs hang, and I'll adjust the stirrups for you." He worked away at the leathers beneath my leg.

"Okay. Thanks, Jack." I held onto the pommel for dear life while Luna's ears twitched back and forth.

Jack adjusted the leather straps with the ease of a man who has been around horses for a long time. Luna stood perfectly still as he set my feet into each stirrup.

I looked away from the ground toward Tomás, who mounted Romulus in one effortless leap.

The crazed horse lifted his head and whinnies, his nostrils flaring, his feet stamping. Luna's ears pricked to attention.

"Now, hold the reins between your fingers and your thumb, not too tight. Let them rest on Luna's neck, just so." Jack patted my leg and stepped away.

"Okay. I can do that." Perched on Luna's back, the top of

the ground seemed a long way off. I could climb a rock face but feared falling off a horse.

"Now, give her a bit of heel, and you'll be on your way." Jack encouraged Luna, clucking his tongue.

And then we were off. With a giddy-up and a quick lope, Luna followed Romulus into the mountains along a dirt trail thickly layered with pine needles. The path narrowed as the horses ascended the sloping terrain. I breathed in the still air and the piney scent of balsam. This was a primeval forest, one not yet succumbed to the lumberman's axe. I marveled at the standing dead: the thick girth of ancient trees and a forest floor blanketed in green moss. I looked up but could not find the sky, hidden above a mesh of branches. It was a place of shadows, eerie yet beautiful all at once.

Riding a horse was more complex than I remembered. There were many factors to consider: looking ahead, keeping my feet in the stirrups, aligning my hips with Luna's some-what choppy gait—I tried not to bounce. At least I didn't have to steer; Luna knew where she was going—back to the barn.

"Tomás, is this the only way to Rosalia's house?"

"Yes, it is." Tomás turned in his saddle and grinned at me. The laughter had returned to his eyes. "Are you having fun yet?"

I was about to answer when my breath caught in my throat. Luna's haunches dropped and then shot forward. My feet left the stirrups as Luna scrambled up the final slope, hot on Romulus's tail—it was a race to the finish. I grabbed the saddle horn and squeezed my knees against Luna's round belly, pitching forward and burying my face in her snowy white mane when she abruptly stopped. Looking up, I met Rosalia's piercing black eyes, Tomás's grandmother.

We had arrived.

———

"Dearest Tiegan.

How are you doing sweetheart? Your father and I miss you. I can't believe Christmas is right upon us. It's just not the same without you.

Your father and I are after keeping busy. Every night this week has been Ceilidh festival or a kitchen party to attend. We're after a wonderful turnout at the seniors residence yesterday. As I live and breathe how those old folks know how to kick up their heels. What a time.

Be still my heart, Tiegan, and don't you dare say a word to your father, but I'm after telling you about old Mr. Patterson. He owned the woolen mill down in the harbor. Now there's a man who knows how to step it off.

Well, I'm off now, sweetheart. I signed up for a Zumba class at the Rec center, with Vera's mom. Did I tell you about that?

Love,

Mom

Xoxo

PS. Your father says hello and to keep sending pictures. They're just dandy. He also mentioned something about old brooms knowing how to sweep the right places. Do you know what he meant by that?"

15

"My six-word love story: I can't imagine life without you." —
Unknown

Tiegan

"Let me help you, child." A voice that wouldn't take no for an answer greeted me, firm hands offering salvation from my precarious position. I curved my lips into a faint smile, sliding from Luna's withers. I landed on both feet, but my legs buckled. I felt boneless as if my body was no longer part of me. I tried to speak, but my words came out as gibberish. I sank onto my knees, digging my fingers into the hard dirt and staring through a curtain of darkness.

"Tiegan? Are you all right?" Tomás knelt, gripping my shoulders, his thumbs pressing into my collarbone.

I looked into his worried eyes as he lifted me off the ground and onto my feet. I threw myself into his arms, melding into his body. My hunger was beyond anything I had ever felt—my throbbing core, a pulsating ache—for

Tomás. I tucked my face under his chin, inhaling his scent deep into my lungs.

"I'll tend to the horses, Grandson. Take the girl into the house." Rosalia's voice faded away with the clip-clop of the horse's hooves.

"How about we ride that wild pony, sugar boo?" I pressed my lips to the pulse of Tomás's throat, my hand drifting to the package between his legs. I plowed my other hand through his hair and yanked his mouth to mine, sliding my tongue between his lips, licking his teeth, and suckling his tongue. I stroked the outline of his swelling erection—my pussy flooding with liquid heat.

What did I say? Wild pony? Sugar boo?

"This is not the time, *meu amor*." Tomás rested his lips on my forehead. He stepped backward, sweeping his hands down my body, brushing dirt and debris away from my clothes.

I gazed around the farmyard, taking in the neat structures: the low-roofed barn and the open stable. Chickens pecked at the dirt. Long-eared goats foraged in the underbrush of the nearby forest. One stood out—a shaggy black creature, horned and bearded, gazed at me with knowing yellow eyes.

Rosalia, a wiry woman with a weathered face, returned from the barn.

"Tomás Ferreira, is this how you act in front of your grandmother? Introduce me to this lovely one." She looked at me with a sharp, birdlike gaze, her raven black hair cascading down her back in flowing streams.

"Grandmother, this is Tiegan." Tomás smiled from me to his grandmother. He stepped away and presented me.

"Welcome to my mountain, Tiegan. I hope the ride in was not too difficult." Rosalia's dark eyes pierced into mine. She took my hand in hers.

"Thank you. I thought I did well, at least until that last bit." I found my voice. "I've heard so much about you, Rosalia. It's nice to meet you."

"Good things, I hope?" Rosalia dropped my hand, turning her fiery gaze to Tomás.

I'm not sure if she was asking Tomás or me that question. I seized the moment to study Rosalia. There was a family resemblance, but I had to look hard to see it. There was nothing soft about Tomás's grandmother.

"Come, both of you. The tea is brewing."

I wrapped my hand around Tomás's arm, reluctant to let him go, butterflies fluttering in my stomach. A warning sign of looming disaster?

We followed Rosalia beyond the barns and through a stand of wizened olive trees, heavy with glossy black fruit, ripe for picking.

Rosalia's home blended into the wild landscape. Thorny vines climbed rubble-stone walls, snaking onto the slate roof as smoke curled from the chimney. I followed Tomás inside, past thick windowsills and square rooms, across wide plank floors covered with durable woolen rugs. A ceramic cook-stove took center stage in the kitchen, with a cauldron simmering on the stove. Tomás lifted the lid, allowing the fragrant aroma of root vegetables and braised meat to escape. He stirred the pot with a long wooden spoon.

"Paprika stew, Rosalia?" He tilted his head in question.

"Of course, Grandson. I knew you were coming." Rosalia wrapped her arms around his waist and rested her face against his shoulder.

I saw it. Tomás was Rosalia's world, and I was an intruder.

———

Rosalia poured the promised tea into three bone china teacups. The tea was aromatic: citrus with hints of blueberry.

"Thank you," I looked up as Tomás spoke.

"Grandmother, we need your help." He reached for the sugar bowl.

I grinned at the generous spoonful Tomás added to his cup.

He caught my drift and smiled back at me.

I breathed easier. Somehow, that simple glance eased my anxiety.

"What help would that be, Grandson?" Rosalia's gaze flickered across the table, resting on me.

"I have found the woman I love, Rosalia." Tomás pressed a soft kiss to my ring, to the marble of sea glass, gazing deep into my eyes. "I would like your blessing."

"I see. I sense there's more?"

"Yes, Grandmother, there is. Tiegan wears an amulet with waning power. One her grandfather protected her with as a child."

"I have nightmares. I have had them since I was a young girl. Tomás thought you might help." I looked from Tomás to Rosalia.

"May I see it?"

I lifted the chain over my head and placed my medallion in her outstretched fingers. My stomach twisted; I felt bare without it, vulnerable.

Rosalia examined the medallion, inspecting each side. She rubbed the coin with her thumb.

"Give me your hand, child. Your left hand."

A memory played in the back of my mind, teasing me, shimmering in the light while hiding in the dark. It was a sensation I'd known before. Some might refer to it as déjà vu.

I've always attributed it to lack of sleep, a vivid imagination, and perhaps my nightmares.

Rosalia rubbed the center of my palm with the pad of her thumb.

My palm burned, flames shooting through each finger. I jerked my hand away—Rosalia's gaze clashed with mine.

"I'm sorry, Rosalia, but you're hurting me."

"There's no need to apologize, child." She placed her palms flat on the table before standing up and walking toward a back door leading to a porch, where a large white dog with thick, wavy fur had been waiting.

It occurred to me that this animal could be a wolf rather than a dog.

The wolf-dog bounded across the kitchen—his massive head hung low, his hackles raised, and spittle flew from an impressive mouthful of yellowed fangs.

My heart was in my throat. I expected an immediate attack.

"Rosalia, what is going on here?" Tomás rose from his seat, looming over the table, his voice filled with rage.

I wanted to dive across the table into his arms.

"Anjo," Rosalie uttered the dog's name.

His beady yellow eyes released me as he followed Rosalia to the back porch, where he made the necessary circle before lying down.

My lungs burned from holding my breath.

"Tomás, sit down. There is something I must tell you. Something you must know." The weight of Rosalia's gaze bore down on me.

"Child, a *mullo* caused your nightmares." She traced a cross from her forehead to her chest, from her left-to-right shoulder.

Tomás exhaled a sharp gasp of breath, his fingers tightening on mine.

"What's that? What's a *mullo*?" I looked from one to the other.

"A *mullo* is a spirit. When a body dies an unnatural death or a bad death, that person's spirit will return to the land of the living."

"A spirit? Whose spirit?" My voice rose.

"Rosalia, what are you saying?" Tomás stared at his grandmother.

"Do you mean a ghost?" My pulse hammered in my head. My mouth dried.

"No, child. A ghost *mullo* will not cause trouble. A ghost *mullo* visits the people it loves and longs to be with. No, this is a vampire *mullo*, another entity altogether. This *mullo* has entered your body and infiltrated your very being. She has become one with your soul."

"But there's no such thing as vampires...is there?" I swallowed hard. I attempted to rise, but Rosalia gripped both of my wrists with her bony hands, pinning me to the table.

"I can help you, child. There are ways to kill a vampire's soul." Her eyes flashed with dark light, her voice grim.

"You want to kill the vampire?" My flesh rose into a million goosebumps.

"Do not doubt me, child. Anjo confirmed it. The dog can sense vampire spirits. I would not have allowed Anjo to hurt you."

I was not so reassured. I was still struggling with this nightmare of horror Rosalia expected me to believe.

"What are you saying, Grandmother?"

"You've been tricked by the *mullo*, Grandson. This woman will not fulfill the prophecy." Rosalia's dark eyes flashed in Tomás's direction.

"No, Rosalia! You are wrong!" Tomás smashed his fist on the table.

The blueberry tea slopped over the gilded rims, filling each saucer.

"Grandson, open your eyes." She hissed like a cat, rising from her seat and leaning over the table. "This *mullo* is the spirit of Sylvie. It is Sylvie who visits this girl in the early hours of the morning, possessing her body—enticing you with sexual favors."

And just like that, I knew it was true: the dreams, the sleepwalking, the nightmares—the intense physical attraction I felt for Tomás. Sylvie, the Southern belle. Who else would murmur, Sugar Boo? Those words were not part of my vocabulary.

A memory whispered in my mind—words my grandfather spoke many years ago: words of fire, hell, and brimstone, the casting out of evil, the bursting of spirits.

I had to accept Rosalia was correct—about everything.

"That's enough, Rosalia! Have you lost your mind? Do you take me for a fool?" Tomás's voice bounced off the walls, an echo in my mind.

I was somewhere else, wandering through dense fog and heavy mist.

"Tiegan? Tiegan, let's go. I will not listen to any more of this—this ridiculous nonsense."

I stared into Tomás's face. His eyes were angry, his mouth drawn into a straight line. I rose from my seat—a broken toy, a plaything, used and abused by a dead woman's vampire spirit, with no one to blame but myself. Maybe that's not entirely true—I could blame Sylvie. "Tomás, I want to speak with Rosalia."

"No, Tiegan, I will not leave you alone with... this woman."

"Tomás, it's fine. I'm fine. Leave us."

"A moment, Tiegan, and no longer." Tomás stalked out of the kitchen. In the doorway, he turned, facing me. "Do you remember what I said earlier?" Tomás held me in the fierce grip of his gaze. "I love you, and nothing said here today will change that."

Rosalia's hands trembled, her face paled. She stared after Tomás.

"Rosalia?" She didn't seem to hear me. I wanted to feel sorry for her, but right now—I needed clarity. "Rosalia, I believe you." I touched her arm.

"I'm sorry, child." Her gaze leveled with mine.

"This spirit… I've always felt something but didn't know what it was." I opened my mouth to say her name but couldn't. I squeezed my hands together. "Sylvie has been with me for a long time. I know what she wants, what she has always wanted. Sylvie wants Tomás. What did you mean when you said you could kill the vampire? What would happen?" The clock on the wall ticked away, second by second, and I worried Tomás would burst through the door at any moment. I had never seen him that angry.

Rosalia stared at me for what seemed a long time.

"Iron can kill a vampire. Killing a vampire's spirit is more complex. When the moon is full, you will return here. This mountain is a sacred place, and you will be safe. I will prepare an iron pin." Rosalia placed her palm over my heart, holding me in place. "The pin will pierce your heart, freeing you. Your life will be yours, and your nightmares will end." Her shoulders straightened, and those dark eyes pierced mine. Her voice lowered. "You will leave this mountain—you will leave Portugal. You will leave my grandson alone." Her hand fell from my chest.

I sank back into the chair, squeezed my eyes shut, and pressed my lips together. I had one more question: "What will happen to Sylvie?" I met Rosalia's fiery gaze.

"Sylvie will return to the Valley of the Dead, and this time she will stay there."

I walked through the foyer, shutting the heavy door behind me. Pain gnawed at my gut. I was that little Spartan boy, the one of legend—brave on the outside yet dying on the inside.

Tomás waited in the courtyard with Romulus in hand, the horse pawing at the ground, eager to take flight. I ran through the olive trees into his arms, feeling the protective embrace of his shadow. He murmured words of love in a fierce voice, filling my heart. I clung to him, unwilling to let him go.

He lifted me onto the horse and settled himself, wrapping his arm around my waist and tucking my head under his chin. I glanced back and couldn't help but notice my little lavender plant, sitting lost and forgotten in the doorway of Rosalia's stone house.

———

We were high above sea level. My heart pounded in my chest, and my breath quickened. The trail Romulus chose was narrow and overgrown with thorny brambles.

"Where are we going? Are we lost?" My sense of direction told me we were going the wrong way.

"No, we're not lost. There's a place I want to show you."

I leaned into Tomás's chest, relaxing into Romulus's easy gait. I wanted to forget the words Rosalia said, but I couldn't. I didn't know what to do or what to think.

The horse halted in a clearing, and I gazed upward, spellbound by the union of heaven and earth. Where one began and the other ended was indistinguishable. In this place, they were one. A waterfall thundered over a granite shield, cascading from high in the clouds into a basin of tranquil water shaped by the currents of time.

Mist drifted above the water. This was an enchanted place.

I slid off Romulus and landed with both feet firmly planted on solid ground. He unsaddled the magnificent horse, leaving him to graze on nearby patches of green grass.

"What is this place?" I turned away, gazing into the translucent pool of water. The tang of moss and forest filled my mind. An ancient aroma evoked a memory I had always known: moist earth and blood of the stone.

"I would come here as a boy and gaze at the clouds. I wanted to share this place with you." Tomás circled his arms around my waist.

I truly saw him for the first time. Sylvie led me to Tomás. I was here because of her—I wanted him because of her. Would I have changed any part of this journey if I'd had the chance? Rosalia's words echoed in my mind, "She is not the woman you are waiting for, Tomás."

"It's beautiful, Tomás. Thank you for taking me here." I gazed into his essence, swallowing back hot tears.

"Tiegan, I want to apologize to you."

"Apologize? For what?" I looked into the rising mist of the fairy pool.

"For all of it: curses, prophecies…vampire spirits. All those things Rosalia said—about Sylvie. I love you, Tiegan."

"I love you too, Tomás." How could I deny the grip Tomás Ferreira held on my heart? I couldn't, not anymore.

"Really?"

"Yes." I placed my hands on my hips, jutting out my chin.

Tomás swept me into his arms, crushing my lips with his kiss.

I kissed him back, sliding my hands under his shirt, under the waistband of his jeans—my goal—to relieve Tomás of all pieces of clothing. I wanted him there—in that place.

Within moments, we were naked in this verdant oasis, the

creatures of the forest our only witness. Tomás stood before me, magnificent and so very beautiful, his shaft as hard as the stone of this place. His eyes were hypnotic, and I was in thrall. I stared into the kaleidoscope: dark chocolate, a flicker of light, a strike of gold. My breath caught.

He knelt before me on the cushion of moss, his hands coursing the curves of my body, his lips grazing my breasts, my belly, my sex.

Silent whispers filled my mind—stories of doubt, heartache, and pain.

"Tomás…I need you." Did I say that? Or did Sylvie? My doppelgänger. Was she a friend or a foe? The bane of my existence or my lifeblood? What would I be without her? How would I even know?

His lips trailed in a downward, circling my clit, drawing on that tender piece of flesh. He lifted my leg over his shoulder, opening my core to his hunger, clasping my bottom in the spread of his hands with carnal force, sure to leave bruises.

I tangled my fingers in his hair, racked with an explosive surge of pulsating ripples. I cried out, whispering his name.

"I love tasting you, so sweet—like flowers, like honey." He buried his tongue into my weeping pussy, spearing hard and fast, taking me to that mindless place.

A sharp pain, a dull ache, and an acute awareness strangled my heart. I loved him—I had always loved him. I sank to my knees and joined him on the mossy bank, lying back on the bed of moss, pulling him with me. Our legs, our hands intertwined—our lips brushed.

He filled me, easing in and out slowly and steadily. It was an exquisite sensation but not enough to satisfy my rising hunger.

"More, Tomás. Fuck me harder." I raked my fingers over

his back. My pulse hammered in my head, making me forget —I was not the one.

I was on the brink of release, my pussy pulsing with quivering waves, and then in one quick motion, Tomás repositioned, and I was on top, his cock reaching the end of me. My breath raged, and my heart hurt. How could I say goodbye?

"I want to watch you." He growled, tilting my pelvis, rolling my sex over his shaft, tantalizing every heated tissue.

"Faster. Don't stop." Flames licked my thighs, and nerve endings flared.

His grip tightened, and a groan rumbled in his chest. He quickened, and his shaft jerked. He cried out, a carnal shout to the gods above.

Undulating into the ebb and flow of each explosion, racked with the trembling sensation of orgasm, I fell onto him, pressing my lips to his throat, to the shadow under his jaw. We stayed fused, lost in our world of one. After two long moments, I lifted onto my elbows and gazed into his beautiful face. "You finished."

"I know."

"And you're okay?"

"I'm more than okay."

"That's not what I meant, Tomás."

"I know what you meant."

"After what Rosalia said? That I'm not the one?"

"None of it matters…not to me…not anymore." He cupped my face, pressing his lips to my forehead.

I had no words, no rebuttal. I wanted to believe.

"Tomás, can we go in the water?" Since we arrived, the crystal water of the faerie pool had been calling me. An ethereal essence, a spirit voice murmured in the shadows.

"You want to get in the water? It's not warm." He stood up, his hands spread across my backside.

"Yes, I want to." I clung to him, my legs wrapped around his waist, gasping as icy mist and frigid water enveloped us. Tomás waded through the shallows into the depths. He doesn't let go of me, but then I realized why.

Out of sight, a sheet of velvet-covered rock lies beneath the surface. I felt the energy of the cascading water—caught in a vortex of wet mist—on the other side, in a different place.

"You feel so good," Tomás murmured, tightening his grip on my hips and sliding my bottom to the edge of the precipice. "I love being inside you."

I inhaled. Mother Earth had shared one of her sons—a warrior of the mist, a mystical king with the physical presence of a god. Penetrating black eyes pierced mine, sinews of muscle roiling beneath translucent skin. I blinked, and the mist king vanished—Tomás's beautiful face came into focus. I trailed my fingers down the sides of his face, the angles of his jaw, reassuring myself he was real. Or was I playing hide and seek with a reality I didn't want to confront?

Like the crashing tide of an angry ocean, he crested in and out, each surge striking hard and fast. My breath staggered, and I braced the soles of my feet on the face of the rock wall, the cold water numbing the folds of my vagina. A switch had flipped. Mindless with arousal, I spurred him on, raking my fingers down his back, sweeping my tongue between his lips, my screams buried deep in his mouth.

I didn't want to leave the solitude of the mountain pool. I could have stayed in a make-believe world where reality did not exist.

———

"What about the curse? You don't believe it anymore?"

"For years, Rosalia poisoned my mind and Anca's with all of this nonsense. Curses? Prophecies? And now vampire spirits? It's too much, Tiegan. How can I believe any of it?" Tomás shifted gear as the Land Rover carved the last switchback.

"I don't know, Tomás."

"Sylvie died a long time ago, and it broke my heart. But you're right; Anca was right. Sylvie died from complications. I've been chained to this belief my entire life. I will not let Rosalia destroy our future." Tomás talked himself into it, validating this new way of thinking.

I gazed out the window as we drove toward Carvoeiro. The landscape had changed in more ways than one. Sylvie's spirit—though I won't call her a vampire—was a part of me. Yes, she caused chaos, but at least I understood it. I knew what Sylvie wanted, what she had always wanted. Sylvie wanted Tomás and had shared him with me.

If Rosalia was right about Sylvie, then she was right about everything else. And that meant somewhere out there was Tomás's true soulmate: his invisible thread, the one person who would make him whole—and I was not that person.

I pressed my teeth into my lower lip, realizing what we had done. My vagina pulsated from the heat of Tomás's bare cock, my core slick, wet with his seed. I silenced the noise; I had nothing to fear—I had taken precautions. I felt for my medallion. It was gone.

"Oh, no…I forgot my necklace." I remembered—I gave Rosalia my medallion, but she didn't return it.

"Do you want to go back? We can make it before nightfall." Tomás swerved the Land Rover off the road, braking on the shoulder. Clouds of red clay rose from the dry earth, enveloping the Land Rover in dust.

As much as I wanted my medallion back, I no longer needed it. I wasn't afraid anymore.

16

"If you're on thin ice, you might
as well dance."—Unknown

Tomás

You're wrong, Rosalia. Do you not see what I see? I smashed my fist on the bar top. What had I become? A madman, a ranting fool pacing the floor, talking to myself. When did the contractors leave? And Eli? How many hours ago? I paced the perimeter of the dining hall, from wall to wall, corner to corner, every familiar footfall—my sanctuary—my prison.

Those moments—making love on the mountain. Two incredible times. It was more than incredible. Spilling my seed inside you, sweet Tiegan?

You are mine, and I am yours. You fill my soul, *meu amor.* And now? How could I face tomorrow and every day after that?

What had I done?

She would forget—she would be happy—with someone else.

Her whispers trailed after me through the kitchen and up the stairs to what had once been a studio apartment and was now my office. My cell phone vibrated and chirped on the desk. I turned sideways and slammed my fist into the painted concrete wall.

I promised you the world. I made you believe.

I studied my bloodied knuckles and stared through the window at everyday people living everyday lives. That's all I ever wanted. And now? The truth slapped me in the face—undeniable truth.

I have to take it back. I have to end this before it's too late.

My throat closed. My vision blurred. Eli was right. How could I let her go? How could I not?

The cell phone chirped.

I'm sorry, *meu amor*. I'm so sorry. How do I live without you?

"Hey, man. Thought I heard you up here." Eli leaned in the doorway, his arms hanging loosely at his sides.

"It's your day off, isn't it?" I ran my hands through my greasy hair—sour odors wafted from my armpits, curling my nostrils. Removing the shower during the renovations was a poor choice. I gazed at the blue blanket strewn over the sofa, at the big screen television on mute.

"Thought I'd check the lines. The connections. Have you been here all night?" He glanced over his shoulder as he opened the mini-fridge and twisted off the lid of an orange juice bottle. "They're good, no leaks."

"Great. That's great." I stared at him through tired eyes and walked to the bathroom. I bent over the sink, splashing water on my face.

"You look terrible, man—like death warmed over." He lifted the bottle and took a swig.

"Hmm. Death cures everything, doesn't it?" I tossed the towel into the bin.

"What? What's up, man? Something wrong in paradise?" Eli's eyebrows rise.

My cell chirped, vibrating on the desk.

"I have to get this." I nodded at the phone. "Thanks for checking in." I turned away from Eli's penetrating gaze and took the call.

"Tomás? I've been trying to get you all night. Where have you been?" Anca's voice was hurried, and car horns blared in the background.

"Good morning, Anca. What can I do for you today?" I leaned back in the chair, stretching my legs and crossing my ankles, readying myself for what I expected would be a lengthy conversation.

"Did you know your father is in town? Why weren't you picking up?" She demanded answers to both questions.

"I saw him in Monchique." Our father—that caught me off guard. She referred to him as mine, not hers, trying to provoke me. I wouldn't sway, not this time. That argument was becoming tiresome. I saw the old man working with a bear—Rory's younger counterpart. Watching that bear dance the same steps I had taught Rory, my mind went blank. The sight of the bear affected me most, not my father, never him.

"And you didn't tell me? Why didn't you tell me? We're meeting for lunch today, and I want you to come." Anca's voice squeaked.

A car door slammed, followed by muffled silence.

I assumed she was on her way to Carvoeiro.

"I can't." I closed my eyes and yawned, picturing Anca— smoke curling from her ears, her eyes blazing. I turned my head from side to side and cracked my neck.

"You aren't coming? Please come, Tomás. Should I pick you up?" Her voice shifted from pleading to insistent as the engine roared to life. "Why are you always such a dick? Can you answer that? Tomás?"

I chuckled inside, not daring to voice my laughter. One thing remained the same: I could never please Anca. She was like my father.

I locked the backdoor behind me, stuffing the keys in my pocket, sunlight blinding me. "What the fuck?"

"What is it? What's wrong?" Her voice rang in my ears.

"Someone stole my car." I canvassed the street, looking one way and then the other.

"No way. Are you kidding? The car? The four by four?"

"The SUV Goddamn it. I have to go."

———

T*iegan*
The stadium, fashioned after the old bullring in Madrid, was a masterpiece of Moorish revival. Domed towers flanked each cardinal point and featured a retractable roof. The air was crisp, and stars twinkled in a black velvet sky. A shiver ran down my spine as the matador swung a cloak of red silk, taunting the black bull. The bull stamped his feet, lowered his massive head, and bellowed— my initiation to Portugal—a bullfight.

Tomás bought tickets for the evening event and invited Anca, planning the entire night, which included an early dinner at an Italian restaurant followed by the bullfight. He mentioned wanting to make it up to her but didn't specify what he meant by that.

In Portugal, the bull would survive. According to Tomás, the bullfight was a test of wits between man and beast. I remained unconvinced.

This bull was not a puro, which meant the bull had fought before. This bull was skilled in the art of stealth and practiced in cunning. The bullfighter would have her hands full.

I stared, spellbound, as the matador performed an intricate dance, darting from side to side of the silken cape, to the crowd's cheer, to the bull's fury. She barely escaped the horns of the enraged beast.

The bull charged again in a rush of agility, forcing the matador into the wall. The matador gored and possibly disemboweled, and the bull would have its just reward? But the matador leaped up, bounding over the rail, and the bull's horns crashed with a loud bang. The crowd responded in a frenzy of madness, the ripple effect of group contagion. They cheered, rising from their seats and waving their fists in the air, a fabulous show of appreciation.

"So, what did you think, *meu amor*?" He looked amazing, as always, wearing tapered jeans and a black leather jacket.

"Well, I'm glad the bull didn't die." I grinned, truly relieved.

"I think the bull enjoys himself." He informed me in no uncertain terms.

"You do?" I lifted an eyebrow.

"Yes, the bull is a savage animal looking for a fight. It will always attack."

"Hmm…okay, if you say so. I'm not sure I agree."

"A bullfight is the ultimate display of macho testosterone," Anca's laughter echoed behind us as we walked through the circular passage and descended a spiraling staircase into the expansive halls of a grand stadium.

"For man and beast." I giggled at Anca.

"Yes, that's right." Tomás placed his hand on my lower back, staying close by.

I had grown used to his hovering presence.

"Come on! Hurry, or we won't get a table," Anca called out as she rushed ahead, leading us through the gothic-shaped doors of the Campo Pequeno.

An open-air tapas bar bordered the terraced gardens, and

that's where Anca headed. She was right—bullfight fans filled the tables, not wanting the evening to end.

We found seats at a small table on the edge of the piazza. I leaned back, admiring the domed turrets, horseshoe-shaped windows, and romantic architecture of Lisbon's bullring illuminated by the moonlight. It was truly spectacular.

"Tomás, we need beer." Anca drummed her fingers on the tabletop. "Where's the server?"

"Tiegan, what would you like?" Tomás ignored his sister.

She made a fist, punching her brother square in the chest.

"Ow! What was that for?" He looked hurt.

"The night is still young. After we eat, we should go dancing. Hey, it's not like you have anywhere else to be. Besides, I want to check out the fancy new wheels." She smirked, referring to the electric vehicle Tomás had picked up yesterday.

"Tiegan?" Tomás asked a second time, and then his eyes darkened, and the corner of his mouth quirked—a satisfied man well-fucked, and Tomás's brand-new vehicle, a full-size model with extra legroom and tinted windows—well-christened.

"Sure, beer is fine." I swallowed the ball of desire coiling in my belly. The drive to Lisbon felt long, and halfway there, I wanted—no, I needed—release. I couldn't wait another mile.

"I'll be right back." He leaned in and kissed the top of my head, his fingertips gliding along the contour of my jaw.

All I wanted was to return to the hotel and taste him again.

"I haven't seen Tomás this happy in a long time." Anca's gaze followed her brother as he weaved through the tables toward the bar. "I'm glad you found him, Tiegan."

I blinked, overwhelmed by a rush of emotion. Tomás stood in line, absorbed in a lively conversation with a man in a blue sweater. I twirled the sea glass ball on my finger.

"Tiegan, are you okay?" Anca placed her hand on mine.

"I met Rosalia last week." I gazed into her eyes, which were more green than brown, reflecting the color of her emerald sweater dress.

"Oh…and how did that go?" Her voice held a massive hit of sarcasm.

A tear fell, and I wiped it away with the heel of my hand. I didn't know where all this emotion was coming from.

"Jesus. What did my grandmother say?" Her eyelashes lifted.

"She said I'm not the one," I repeated the words that ran through my head—every moment of every day.

"Oh my fucking God, he still believes that? Jesus fuck, I knew he would screw this up. I just knew it." Fury raced through her words as she leaped from her seat.

"Anca, no. Wait." I reached for her arm, yanking her back just in time.

Tomás caught my attention from across the patio, raising his eyebrows in question.

I smiled, and he returned to his conversation with the man in the blue sweater.

"Tiegan, let me talk to him. This is fucking bullshit."

"No, it's not like that. Tomás told Rosalia she was wrong."

"Oh. Well, thank fucking Christ. It's good then, right?" She nodded her head up and down, waiting for me to agree.

"No, it's not good." I pressed my lips together. Should I tell Anca everything?

"Look. Tiegan, don't let my grandmother ruin things between you and Tomás. Please, I beg you."

I moved carefully, hoping to prevent Anca from going on a rant. She would criticize Tomás from every angle.

"What about Sylvie? She died because of the curse." My voice cracked, and I looked into my plastic cup.

"No! Oh my fucking God. Did he tell you that?" Anca's voice sang in horror.

"You don't believe it?" My bottom lip quivered. It was all I could do not to burst into tears.

"Dammit. Those are the fantasies of an old witch. Rosalia has ruined my brother's life. I don't get it. He can't seem to break free. I think the old witch put a spell on him herself. Every summer he spent on that mountain of hers. Not me. No way in hell. I wanted nothing to do with that mountain. It was different for Tomás. He was always the chosen one." Her expression shifted from anger to pity.

How could I tell Anca that Sylvie's vampire spirit lived within me? She would think I was batshit crazy. Maybe I was. According to her, Tomás drank the fruit punch too many times.

"When Tomás found Sylvie, I thought he would finally be free. But then Sylvie died, and Rosalia's had him in her clutches ever since. I'll talk to him." Her voice told me she would do more than talk to her brother.

"Anca, no." I clutched her wrist, imploring her. "Please, Anca. Don't." This was not the time or the place to air dirty laundry.

She sat back in her chair, her gaze flicking toward her brother.

I looked, too. I couldn't take my eyes off him—a jolt of heat made my lips part and my mouth water. He was stunning, from the chiseled line of his jaw to those piercing eyes. But it didn't stop there. Beneath that black T-shirt were rippling muscles I wanted to lick. The air crackled, charged with magnetic energy—my breasts grew heavy, the ache grew, and my thighs tingled. It was a full-body response to the man in black.

Anca's gaze returned to me. She pinned her lips together and nodded.

17

iegan

Holiday tunes floated through the sound system of the small cafe across the road from Vera's boutique. The cafe was an easy go-to for a latte or a strawberry tart. This morning, we sat in the window seat so she could keep an eye on the front door of her shop. At this time of day, shoppers were few and far between.

"You're saying Tomás's wife died because she wasn't his true soulmate? From a curse? And you think you're possessed? By a *mullo*? Is that what you called it?" Her forehead creased with concern as she looked across the table.

I nodded, glancing around the cafe. Did I care what people thought? No, but I would rather not announce my nightmare to the world at large.

"Are you feeling all right, hon? Does this have anything to do with Aaron?" Her voice gentled, calling my attention back to her.

"What? No. Why would you think that?" I squared my

shoulders, understanding her implication. I hadn't thought about Aaron in days. No, this had nothing to do with him. If his mullo was haunting someone, it wasn't me.

"Tiegan…you've been through so much. Maybe you should talk to my therapist. She has a great way of putting things into perspective." Her voice faded in and out of my mind.

"No, Vera. There's nothing wrong with me." I gazed at the small vase in the center of the table, overflowing with sprigs of holly and bright red berries.

"I don't know, hon. Hey, how about a holiday? Let's take Lola to Barcelona. Do the museums—Picasso, Gaudi. The coffee's to die for. Oooh, we could walk La Rambla. It would be such fun." She squeezed my fingers, her eyes bright.

"No! I don't need another holiday. I'm fine."

How did I make Vera understand? How could I expect anyone to understand?

Vera pressed her lips together as if there was more she would like to say. She stared me down for more than a moment and then exhaled a long breath. "So this *mullo* is Tomás's wife?"

"Her name is Sylvie." She was a part of me. Oh God, maybe Vera's right. Maybe I was crazy; I heard voices and saw things that weren't real. How did I end up in this place? How had I gone from being a local hero to a hot mess?

"And this Rosalia woman wants to pierce your heart with a steel pin? Is that what you said? Jesus, Tiegan, this is some crazy-ass shit—like those nut jobs back home. Remember?"

I did remember.

The day I arrived in the Algarve and met Tomás was All Saints Day, the Day of the Dead, or Samhain. It was the day the door to the otherworld swung open, and all beings traveled freely: ghosts, faeries, demons, and newly created souls.

On Cape Breton Island, a modern pagan cult following

the teachings of the druidic religion lit fires to honor the dead and assist them on their journey. The sacrifice of a white cow was part of their celebrations. Thanks to one fervent cult member, social media, and a well-placed live podcast, an ancient grove of oak trees hidden deep within the Anse Valley Highlands attracted the world's attention. Solar-powered, infrared security cameras now monitor access to the trailhead.

"Don't you see? My nightmares. My medallion. Grandpa gave me that medallion. He was trying to protect me. He must have known." I tapped my fingers on the table—that day now held new meaning. "The attraction I have for Tomás—I don't know. It's not just sex, Vera—it's phenomenal sex, and I crave it, every moment of every day."

"Nothing wrong with that, hon." Vera's laughter lightened the mood.

"Tiegan?" His voice prowled beneath my skin, the whisper I turned to in the dark of night. I thought I had imagined it, as I had many times before, but I hadn't. He stood beside me, just out of sight. "Good morning, Vera."

"Tomás? What is it? Is something wrong?" I looked over my shoulder, catching his ready smile. I woke to those luscious, soft lips ravishing my core, burrowing deep into my sex. I blushed at the climactic memory and the sudden surge of heat flaring between my legs.

"I'm afraid so. A wildfire is burning out of control on the mountain's north side. They're evacuating Monchique." Tomás was ruggedly handsome in his signature black T-shirt, ripped jeans, and construction boots.

"Oh my God, how bad is it?" Vera and I echoed the exact words.

"Bad...I can't find Rosalia. She's not answering her cell. I'm going up there to ensure she's okay." His eyes shadowed with concern.

"I'll come with you." I rose, my chair scraping across the floor. I remembered—the long trail through the thick forest —the only way to and from Rosalia's sanctuary.

"No, Tiegan, it's not safe." He cupped my shoulders, towering above me.

"But I want to help." I swallowed back the need, the desire.

"No, I won't put you in harm's way. It's too dangerous. Eli's coming with me. I'll call as soon as I have news. The last time I spoke with her…the things I said." His lips were hard, his gaze searching.

"What about Jack?" I thought of the nice man who helped me with the horse.

"There's been no contact with either one. I'm sorry, I have to leave. There's no time to waste." He nodded and then turned away.

People in the cafe rose from their seats, engaging in conversation. The atmosphere changed from a relaxed morning to a chaotic frenzy.

"Be careful. Promise me," I said as I followed Tomás to the sidewalk, wrapping my arms around him and burying my face in his chest. I didn't want to let him go.

Eli waved from the passenger seat of Tomás's truck as they drove away.

In my need to be with Tomás, I had forgotten about Vera. Her gaze lingered on the summit of Mt. Foia, watching the thick yellow smoke billowing into the air.

"Tieg, I'm going to close the shop and go home. I need to keep an eye on things in case this fire spreads. Do you want to come with me? You can stay as long as you want." She searched my eyes, her gaze hopeful.

"It's okay. I'll be fine." I gave her a quick hug. "I'll call you later, alright?" As much as I appreciated her concern, I declined. She was my best friend, and I had dragged her into my nightmare without considering how it would affect her. She had enough on her plate and didn't need me adding to her troubles. Whatever was ahead, I could handle. I offered her a reassuring smile as she walked away.

———

Church bells tolled. The town was quiet, almost deserted, the townsfolk glued to their televisions and computer screens, watching up—to—the—minute footage of the blazing mountain. Flames licked the countryside, threatening everything and everyone in their deadly wake. The army had deployed to help with the evacuation.

Shifting winds fanned the flames and ignited new fires, sending smoke down from the mountain. Fingers pointed at hydro lines and a deadly forest—at the unregulated growth of eucalyptus, commonly called tinder trees with their long strips of bark floating in the wind—as the cause of this fire.

Three days passed.

———

The sound of tapping woke me. Jumping out of bed, I rushed through the dangling string of beads and threw open the green door. João's eyes widened as they took in my disheveled look, complete with pony pajamas and bare feet.

"João, why aren't you at school?" I looked past João toward the mountain peak, where smoky plumes choked the sky. I blinked, my eyes stinging and my throat itching.

"No school." João shook his head back and forth. "Because of the fires. Mama sent me—chickpea with ham." João offered a plastic container of soup and a round of freshly baked sourdough bread. I had been the regular recipient of care packages from João's mama ever since I sketched the portrait of João and his avo.

"Right. Of course. How are you, João? How's your mom?" I opened the door and let the boy pass through.

The cat jumped off the sofa, winding around João's legs.

"Mama won't let me go fishing. Does he have a name yet?" João tilted his head, giving me that sly smile nine-year-old boys were famous for.

"Hmm, I might call him João." I poured the soup into a saucepan and turned the burner on low. This is an ongoing conversation: why does the cat not have a name?

"That's my name." João laughed—a belly laugh echoed off the domed ceiling.

"Okay, you pick a name." I chuckled and tousled the curls on top of his head.

"I get to pick?" He threw himself onto the sofa and stared at the domed ceiling.

"Yep, you pick."

"Al…"

"Al?"

"Yep, Al for the Algarve. That's where he's from. His name should be Al."

"Al."

"He looks like an Al." João nodded his head up and down.

"Okay—Al, it is."

He lifted the newly named Al into his arms, the cat's long body reaching João's knees. He kissed his furry head.

The loud rumble of a low-flying engine shook me from my musings. I rushed to the balcony and threw open the doors. "João, look!"

We leaned over the railing together, watching in awe as a large yellow plane—a water bomber—dove from the sky. There was no wind; the ocean's surface resembled a pane of reflective glass. The engine's drone emitted a rumbling, ratcheting sound as the seaplane leveled out. Probes emerged, scooping water into the plane's empty belly. Thirty seconds later, the plane ascended, carving into the sky and banking inland toward the mountain and the still-raging fire. In its wake, another water bomber arrived, repeating the same process.

"*Avo* said they would come. They came last time."

"How many fires have there been, João?" I glanced at my phone. I couldn't help it. I looked every five minutes.

"Lots, when I was little."

"Should we have soup?" I walked back to the cooktop and stirred the saucepan. This was another ritual—we shared the goodies João's mama had prepared.

"Yes, please. Chickpea is my favorite." João sat at the table, drumming his fingers on the checkered tablecloth, while I ladled the soup into two oversized bowls. I cut the bread into thick, heavenly slices.

"The Christmas Market's next week." João jammed a mouthful of bread into his mouth. "I can't wait to see the bear."

"What bear?" I glanced at João with a quick look of surprise. Could it be the same man—Tomás's estranged father? How many bears could be dancing their way through the Algarve?

"The dancing bear. I saw him in Monchique." João bent like a pretzel, weaving a stick with a dangling ribbon back and forth on the floor. Al snatched the ribbon, enjoying the game. "I know a joke."

"Oh, really? Tell me." I leaned back in my chair, my mind racing with too many thoughts at once.

"Okay." João grinned, his eyes wide. "How do you make holy water?"

"I don't know, João. How do you make holy water?"

"Boil the hell out of it!" João chortled. I laughed at the sparkle in his dark eyes, at the grin on his face.

"That's a good one, João." I ladled more soup into his bowl.

———

Rain pounded the rooftop, overflowing the gutters and washing the windowsills. I had forgotten to close the shutters. A voice in my head urged me to wake—but my body felt heavy and my mind sluggish. I wanted to snuggle under the soft duvet and go back to sleep. Instead, I jumped out of bed and fell to the floor, tangled in the sheets. I lay in the darkness, my face resting on the hard floor.

"Tiegan?" His voice whispered, drifting through the darkness.

My nostrils filled with a sharp stench—wildfire, a mix of black soot and oily residue. Water droplets dripped from his hair, cooling my face—I licked my lips and savored the rain, my heart swelling with joy—he was safe.

"Tiegan? Are you all right? You must have fallen hard, *meu amor*. I heard a thump." He crouched beside me on the floor, unclothed and gloriously naked.

I ran the palms of my hands over his bulging thigh muscles. Grit coated his skin, and particles of ash mixed with sweat.

"You're back. What happened? Where's Rosalia and Jack?" I sat up, my knees underneath me.

"They're all okay. Rosalia, Jack, the horses. We kept the fires away from the barn and the house." His voice was tired.

"Is it over?" A draft crawled over the floorboards. Outside, the wind howled, gusting sideways, slapping the walls of Vila Algarve with sheets of rain, but I was in a world of my own making. I snuggled closer.

"It's over, and this rain will extinguish hot spots or flash fires. Tiegan? Are you okay?" He stroked my hair, lifting my chin to meet his gaze.

"I'm glad you're here, that's all." A sigh escaped my lips—my blood hummed.

"Let's get you back to bed. I'll join you in a few minutes." He scooped me into his arms and dropped me onto the bed. Leaning in, he pressed his lips to my forehead.

"No, Tomás. Stay with me." I drew my hands along his thighs, cupped his balls, and squeezed gently.

A bolt of light cracked the sky wide open. I saw what I wanted to see.

"And I want you, but I've been dirty for too many days. Let me wash up. I won't be long." He gave me one forehead kiss.

"You're not leaving me." I followed Tomás into the bathroom—into a cloud of steam and a shower of rain. I reached for him, plunging my hands through his hair and meeting his lips.

Our tongues collided as he delved deep, leaving not a morsel untouched. He gazed into my eyes. "Do you know how much I've missed you?"

I folded my arms around him, pressing into his swelling erection. Arrows of heat shot through me as the ball of lust unraveled.

He drizzled a healthy dollop of sandalwood, and an amber body wash over my backside, his hands skimming my shoulders and back, soaping my skin with the rich scent of bergamot and juniper berries.

"Tomás," I murmured his name, a yearning moan rising in my throat. I was weak-kneed and oh-so hungry.

He dragged his mouth down the side of my face while his

fingers played—with the underside of my jaw, with the curves of my breasts, to the soft skin below my belly, rising again to cup my breasts and to pinch the inflamed nubs.

And then he knelt before my thighs and paid homage to my pussy. With soapy, slippery hands, he dragged his thumbs through my labia, separating the needy folds. He lavished my flesh with teasing nibbles and hard pulls, drawing my clit between his teeth and lapping the hood with a hard tongue. He splayed his fingers across my bottom, squeezing my ass cheeks.

When he eased the pad of his thumb deep into my pussy and flexed that hard digit—faster and then faster. I lost myself. My eyes rolled back in my head, and I cried out. I shoved my fingers into his hair and guided his lips, my lust for him gathering storm. Seconds more, that's all I needed. An ache flowed from my head to my toes and back again. I lifted my face into the spray of hot water as my climax reached a rolling peak.

Tomás rose to his feet, closing his hands on my face. "Do you know how much I love you?"

"That was incredible, Tomás. Thank you." I gazed into his eyes. There was so much I didn't want to see.

"What? You don't have to thank me. I love you. I've missed you." He pressed his lips to my forehead, his shaft hard against his ridged belly.

I turned away, planting my hands against the shower wall. I dropped my head and widened my stance. "I love that you love me, Tomás."

"What does that mean, *meu amor?*" He knew what I wanted and what I needed.

"It means everything." Water pellets beat down, stinging my flesh.

His fingers brushed my hair back, his lips pressing against the nape of my neck, moving from my earlobe to the underside of my jaw. One finger skimmed from the entrance of my pussy to the puckered rim of my anus, circling the tight bud.

"Tomás, no. I don't…I don't do that." My butt cheeks flinched. My pussy shuddered.

"No?" His damp hair brushed against my face as he leaned in, kissing the corner of my mouth.

"No, I never have." I swallowed hard, biting down on my lower lip.

"Then I'll be the first?" He trailed his hand over the flat of my belly to the folds of my sex, fingering my outer lips. He nibbled my earlobe.

"Yes, but…won't it hurt?" I leaned into his exploring mouth, my eyes closing.

"I would never hurt you." He eased two thick fingers into my pussy, grazing my clitoris with the pad of his thumb.

"I know, but will it hurt?" I gasped at the penetration—my arousal flared.

"It will be uncomfortable for a moment. And then you will like it, I promise." He suckled my tongue and my lower lip.

"What if I don't like it?" I sank against him, aching for him.

"Then we will stop." His breath mingled with mine. "I want to possess every part of you. Will you let me?" He gazed at me through half-slits.

"Yes." I didn't want to say no. I wanted to give him everything.

He sank onto his haunches, parting my ass cheeks with the brush of his thumbs, and then his tongue seared that dark entrance with long, hard licks. That thick muscle snaked past the tiny pucker, prodding the soft tissues and pumping into me. "Do you like that?" He leaned back, his breath warm against my heated skin.

"Yes." This was a new world of sensation. I bent my mind in a new direction, embracing the unknown.

"Stay here, *meu amor*." He stood, cupping my shoulders and holding me for a brief moment.

"Where are you going?" Curtained in the pounding spray, I listened to drawers opening and closing—my mind spinning.

"We need to do this right. I don't want to hurt you." He gathered me into his arms, his cock throbbing against my clit.

I circled my arms around his waist, pressing my face against his chest. We stayed that way for a long moment.

He reached behind me and flipped open a plastic bottle of waterproof lube. He greased the folds of my sex, my clitoris, and my anus with slippery gel. "Turn around, *meu amor*. Lean against the wall."

I followed his instructions, standing spread-eagled, my back arched.

"I'm going to press against you. Are you ready?" He swept his palms over my flesh, squeezing my bottom.

"Yes." My anticipation built, my need quickening. My pulse hammered in my head.

He rested one hand on the small of my back and then, with gentle force, fed the crown of his cock into that dainty cavity. Time stood still as his shaft slipped past the anal ring.

I gasped, a shiver dancing over me as the sphincter clenched down, denying him.

"Are you all right?" He stilled, trailing the backs of his knuckles in circles over my bottom—tantalizing, soft strokes that teased my mind.

"Yes." I cried out, teetering on the edge of pleasure and pain.

"Breathe, Tiegan. I love you. You're everything I want."

His hand rested on my shoulder, his thumb stroking my throat.

"Hmm." The nerves inside my cleft swelled, and my thighs quivered.

"Do you want to stop?"

"No…more, give me more." I braced my palms on the hard wall. I was ready.

His cock inched inward, and then in one stroke, he filled me. A rigid column of flesh, harder, thicker than ever before. The thrum of each vessel, of each vein, pulsated inside me. It was an excruciating pleasure.

I gasped for breath, my arousal a tightening fist coiled in my belly. My anal channel contracted, sucking him inward, a deep tissue massage rubbing places I didn't know needed rubbing.

He sensed my arousal and, with his hands on my hips, withdrew halfway and then filled me—one, two, three gliding strokes.

I cried out as a delectable pressure built, spreading heat through my entire body. My bones locked, my clit swelling. I let my fingers drift to the aching nub in a frenetic dance of heated desire.

He twined his fingers with mine, cupping my fleshy mound, lifting me, and arching my bottom, pumping into me —hard, driving strokes that pressed deep. "Come with me, Tiegan." His voice resonated, a deep bass note bouncing off the tiled walls.

I let myself go to the sensations rolling over and through my body, the rocketing tremors. White dots flashed beneath my eyelids, my breasts tingled, and my sex ached—a full-body orgasm, an overload of sensory stimulation.

18

"One day, you're the best thing since sliced bread. The next, you're the toast."—Unknown

Tiegan

Bianca's Brew Pub's grand opening was a resounding success. The restaurant's new look featured a slick industrial design with trestle tables, hanging Edison lightbulbs, and a polished concrete floor. Stainless steel vats gleamed behind a glass wall, while digital menu boards hung from the ceiling, promoting select brews and an unpretentious family menu.

The servers wore matching black T-shirts embroidered with Bianca's new logo—a silhouette of a sea witch, a bruxa. They balanced trays of complimentary appetizers and beer flights, featuring five pewter mini-mugs on live-edged cedar planks. The staff ensured no one went unattended or empty-handed.

"Tomás, what can I do to help?" I met him in the aisle, resting my hand on his muscled arm.

He pulled me against his chest and kissed my nose. Tomás

needed a haircut, but those unruly, tousled locks only enhanced the bad boy image and made him even more attractive, in my opinion. I held him close, savoring the moment. These past seven weeks had been a whirlwind in many ways. I hadn't meant to fall hopelessly in love when I stepped off that airplane.

"Not a thing, *meu amor*. Everything is under control. Where's Vera?"

"She'll be here soon."

"Good. Find a table and enjoy yourself. I'll be with you in a few moments."

I knew that wouldn't happen. Tomás operated alone, greeting each patron individually. Congratulatory words and compliments flew faster than the storage tanks could dispense the craft-brewed liquid gold.

I found an empty table in a corner by the window. I wanted to feel happy, but I was an eggshell about to crack inside. A familiar voice called to me—Catarina, sporting a purple ponytail and black stiletto fingernails, fit perfectly into the trendy new digs.

"Hi, Tiegan. How are you?"

"Cat. Congratulations on the promotion!"

Catarina was now Lead Server, overseeing all wait staff at the new Bianca's.

"Thanks. Have you looked at our new menu?"

"No, not yet."

"The Bison Sliders are yummy and come with parm and truffle fries. Pairs well with the Sea Hag: a cream ale with a nice caramel finish.' Her eyes danced with excitement.

"Wow. Sounds amazing."

"But you might try the sangria—Eye Candy. It's lovely to look at." She nodded her purple head.

I giggled. How could I say no?

"Eye Candy, please." I leaned on my elbows, taking in the

scene before me—milling people, filled tables, cheerful noise. I hummed a tune—classic rock playing in the background. The song took me back to my childhood: squashed into the bench seat of my dad's pickup—Vera and me—head thrashing and strumming imaginary guitars to a song on the radio to make my dad laugh.

"Tiegan! Wow. Look at this. Tomás must be thrilled." She slid into the booth—her face flushed, her eyes shining too bright.

"Yeah, I'll say. Not bad for a soft opening, eh?"

"Your paintings are fabulous—my God. I did not know. I love the one of Derek and that old car. And the pregnant lady with all the lavender? Just wow."

"Thanks." I hoped Tomás felt the same. He had yet to comment. Those last few days had been a whirlwind of setup, deliveries, and staff training. Eli engineered the artwork pickup and delivery, and I helped him hang each colorful portrait. The subject matter of each piece was likely not what Tomás had expected. I had immortalized the memories of my trip to the Algarve with the people of the Algarve, and they now hung proudly on the walls of Bianca's.

"Guess what? Steve and I are finished." She waved an empty ring finger at me from across the table.

"Oh my God, Vera! When did this happen? What happened?" I tipped my head back, staring at her.

"We had a long talk, and I gave him back his ring." She shrugged.

"Are you all right?" I arched my eyebrows and waited.

"Well, you know things weren't exactly perfect." Her lips quirked.

Oh yeah, I knew.

"There's someone else." Her face flushed a light shade of pink.

"What do you mean, someone else? He cheated on you?" I straightened in my seat. She had my full attention.

"It's okay, Tieg. Like I said, there's someone else." Vera smiled and then laughed. It was a happy sound.

"You mean you've found someone else?" My mouth dropped open.

"I don't know how it happened. I wasn't looking. I thought I was happy, and then." Vera snapped her fingers, lifting her shoulders into an exaggerated shrug. "I had to call it off, Tieg. What else could I do? How could I marry Steve when all I can think about is him?"

I pressed my lips together and tried not to laugh. With Vera, everything was black and white—no shades of gray existed in her mind.

"Okay. So who is it? This other guy?" I giggled, arching my eyebrows.

"Tiegan, he doesn't even know I exist." Her gaze fell to her lap.

Somehow, I doubted that…

We were interrupted by Eli, who slid into the bench seat beside me, bumping my elbow on purpose.

"Ladies. How are we today?" Eli tousled my hair. We had developed a sense of camaraderie—Eli and me—ever since my near-death hit-and-run. "Your portraits are a huge hit, Bug."

That's what he calls me: Bug. I liked it better than Miss Tiegan.

"You think Tomás likes them?"

"Of course, he likes them. He likes everything you do."

"I love the new logo, Tieg. A sea witch. So cool…" Vera nodded.

"Thanks." I couldn't take full credit; my inspiration—the old fishing boat moored in the sand on Carvoeiro Beach and the sea witch—a fisher's good luck charm, idolized on the prow. Our bruxa—Bianca—sang and danced on the crest of the waves, the darkness carrying her laughter to those who listened.

"Hi, everyone. Can I offer refreshments?" Catarina placed a flight of specialty brews on the table and my sangria—Eye Candy—a brilliant shade of scarlet in a tall glass, topped with citrus and a pink-striped organic straw, the beverage deserving of a playful moniker.

"Thanks, Cat." Eli's grin reached his eyes.

"These are the lighter beers." Eli caught Vera's eye. He pointed to the second one in the middle. "Try that one, the White Witch. It's a white beer brewed with orange peel and coriander."

"It's almost spicy." Vera peered over the rim of the pewter mug at Eli.

"I'm working on another recipe, unpasteurized and organic. I'd love your opinion on the flavors if you want to try it." His voice drawled, soothing to the soul.

"I'd love to." Vera set her mug on the table, rising from the booth.

I couldn't help but notice how Vera's cheeks were a little too rosy.

"Bug, are you coming?" He glanced over his shoulder.

"No, go ahead. I'll catch up with you later." I lifted an eyebrow and smiled.

"Tieg, are you certain?" Vera locked eyes with me, a smile spreading across her face.

"I'm good. You go ahead." I watched them, recognizing what a perfect couple they were. Eli's easygoing nature complimented Vera's energetic style. Opposites attract, or so the saying goes.

With Eye Candy in hand, I wandered through the milling crowd. I made my way to the entrance doors and gazed into the night. Neon angels glowed from each streetlamp, and an artificial Christmas tree twinkled with sparkling white lights in the center of the town square. Tomorrow at noon, the Carvoeiro Christmas Market kicks off the holiday season. I wondered if the man with the dancing bear would attend.

I turned away from the picturesque scene, drawn by the melodic trill of a woman's laughter. The distinct sound reminded me of silver bells on a horse-drawn sleigh.

In the farthest corner of the restaurant, a woman caught Tomás's attention. She wore leather: a blood-red catsuit paired with over-the-knee suede boots—lustrous strands of black hair cascading over her shoulders. She was nearly as tall as he was. The green-eyed monster whispered in my ear as the crowd parted while I walked toward Tomás—I overheard the tail end of their conversation.

"The storage tanks lend a sense of legitimacy, authenticity. Undoubtedly, your customers will appreciate the technical skill of crafting such a fine brew. I certainly do." The woman's voice dripped with honey as she traced her hand down Tomás's shirt sleeve.

"Yes, that's an excellent point. The quality of our product and a welcoming atmosphere are key to our success," Tomás nodded, engrossed in conversation.

I joined them in the crowded aisle. Sensing my presence, he broke away from the woman.

"Tiegan." Tomás took my hand and pulled me to his side. "I'd like you to meet Astrid Lopes. She's with the press."

It was then I noticed the camera hanging around her neck.

"Ah, yes. The artist. Anca told me all about you. Your paintings are spectacular. Each one is a living portrait—they speak to people. Perhaps you have time for a few questions?" She didn't flinch.

"A friend of Anca's? I focused on Astrid Lopes, taking

note of her eyes—diamond-shaped orbs, emerald green and webbed with gold.

People stared, checking out the woman drenched in fragrance and poured into tight leather. I gagged.

"Ladies, if you'll excuse me. I have somewhere I need to be." Tomás pressed a light kiss on my forehead.

I searched his face for something I wanted, something I needed. I stared after him as he picked his way through throngs of people and disappeared through the swinging kitchen doors.

"Now, that's a tree I'd like to climb." She purred, not missing a beat.

"Pardon me?" My mouth dropped open.

"Oh my God, I love the names of the craft brews. I can only guess who the Knotty Buoy is fashioned after." Astrid batted my arm and winked.

"Tomás said you're with the press?" I resisted the urge to slap this woman.

"Yes, I'm doing a feature on dining in the Algarve." Astrid lifted her painted lips into a wide smile. "Bianca has a definite buzz: a quirky atmosphere, great music…a place people can unwind. And a brewpub, of all things. Not common in this country. It's nice to see an entrepreneurial man invest his passions locally."

"It's been a dream of Tomás's for a long time." My voice hitched.

"Yes, so he said…family recipes and whatnot. He's a passionate man, isn't he? I'll bet he fucks like a God." Her sultry voice followed him through the sea of heads.

I swallowed the wrong way and choked on my sangria.

"Oh my goodness, are you okay?" Astrid placed her hand on my forearm, looking down at me from the tips of her stiletto heels.

"Thanks, I'm fine." I stood straighter. Damn.

"Well, my, my. Look at the time. I'd love to stick around, but the club scene is calling my name. Only so much a girl can accomplish before dawn shows her pretty face, and the list is long. Work. Pleasure. Work. All the same in my world. Would you tell Tomás I'll be in touch?" Her laughter resonated in my mind, and the bells were ringing.

My head hurt—a tight sensation on the left side of my brain that wouldn't go away. I searched the crowded floor for Tomás and found him in the brewery, explaining the craft beer production process to a small group of interested listeners. I said my goodbyes and walked home alone. I didn't want to talk to anyone. I didn't want to be friendly. Even the twinkling lights did nothing to improve my mood.

I climbed the stairs to my apartment. Al greeted me with a meow, demanding his dinner. I walked through the dark rooms, not bothering to turn on the lights. Somehow, the darkness felt comforting. I downed a glass of orange juice along with two painkillers and collapsed into bed.

With the cat nestled on my chest and the window wide open, my eyes fluttered shut. I tried to release the day's troubles. I wanted to sleep, but that elusive state wouldn't come. I teetered on the edge between here and there. My mind wouldn't rest. Whispers chased me to the borderland, and it was there I had that aha moment. Words Rosalia spoke stirred in my mind, and I was struck by the obvious, the missing piece to the puzzle—something Tomás hadn't shared.

She is not the woman you are waiting for, Tomás. This woman will not fulfill the prophecy.

It played in my mind, a never-ending loop, over and over again. Fulfill the prophecy? What prophecy? What did Rosalia mean? That dark space lured me to the other side, and sleep finally came.

———

The crowd applauded the bear's erratic dance. When the music paused, the bear stood tall, rising to its full height. I reached into my pocket for some coins, waited for the crowd to disperse, and then dropped my money into the hat—a black felt fedora with a leather band and a feather embellishment, the inner rim embroidered with intricate threads of gold. The coins clinked as they landed. He took my hand, patting it like an old man would, his chocolate eyes searching mine as he spoke in a language I didn't understand.

"Kavan." The man whispered in my grandfather's voice.

"Grandfather?"

"Brave one." His voice drew me deeper into the shroud.

I was neither here nor there; I was somewhere in between. Time stood still—the lines of reality blurred.

———

Dawn's pink light filtered through the bedroom window. I woke to laughter, silver bells, and emerald eyes. My heart pounded, and my skin felt clammy and cold. I threw my arm across the bed, reaching for Tomás, but he wasn't there. I found his side of the bed not slept in.

19

---

*"Dear Life: will you at least
start using lube?"*—Unknown

iegan

"Tiegan, wake up. It's almost noon, *meu amor.* Why are you still sleeping?" The soft rumble of his voice caressed my mind, the mattress dipping beneath his weight.

I tossed my arm over my head, my eyelids unwilling to open.

"You sleep like the dead." Tomás lifted my hand and brushed his lips over my knuckles.

I could feel the smile on his lips.

Sleep like the dead—Morpheus, the son of sleep, the God of Dreams. Could Morpheus be the one responsible for my nightmares? And not Sylvie?

"Do you want to go to the beach? It's a beautiful day." He released my hand, the bed creaking as he stood, walked to the window, and threw open the shutters, inviting in the ocean breeze and the salty brine of the early morning.

"No." I winced in the light, my mind drifting in the turquoise waters of December. Only the brave or the foolish would think of such a thing. And I was neither brave nor foolish.

"Why not go sightseeing? We could drive to Silves to visit the castle." He lingered in the doorway, still wearing last night's clothes, jeans, and a black T-shirt haphazardly tucked beneath a leather belt.

I crawled out of bed in a zombie-like state, with my eyes half shut. I shuffled past Tomás, who was now grinding coffee beans. The grinder—a present from Tomás.

"Coffee will be ready in two minutes." His dark eyes locked with mine, and he grinned, his expression light and happy.

"Okay." I gazed at the stubble on his chin and that luscious mouth capable of giving such pleasure.

I crossed the tiled floor to the bathroom, turned on the faucet, and stepped into the shower—encapsulated in steam and lost in the white noise of rushing water. I washed my hair once and then twice, rubbing the conditioner through the ends. After wringing out the excess, I left my oasis and stepped onto the bathroom floor, water pooling around my feet. I stood before the clouded mirror, wiped away the fog, and inspected my reflection. I had gained weight since arriving in the Algarve. My hip bones no longer stuck out. I thought that was a good thing. I knew my mother would say so.

"Coffee's ready. Should I make toast?" His voice reached me, muffled and oh so sexy.

"I'm coming." I slipped into my jeans and a brand-new Bianca T-shirt, form-fitting and long-sleeved, that hugged my new curves perfectly. I followed the enticing aroma of dark roast coffee, where a steaming mug awaited me. I leaned against the counter, blew on the rising steam, and took a careful sip.

"We could take the bike." He glanced up, a curl of black-strap molasses resting on his forehead.

"What?" I gazed at his tousled hair and the circles under his eyes.

"To Silves. To see the castle?" He slathered butter on a piece of toast.

"Oh, sure. I suppose so." I sat in the chair, smoothing the wrinkles from the tablecloth.

"Good. I'll have Eli look after today's deliveries, and we will spend the day together." He smiled, the muscled lines of his face softening.

My mouth watered. That was the effect he had on me.

"Tomás?" I pulled my damp hair into a messy bun on top of my head.

He looked up.

"Rosalia said I wasn't the woman who would fulfill the prophecy. What did she mean by that?" I watched him, captivated by his movements, an innate animal grace.

"I'm done with all of that. Ghosts, vampires, and God knows what other faerie demons Rosalia might dream up." Tomás rolled his eyes. The butter knife clanked, landing in the sink.

"What is the prophecy?" My voice reached every corner of the room.

His jaw ticked, and his gaze drifted to the open window, to the blue ocean view. I knew then there was more.

"How many times do we have to talk about this?" He scowled at me, his brows creasing. "I don't believe any of Rosalia's crazy stories. Why do you?"

"You think your grandmother's crazy?" I chewed the corner of my lip.

"Rosalia has her beliefs. Let's leave it at that." He sorted through the refrigerator and found what he was looking for —jam, homemade fig jam, compliments of João's mama. "Can we let this go? I love you, and you love me. That's all that matters, right?" He crossed the floor in two strides and quickly kissed my forehead.

"I talked to Anca. At the bullfight." I reached for his hand.

"And how did that go?" His deep chuckle ignited a fire in my heart.

"She thinks Rosalia's a witch." I loosed a breath. My knees trembled even though I was sitting.

"Maybe she is. I know what Anca told you." He sat in the chair opposite me, resting one arm on the table.

"You do?" I swallowed the lump lodged in my throat.

"Of course I do. She thinks I am bewitched; I am under Rosalia's spell. It turns out Anca was right all along. Happy now?" His eyes searched mine.

"No, Tomás, I'm not happy." I pulled away and crossed my arms.

"Can't you let this go? Why does it matter so much to you?"

"Because of Sylvie." There, I said it. Sylvie was a part of me. How could Tomás not see it? How could he not feel it? Her presence awoke every time we made love and every time I touched him.

"I love you. Is that not enough?" He answered without blinking.

"I want it to be." The words hung between us.

"Then why are we having this conversation?" The roughness of his voice scraped the edges of my mind.

"When we met, you believed Sylvie died because of a curse." I managed even though my lower lip quivered—I needed to cry.

"There's no curse and no prophecy," Tomás leaned in closer, his breath minty fresh. "I love you. Do you love me?"

There was so much more I needed to say, but I couldn't find the words.

He cupped my face in his big palms, slanting his lips over mine—filling me with the taste of him, the scent of him. Then he pulled away, an easy smile spreading over his face.

My blood hummed, and my bones vibrated, an unearthly shudder flowing through me—quelling the fire my sole aim.

His phone chirped from across the room.

My gaze followed the sound to the armchair, to his leather jacket. He made a frustrated noise and rose from the table.

"There's a problem with a dispenser. I'll be back in a bit, okay? Tiegan?" He slipped into his jacket and put his phone inside his pocket. He was out the door before I could turn my head.

"Okay." My vision blurred, but my thoughts remained sharp. I was merely a plaything, a diversion from his chaotic life—an easy hookup. That much was obvious, at least to me.

———

"Tell her, man." Eli's soft voice stopped me in my tracks.

A shiver shot from my palm to my elbow, radiating from the sparkling chrome of the swing door into Bianca's newly renovated kitchen. Who was she? Was I the one Eli referred to?

"Tell her what, Eli? What would you have me say?" Tomás's enraged voice sent shivers down my spine.

"Everything. All of it. The truth." Eli's voice conveyed a hint of exasperation.

I hugged the paper tote filled with croissants to my puffer vest. I had dressed hurriedly, pulling a black toque over my head, the pink button-up vest my latest find from Vera's shop. I wanted to surprise Tomás and apologize. I hated how I behaved this morning—clingy, needy, and whiny. I didn't recognize that person.

"None of it matters. Not anymore," Tomás's response was as clear as mud—to me, anyway.

A black mood followed me home last night, the same one I woke up with. Even now, darkness played havoc with my mind. My emotions—up and down like a toilet seat.

"What does that mean?" There was confusion in Eli's reply.

"I don't want it…any of it." Tomás's voice hitched.

I could picture his dark gaze, his fingers running through his hair.

"Look, man, the kumpania has waited too long." Eli's tone carried a note of disbelief.

"It's over, Eli. I'm leaving the Union. I'm done with it."

"What? Why? You can't do that." Eli argued with him.

Why was he so invested in Tomás's future?

I combed through the days and weeks of the time I had spent with Tomás. What was the kumpania, and what was this union they referred to?

"I can, and I will. There are many people more qualified than I who would happily step up. It's time." Tomás voice dropped to a whisper.

I held my breath, straining to catch a conversation I had no right to overhear, yet my feet remained frozen to the floor.

They snapped at each other, back and forth.

"You can't walk away. Not from this."—Eli.

"Watch me."—Tomás.

"So, what will you do?"—Eli.

"I'll do what I am doing."—Tomás.

"And the little bug? What about her?"—Eli.

"Jesus, man. Leave it alone."—Tomás.

My mouth went dry. Whatever this was, it concerned my relationship with Tomás.

"You will deny the prophecy? Your people? She's the one, and you know it."—Eli.

"Yeah? And what if she's not Eli? What then? Tiegan will die, just like Sylvie."—Tomás.

I inhaled and forgot to exhale. I saw it now, so clearly—Sylvie. This had always been about Sylvie. The truth was right in front of my face all this time, and I couldn't see it.

My stomach coiled into a fist as I slipped down the aisle between rows of shiny tables and escaped—from Tomás.

I staggered ten paces to the complimentary trash cans the town of Carvoeiro provides for local pedestrian use. Gripping both sides of the steel bin, I hurled the remains of this morning's breakfast into the wide-open maw.

Just like Sylvie.

Shadows danced, and the ground warped beneath my feet.

His words struck a knife through my heart. Rosalia was the only authentic voice in this nightmare. Tomás knew Rosalia spoke the truth, yet he lied—how many times? I let that fact sink in. I wiped my mouth with my sleeve.

Pinpoints of light flashed through the black clouds.

"Child, are you all right?" A voice distracted me—a low, rumbly voice, so like Tomás's.

The man looked different without the bear by his side. Taller than I would have expected: light-framed, gnarly but well-knit. His bony face gave him a rough look as if he had missed a few too many meals. He took my arm, guiding me to the white and blue bench at the edge of the cobblestone square overlooking the ocean.

"You're very pale, child. Should I call for a doctor?" The man towered above me, his brows creased.

"No, thank you. I'm fine. Please, would you sit with me?" I

wrung my hands together, beads of sweat collecting between my shoulder blades.

"Yes, of course." His chocolate eyes peered at me, filled with concern.

"I know who you are." I swallowed back the bile, my breath sawing in and out. This man could answer my questions.

"Have we met?" He tilted his head to the side, studying me as I had studied him.

"No, we haven't met." I let go of the pain and the fear and swallowed hard. "I have questions about your son. I need your help."

"My son?" His eyes locked on mine.

"Yes, please forgive me. There are things I need to know. That he won't tell me." My voice caught, and I gripped my knees with both hands and stared into the sea.

The cresting waves pounded the sand with ribbons of white foam. Clouds flew across a brilliant blue sky, and I wondered if it might rain.

"What's your name, child?" He sat next to me on the bench, his gaze fixed on me.

"Tiegan, Tiegan Moss." I looked into his eyes and saw only concern.

"I am Joseph Ferreira." He bowed his head in greeting.

A seagull landed at our feet, followed by two more. They screeched. They battled each other for scraps in the sand.

"Rosalia says I am not the one. Please, would you tell me what she meant?" There was no need to explain. This man would know the truth.

"Look at me, child." His soft voice murmured.

I gazed into chocolate eyes, flickering with gold.

"And you believe Rosalia?" Joseph blinked, a soft smile lifting his lips.

"She said I am not the one who will fulfill the prophecy. What is the prophecy?"

"And my son will not tell you?"

"No."

"Ah." Joseph sighed and leaned back on the bench. He extended his legs and crossed his feet. "I am not part of my son's life. I should tell you it was not my choice. It was Rosalia's."

"What? Why?" I glanced at him.

"That is not something I can share, but I will tell you Rosalia can be a formidable woman." He threaded his fingers through brown locks. So, like Tomás, it hurt my heart. "The prophecy was cast upon my wife, Rosalia's daughter when she was a child, and with the prophecy came a curse."

I nodded. I knew all about the curse.

"Angelina cannot remember what happened that day. There was a celebration in Scotland to crown a new Gypsy King. Rosalia was among the crowd. That is when a *chovihani* laid hands upon little Angelina. She whispered words for all to hear—a curse of death and the prophecy of a new line of kings. Angelina fell to the ground, and when she woke, she bore a scar across her breast. Rosalia tried to remove the curse from my Angelina and, years later, from the children, Tomás, and his sister, Anca. But the spell proved too powerful, even for Rosalia."

The world of black magic, superstition, and myth exists. But I knew that already, didn't I?

"Fate has destined Tomás to become our people's leader once a healthy child is born to him." He patted my hand.

"A baby?" Joseph's words hit me, a hard slap on the face. I stared at him, my eyes round. "What will happen when this baby is born?"

"Our people will unite, and the reins of power will change. It is prophesied."

"How? How will it happen?"

"That, I cannot tell you."

Joseph may not have the answer, but the tone of his voice held no doubt. The urge to laugh bubbled up inside me.

"Miss, you're very pale. Let me take you to a doctor."

"Thank you for answering my questions." I shook my head, refusing his help.

Joseph watched me and then nodded.

"Be careful, child, very careful. Many would not want to see the prophecy fulfilled, dangerous people."

"What do you mean?" I sat up straight, my shoulders tightening.

"The woman who gives birth to this child would be in a precarious position. Her life would be in jeopardy."

I stared at him in disbelief, those near-death moments flashing through my mind. The rush of wind as Eli saved me from the speeding car—the surging waves as the powerboat raced by—the falcon, carrying my soul to the netherworld.

One solitary gull remained, pecking the sand with a hooked beak, tossing fragments of loose shell onto the toes of Joseph's black-soled boots.

"It is a powerful position to lead the Roma."

I nodded my head. Could I envision Tomás Ferreira, the bad boy of Carvoeiro, the leader of the Roma people? The king of a Roma nation? I knew enough about the Roma from what Tomás had shared and what I had learned. After all, I was one of them by blood. I felt that bond, that connection. The Roma existed in a society where they didn't quite fit in. No, that's not entirely accurate—they hid; years of persecution had forced them to do so. Tomás could be their voice, and I could support him. But then I remembered the words Rosalia had spoken.

I was not the one.

A prophecy and a curse. A soulmate and a child. It all made perfect sense.

———

I sat at the end of a long wooden table, my hands curled around a paper cup. The spicy blend of wine, cloves, and cinnamon teased me with the smell of Christmas. My foot tapped to the erratic beat of Jingle Bell Rock, the song blasting from speakers hidden within the giant holiday tree. The Carvoeiro Christmas Market was in full swing.

"Tiegan!" White leather gloves gripped my shoulder, and Vera's gaze locked onto mine. "Are you okay?"

Was I okay? I didn't know where to go or what to do next. I stared beyond the jagged cliff at Vila Algarve, at my apartment. I could be there in under five minutes. I could pack my bags, catch the next flight, and leave everything behind.

"Who was that man you were talking to?" Her golden hair shimmered in the sunlight, complimenting the houndstooth scarf draped elegantly down the front of her cable-knit sweater. She studied me with curious eyes.

"Oh, that was Tomás's father." I had a panoramic view of the town square, which included the still-closed Bianca's. I watched the entrance, embracing my role as an eavesdropper, and wondered if Tomás was still inside. My gaze returned to Vera, admiring the rest of today's outfit: wide-leg jeans, pointy-toed boots, and five-inch heels.

"Tomás's father? Really?" The heels clicked on the cobblestones as she joined me on the bench seat.

"Do you remember what I told you before? About Sylvie? And what Rosalia said?" I stared at the bag of croissants, my appetite lost. "Are you hungry?"

"You don't still think that, do you? That spooky spirits

possess you?" A smile curved her lips as she dove into the paper bag.

My heart seized as the door to Bianca's opened.

"Are you okay? You don't look so good." She placed her knuckles on my forehead, her brow creasing.

"Rosalia told Tomás that I wasn't the one," I whispered as I watched Eli, hidden beneath a black hoodie, walk down the street toward Vera's shop.

"You're not what, exactly?" She inhaled the chocolate-covered croissant, flakes tumbling onto her scarf.

"Not the woman who would fulfill the prophecy. Tomás lied to me. He never told me what the prophecy was or what it meant."

She lifted her eyebrows.

"When Tomás finds that woman, the right woman, the prophecy will come true; well, it will when they have a baby."

"A baby?"

"Sylvie died because of the curse."

"What curse? Oh, come on. How can you believe that?"

"I overheard Tomás talking to Eli. If I weren't the right woman, if I'm not his soulmate, and if I were to have his child, I would die, just like Sylvie." I thought about that a moment longer.

"Eli? What does Eli know about this? Where did you get this from? That man?" Her gaze searched the square for Joseph. "None of this makes sense. You can't believe this." Her eyes locked on mine, the croissant forgotten.

"I'm not his soulmate. That's what Rosalia meant. Someone is, but it's not me." The implication weighed heavy on my mind.

"And you believe this?"

"Well, what would you think if you were me?" I rested my face in my hand, a wave of exhaustion washing over me.

"I think you're on the train to crazy town, but that's okay.

You can save me a seat." Vera's laughter meant to lift my spirits.

"My eyes are wide open. I'm not making this up."

"All right, look—what Rosalia said is true. You're not the one. You're not Tomás's soulmate." Vera stands, brushing her hands down her hips, smoothing away the wrinkles and crumbs from her jeans.

"I'm not." I pulled my toque lower, hiding my ears from the chilly breeze.

"And that man? He told you what? This woman is the key to Tomás's destiny? Okay. What if…what about the car that ran you off the road? And the boat that swamped your kayak? Was that a mere coincidence? A series of unlucky events? Bad luck?"

"You think someone's trying to kill me?"

"I'm saying maybe someone believes you are the one. And that someone who will go to great lengths to make sure this prophecy thing doesn't happen? See?" Vera lowered her voice to an exaggerated whisper. "If I were you, Tieg, I'd sleep with my eyes wide open."

I gulped down the mulled wine, my gaze darting across the square.

"Look, you know I've never been a big fan of Tomás Ferreira. I told you that from the start. But I've changed my mind. He has a good heart, and you, girlie, shine like a lightbulb whenever his name comes up. I've never seen you this happy. Do you want to give that up?"

I didn't want to give him up—I loved him stupidly. Was I insane?

"Honestly, Tieg, this Rosalia; I get she's his grandmother, but wow—Anca's right. Rosalia is a witch—in more ways than one. Tiegan, are you listening to me?" She rested her hand on my arm.

Across the square, a flash of chrome and a reflection of

light distracted me from our conversation. I glanced over Vera's shoulder at Astrid Lopes, the reporter, walking out of Bianca's with Tomás on her arm. Her leopard print jumpsuit showcased ample cleavage, flowing elegantly from a curvy silhouette.

Her voice rang out across the open square, a blend of intonations and exclamations. I watched as she led Tomás under the canopy and into the shadows. She raised her hand, brushing a loose curl from his forehead, displaying perfect posture. I inhaled sharply as her hands cradled Tomás's face. She leaned in, placing a lingering kiss on his lips. I saw her walk away, wait for a break in traffic, and then cross the busy thoroughfare.

"Tiegan? Earth to Tiegan? Where are you?"

"Vera?" I gazed into her eyes and saw my confusion mirrored there.

"Yes, hon."

"I have to go. I'm sorry." I leave Vera sitting at the table. I am at the entrance to Bianca's before the doors close shut.

———

"I s she the one, Tomás?" My voice trailed him through the row of empty tables, my gaze settling on one particular table where the chairs were askew, and two empty coffee mugs sat: one adorned with a cherry red lipstick kiss. Heavy floral notes lingered—ylang-ylang, jasmine, and rose.

Tomás turned, his dark eyes widening.

"Is she your soulmate...your invisible thread? The one you've been waiting for." My voice hollowed. My heart hurt. I watched every line brooding on his face.

His lips parted, but no words came out.

"Is that where you were last night? With her? With Astrid Lopes?"

"Tiegan, you don't understand."

"That's where you're wrong, Tomás. I understand everything. But don't worry, I won't stand in the way of your destiny." I had a flashback to Aaron. I didn't understand him either.

"My destiny? What are you talking about?"

"Come on, Tomás. Stop with the lies, the half-truths. When were you going to tell me?"

"Tell you what?"

"What it all means. The prophecy, the curse. The soulmate—the baby? What Rosalia said." I paused and took a breath.

Tomás appeared to have lost his. His face turned pale. His hands, which had been hanging loosely at his sides just moments ago, clenched into tight fists.

"Well, you don't have to tell me. I already know." At that moment, I faltered. My throat closed. What did I want? I wanted Tomás to close the gap. I wanted him to hold me in his arms and tell me everything would be all right—that this nightmare would go away—that he loved me. But he did none of those things.

Tomás stared at the floor.

"It's all right, Tomás. Joseph told me the truth. The truth you hid from me. He's a nice man, by the way, your father. Perhaps you should talk to him yourself. You might learn a few truths of your own." I nodded my head. It was all I had left, this false sense of conviction.

"You spoke to Joseph? Why would you do that?" His head jerked up, his gaze meeting mine.

"I'm sure Astrid will give you everything you need. Everything I can't."

"Astrid?"

"Do you think I'm a fool, Tomás?" I was a fool for wanting to believe. But this was not about what I wanted. I backed toward the door. "You lied to me—from the very beginning. And look at you. You're still lying." My voice choked. "I bared my soul to you. Goddammit, I let you in. I gave you—everything. What kind of man are you, anyway?" I spat the words. "I will not be lied to or used. Not by you, not by anyone."

I was tired of talking. The adrenaline rushing through my veins moments ago had left me.

"Tiegan, why are you doing this?"

Because I am not the one.

"Look, it's okay. What was this? Really? A holiday fling? Yeah, well, you were a top-notch hello, Tomás. I'll give you that."

"Tiegan, please." He approached one step at a time.

I couldn't look at him: at the mouth, I kissed only hours before, at the hands that held me. I couldn't allow him to come to me. I stuck out my hand like a stop sign.

"It's over, Tomás. We're done." How could I express the emotions swirling inside me? I wanted to feel anger. I wished for rage to mask the pain. My vision blurred as I walked out the door.

———

"Dearest Tiegan,

We got your letter, and your father will be after to pick you up at the airport first thing in the morning. He'll be driving the old truck. The car is right out of commission. We had a silver thaw yesterday, and your father says there's ice in the gas tank. What a kettle of fish.

Love,

Mom

Xoxo
PS. We can't wait to see you! Is everything fine?"

20

---

*"You can't be sad when you're
holding a cupcake."*—Unknown

iegan

I was in the family way: with child, knocked up —a bun in the oven—pregnant.

How did I not know this? How did I not put two and two together? It took too long to realize what was going on with my body. My cycle was crazy, but I thought nothing of it. My eyes would fall shut at the most inopportune times. I lived in a world of hurt—I didn't move or talk to anyone for weeks. I put those feelings of malaise down to one simple thing—heartache. I walked away from the man I loved, and now I carried his child in my belly.

At first, I was in denial, total and complete denial. I didn't plan this. I didn't expect this. How could this have happened to me? I took precautions. I specifically remember reading the label: the hormone-free marvel of the twenty-first century, the latest and greatest in pregnancy prevention, the copper intra-uterine device—the IUD. Well, that was a big fail.

And now, every day, I was more pregnant than the last. I knew that sounded ridiculous; being pregnant just was. I was referring to how it felt. The sensation that pervaded your body: your sense of being changed—you were no longer one. An alien seed wormed its way in and burrowed deep like a tick. It fed on you, sucked the life out of you, and left you sick and tired. But then the little alien made you love it more than your soul. It became your reason for being and building a baby; growing another human being became an all-consuming adventure.

I had not shared the news with Tomás. Why? Because I knew what his reaction would be. I remembered his words about his father; I have no use for a man who walks out on his family. He would feel obligated, and I didn't want his guilt. I didn't want him—like that. But then I remembered I couldn't have him, anyway. I closed my eyes and shut out his voice, the voice I so desperately wanted to hear.

And to complicate things, there was the curse. If I died giving birth to this baby, Tomás would blame himself. So I clung to a sliver of hope—a hope that this was a bad dream— the curse, I mean. If I survived, if the baby survived, I would do the right thing. I would tell Tomás he was a father. I had no other expectations.

I was also alone. Sylvie, my vampire spirit, had abandoned me. I hadn't felt her presence in a long time. I tried to determine exactly when she left. Was it conception? Maybe? The timing made sense. Was that her mission? To take me to Tomás, create a child, and fulfill the prophecy? But that was crazy talk, and I would be mad to believe such a thing. No, I wouldn't repeat that, not to anyone. I was not the one. Rosalia said so. Yet, I wondered, what if Rosalia was wrong about one tiny thing?

Every night, I lie in my bed, waiting to feel that flutter of life in my belly. Not alone. I told myself I was not alone.

My mother knitted baby blankets, tiny hats, and butter-soft sweaters—cotton for the summer and wool for winter. She had embraced the idea of becoming a grandmother. My father was building a cradle in his workshop.

I couldn't bring myself to tell them I might die and the baby might die. It was all too much to bear.

I wanted to come here. I once tried during the heavy winter snowpack, but I turned back when my car hit a patch of black ice and slid like an out-of-control toboggan down a luge track. I spent the rest of that morning waiting for a tow truck to rescue me from North Mountain Road, passing the afternoon at a garage in the peaceful fishing village of Pleasant Bay, waiting for Bob, the mechanic, to replace the bent rim and blown tire on the front wheel of my vehicle.

I had returned—to Meat Cove, the island's tip, the edge of the earth—the place where bald eagles soared and where my nightmares began.

Unlike Portugal, the fierce Cape Breton coast's turbulent ocean was more black than blue. It was a foggy land where sea spray touched the wind and clung to the breeze. It was a place of mud and sand, grass and trees, barrens of lichen, and bogs of bakeapple. It was a place of rock slabs and cliffs where mountains rose from the sea.

In spring, the land was green and filled with all sorts of growing things. Shadows of light flickered through dense deciduous trees, and the only sounds were the twittering of birds, the screech of a hawk, or the soft flutter of a barred owl. You could smell the earthy tang of deadwood rotting on the silent forest floor and the musk of bear scat.

In the summer, tufts of grass, strewn with merry wands, crowned the plateau. It was a place where insects buzzed, and the scent of sweetgrass tickled your nose. And when the tides crept away, clams bubbled up in the mud.

I didn't know what I expected to find, but I had to come. I had to touch the earth. I had to sit on that cold slab of stone, hug my knees, and gaze across the endless horizon where the skies blurred and the ocean ended. I looked upon it once as a young girl and returned now as a woman and mother-to-be. Back then, I did not know I would one day leave my heart thousands of miles away. I sat for a long time before walking away.

Love is a singular emotion. Others claimed it wasn't; they said love was many things and more than that. To me, it was life in its entirety. When I closed my eyes, I could still hear it: the thread of his voice, the sound of his breath. When we made love, that was the one thing I focused on—that sound. Now, it was just an echo in my mind.

Heartbreak was another matter. Heartbreak was a painful death, one you suffered over and over and over again. I was lonely—so very lonely.

If there was an upside, I had learned the meaning of self-care. I had become my own best friend.

I had embraced mindfulness, meditating, and zenned out to the mudras. I signed up for a yoga class to invoke my inner goddess, sending love notes to all those tight places. I learned that pressing your tongue to the roof of your mouth helps with balance—namaste.

I walked to the public pool and swam laps when no one was around at night. I was up to three hundred and forty-two—I did that to forget.

In the mornings, I waddled to the harbor to breathe in the salty air and stare at the sea—I did that to remember.

I kept a journal and wrote in it every day. It was all there: the good, the bad, and the ugly. If I didn't die, if the curse didn't kill me, I would write a novel—a fantastic tale of nightmare, prophecy, and curse.

Last night, I joined a social media mom group, but then I left. I didn't want to talk to other moms. I didn't want to discuss doulas and midwives, breast milk, and formula. I feared I might die.

My state of mind was uncertain. I gazed into the bathroom mirror every night before I went to sleep and made goofy faces. I laughed in the face of death.

I had a lot of shitty days.

To keep busy, I painted. Thanks to my mom and her Zumba lady friends, I had three commissions. Everyone wanted a portrait of their children, grandchildren, or even their dog. Busy hands were happy hands, as my mother said. She also reminded me almost daily that the second mouse always gets the cheese. Go figure.

I was working on another painting but couldn't get it right. It was a self-portrait of Tomás and me, taken from a selfie in front of Bianca's. This one was for the baby, in case I died.

Another discovery, one effect of being so very pregnant— I was in a constant state of arousal. I tried crossing my legs and eating dark chocolate. Not good enough. I craved sexual gratification. I had become an expert at the pre-game and had learned how to bring the ship to port. It was empowering and liberating—a wave ride cresting a tsunami of pleasure. The bathtub had become my playground, a soothing oasis of candlelight and essential oils. I let my fingers do the walking: orbiting the planet, tracing slow circles, and fantasizing. I wore myself out, and when it was over, I needed a nap. Other times, I locked the front door and turned into a six-headed hydra spitting fire. The orgasm—the French call it la petite mort, the little death, for a reason. It was a good reason.

———

It was Thursday night, and the Cameron clan's fiddles swept over the crowd with rapid cuts and melodic grace notes. Vera's mouth hung open; her blue-eyed gaze remained fixed on mine. The server placed a Chardonnay for Vera and orange pekoe tea with milk and honey for me on the table.

"Vera, promise me you will not tell Tomás." I leaned in, as close as my baby bump would allow.

"Are you fucking kidding me? Oh my God! Why are you doing this?"

Her tirade continued, and I deserved it. I kept this pregnancy, the impending birth of this child, a secret from Vera, my best friend. Guilt washed over me, and my face heated. I should have told Vera earlier. Well, on that note, I should have told Tomás. But I wanted to see Vera in person to make her understand and to do that; I had to wait for her to come home to the Island.

"This is because of that ridiculous curse thing. You think you're going to die, don't you? Is that what this is?" Vera sat back in her chair, folding her arms over her chest.

"No! I don't think that. Don't be silly."

Is that what I thought? I was in a state of flux, undecided.

"You're asking me to lie to Eli? You know that, don't you?"

Vera and Eli had become an item. What I asked her to do would be difficult, but I needed her loyalty. I needed her to understand.

"If I don't die, I'll tell him."

"So I'm right. All of this is about that."

"Vera, I need you to trust me." I laid my hands flat on the table, showing no compromise. I believed.

"I don't like this, Tiegan. Not one bit."

"Vera, please…I need you on my side. Promise me."

"All right, you know I will. I won't say anything, but you will once the baby comes. You promise me." Vera's glacier eyes razed mine, but then her shoulders relaxed, and I knew my secret was safe. "He isn't dating anyone, you know. He's miserable."

"You don't know that, Vera." Hope leaped into my mind. Not a flicker but a blinding light, and I couldn't see straight. Why was Tomás miserable? I wanted to find out. I wanted to know. My heart ached at the mention of him.

"I know. Eli tells me everything." She tossed her hair over her shoulder.

"What? Tell me." I took the bait, immediately regretting my words. I didn't want to know––I didn't want to feel.

"Well. He looks like shit. I saw him at the grocery store. He never leaves Bianca's. He's holed up in his office all the time. Have you talked to Anca? I don't understand why you left. You didn't have to leave. Is this why?" Vera pursed her lips together.

"No, I didn't know then."

"Turn your teacup to the left three times and think good thoughts." Her face lit up, and her lips curved into a broad Vera smile.

I looked at her, arching my eyebrows. Vera had a penchant for reading tea leaves. When we were young girls hosting tea parties in the backyard, Vera never missed a chance to interpret the shapes the tea leaves took. And now, I was her querent. I sighed out loud and followed her instructions.

"Okay, upside down, onto the saucer."

I played along.

Vera lifted the cup, cradling it with both hands. "Hmm," she murmured, inspecting the dregs. "This is good, Tieg… there, look on the side. It's a basket." She looked up from the cup, smiling. "That means an addition to the family."

Her enthusiasm filled my heart. I giggled.

"I see a man on the bottom. He's holding an ivy leaf." She turned the cup and shifted her head. An aura of light shimmered around her.

I blinked, and it was gone.

"What does a man holding an ivy leaf mean?" I yelled over the shudder of bows and the toe-tapping, heel-clicking, pounding stomp of the dancers who had taken over the wooden floor of the pub.

"It means there's a man who loves you, that his love is true."

We were almost head to head inspecting the teacup together.

"See, on the other side, that's a sitting hare. That means marriage."

I was blushing, not because the dregs said I would marry my true love, but because the server was standing at our table. He tapped his pen on a yellow pad, waiting to take our food order. Vera was oblivious to the interruption. Nothing distracted her from her game.

"Look, Tieg, here on the bottom edge is a large flower, and on the rim, a butterfly." She straightened her shoulders, looking up, her eyes alight with excitement. "Do you see all these triangles? Tiegan, this is a very good cup. There's love and happiness and everything good."

I didn't know how, but Vera always spun a fantastic tale.

Some days, I can conquer the world.
Other days, it takes me three hours to
convince myself to shower."—Unknown

Tiegan
With talons fully extended, the raptor, a majestic bird of prey, swooped low, striking the earth. The winds whispered, and the eagle soared upward into the clouds. Its victim, a black snake painted orange, writhing in the throes of sudden death, hung from its mighty claws.

"Tiegan?"

A rumbling voice cut through the shadowland of my dreams. My mind stirred—images of Tomás piercing my naked heart—tears welled up, burning my eyes. I reached out, extending my fingers into the dark void, whispering his name. It was only a dream, one I'd had before.

"Tiegan? Are you there?" A low, rumbling voice, nearly a whisper, muffled behind the closed door—a thump made the door frame shake.

My mind snapped into the realm of here and now; my temples pounded, and my fingers tensed. Tomás? My Tomás? Was I losing it? Was I coming unhinged? The knob turned, and the hinges creaked.

"Goddamn, it's dark in here." A dark silhouette filled the doorframe.

I was used to the black of a Cape Breton night. I never left the lights on, and I always drew the shades—to keep the bogeyman out—as my mother often said.

"Tomás? Is that you?"

"Yes, *meu amor,* it's me. I'm here." His voice swooped high and then low.

My chest emptied.

He loomed in the inky dark, close enough to touch. If he took one more step, he would fall on my bed. I reached for his hands and twined my fingers with his. I listened to the sound of his breath, breathing in his smell: sea salt and brine and maybe yeast from the brewery. I wanted to say something, but I had no words.

"Why was your door unlocked? Anyone could have walked right in." He scolded me in a soft voice like one would use to calm a petulant child or a green-broke, crazed horse. His grip on my fingers tightened. His hair fell in front of his face, tickling my bare arms. He pressed his lips to my fingers.

A giggle bubbled in my throat, and I laughed hysterically, crazed laughter. Tears ran down my face.

"Why are you laughing?" The timbre of his voice rose. The floorboards creaked under his shifting weight.

"Like you just did." I gasped, sucking in a half-breath. I giggled. I hiccuped.

"What?"

"Like you walked right in, like a thief in the night."

"Yes, I guess I did." He inched closer.

"What are you doing here, Tomás?" I tried my best to regain some semblance of composure. What had compelled Tomás to cross the sea and travel to the Island of Cape Breton? How had he arrived here? Why had he broken into my house in the middle of the night? Why now?

"Well, um, I have your medallion." He tripped over each word, unsure and almost shy.

"My medallion? You could have sent it in the mail." My hand went to my throat, as it often did. It felt as if a part of me was missing.

"No, I couldn't. Tiegan, I had to see you. There are things you need to know. I need to..." His words spilled out in a frantic rush, his voice breaking. He tightened his grip on my fingers.

"You're representing the Roma at the United Nations next month." I cut him off, my voice raw, my heart thumping. I read the news: a new Roma leader was elected, the torch passed, and a blood ceremony was held in Prague—his destiny was fulfilled. I wondered how that happened.

"Yes. That's true. But that's not why I'm here. I need to talk to you. Tiegan, please, would you turn on the light?"

"I didn't know the Germans had so many Roma treasures —from the holocaust. How will you get them back?" I pondered the question, the situation. The Nazi regime was responsible for the theft of thousands of priceless artifacts from the people they persecuted and the countries they plundered.

"Tiegan, there are so many things..."

"We are talking, and no." I frowned into the dark. I had to tell him, and I didn't know how. What would he say? And what would I do with his answers? My mind spun with a million thoughts.

"Tiegan, please."

"No," I refused, with no apology.

"You are the most frustrating woman I have ever met." His voice smiled, making me smile.

"How's Astrid?" I spat out the words, my voice snapping like the tail of an enraged cat. Al, by the way, purred like a buzz saw at the end of my bed.

Tomás was a hair's breadth away. He smelled so good.

"Tiegan, I swear to you, on my mother's life, I have never so much as laid a hand on that woman or any other woman since the day I met you."

"Why are you here, Tomás?" I inhaled a long, steadying breath. My mind slowed, and I saw things. I could no longer hide in the dark.

"I want to apologize, and I want you to forgive me."

"Forgive you? For what?"

"For what you think you saw. I took advantage of your fears. For that, I want to apologize."

I was not sure what I expected, but not that.

"It doesn't matter, Tomás. You know the truth—what Rosalia said. I'm not your soulmate. That means there is someone else, somewhere out there, who is. You need that person."

"This has nothing to do with Rosalia or what she said."

"What do you mean? I don't understand."

"I let you go…Tiegan, I let you leave because I was afraid."

"Afraid? Afraid of what?" I pinched my eyebrows together.

"Afraid of losing you, like I lost Sylvie," he murmured, his voice haunted—haunted by the spirit of a dead woman, one who would not rest in peace. "I need you to forgive me. I don't want to live without you. I can't live without you. I love you, Tiegan. I have always loved you. Please tell me I am not too late."

Forgive him? There was nothing to forgive. I loved him. I had never stopped loving him. He was here, and that was all that mattered. Who was I kidding? He had me at hello, didn't he? Ha! A giggle bubbled up in my throat, but I wanted to cry.

I bit my lip and held my breath. I had to tell him. I couldn't wait another moment—I guided his hand to my protruding belly. A baby twisted, kicking. I said the words I had practiced so many times: "Tomás, I'm pregnant."

"What? Tiegan… Oh my God. What is this? You didn't tell me. Why didn't you tell me? When?" His voice rose, then faded to a soft murmur.

"Soon," I answered the when and not the why. Reaching backward, I flicked on the light, filling the bedroom with a soft golden glow. I gazed into dark chocolate eyes. He was everything I remembered, from the curl of blackstrap molasses to the hard-angled face to the black button-down shirt—he hadn't changed one bit. "Tomás? Are you okay? Are you mad?"

"You were going to do this? By yourself?" His eyes glistened, and his voice choked.

I nodded. I couldn't speak…

"*Meu amor*, my brave girl… I'm so ashamed for letting you go, for not finding you sooner."

"Am I going to die, Tomás? Like Sylvie?"

"No! No, you will not die."

I needed to touch him. I urged him closer, threading my fingers through his hair, taking his lips in a biting caress. Our tongues collided, exploring and tasting each other. I had imagined this kiss too many times.

"Tiegan, do you love me?"

"I have always loved you."

"Will you marry me? Right now?"

"Now?" My eyes widened.

"Yes, the old way, the Romani way, before the baby arrives."

There was something more I needed to share—one more secret.

"Tomás, it's not just one baby."

"Twins?" His eyes welled with tears as he skimmed his hand across my belly.

I nodded, pressing my lips together, blinking back hot tears.

"Tiegan Moss, you are my love. You are my destiny. I will ask you again and keep asking until you say yes. Will you have me? Will you be mine?" He held my hands. He pressed his lips to my fingertips.

I knew the answer to both questions.

"Yes, I will marry you."

We stayed like that, pressed into each other's arms, but then he broke away and rose to his feet, gazing about my bedroom.

"What are you looking for?" I lifted onto my elbows, staring past him at a painting on the wall of Tomás and me.

"A scarf. Do you have a red scarf?"

"A what?"

"We need a red scarf. We can do this right now. We will become one."

"On the back of the closet door."

I swung my legs onto the floor, straightening my nightgown while Tomás sorted through my closet.

"What do you mean we will become one?"

"It is the old way. A promise a man and woman make to one another." He returned with the red silk scarf I bought from Vera's shop. It seemed like such a long time ago.

"But Tomás."

"If you want a big wedding, we will do that too. But that is not now. I want to make this right for the children. Come, we must go outside."

"What for?" My heart burst, and I smiled.

"You will see."

"Okay, and where do we go to become one?'

"Tiegan, this is a serious matter."

"Tomás, look at me. I'm fat. I'm pregnant." My face flushed, and I stood before him in my nightgown with unicorns, rainbows, and little red hearts.

"You are the most beautiful woman in the world. I love you. I want to be with you for the rest of my days. I want to be your husband." He swept me into an embrace, as much as my protruding stomach would allow.

He was so unchanged. The hard angles of his face, the soft lips, the muscled body I wanted to touch, ravage, and consume. I couldn't ignore the flame of heat stirring in my core, a not-so-gentle reminder of what I had missed. My thighs quivered, and I bit down on my lower lip, squashing my need. He took my hand, and we left the four walls of my little house. We left as two and would return as one.

"Tomás, where are we going?"

A full moon hung in the sky—a strawberry moon, a sentinel of lasting light. While the people of Mabou slept, we strolled hand in hand through wild fescue and dew-kissed grass, and then the meadow transformed into a dense forest.

"A little farther…"

An ancient oak tree stood where the path widened into a slingshot fork. Beneath the boughs of this tree, Tomás paused.

Moonbeams glided through the gnarled branches, creating shadows of heavenly light. Blackbirds, nestled within the foliage, serenaded us with song—they bore witness to our promised union.

"Tiegan…"

It was then I saw the knife. Tomás ran the blade across his bared wrist. I inhaled a sharp breath and stared at the crimson streak.

"Give me your wrist, *meu amor.*"

I held his gaze as the blade sliced my skin—burning like fire. Tomás wrapped the silk around our wrists, over and under and around, knotting the ends, pulling them tight with his teeth. His fingers gripped mine, and our blood mingled, hot and sweet.

Tonight was Midsummer's Night Eve, the summer solstice, the longest day of the year—the day when light and life were most abundant, the day the Lord of the Forest was at his greatest strength. It was also the day of the Faerie, and I wondered if they danced in the moonlight to celebrate our impending vow.

Tomás pressed his lips to my forehead. My breathing steadied, and my heartbeat slowed, becoming one with his. His voice was gentle, melodic, and full of love.

"I promise you, Tiegan Moss, I will be your husband. I will love you. I will respect you, I will make you laugh, I will kiss you when you hurt, I will be your friend, I will be your lover. You are my blood. You are my bone. I am yours, and you are mine from this day to the end of all days."

———

The skies flickered pink, streaked with golden hues, birdsong rising in concert outside the bedroom window.

I opened my eyes and wondered if it was all a beautiful dream. I rolled onto my side, running my fingers across the indented pillow where Tomás laid his head. I remembered— the words we spoke, the vow we made, the crush of our first kiss.

Tomás made breakfast: dishes clanked, cupboards opened and closed, the microwave beeped, the fridge door opened, the coffee pot brewed on the stove, the cat meowed—everyday things I would never take for granted again.

I ran my hands across my belly. The babies were quiet. Did they know their father was here? I squeezed my vaginal muscles tight, savoring the contractions, the pulsing thrum racing through my sex, the tingle of our lovemaking, and I wanted him all over again.

*"Like dreams, small creeks grow
into mighty rivers."*—Unknown

T*iegan*
"Well, now. I hope you have brought your appetite. Supper's on the stove." My mother's voice welcomed us with down-home enthusiasm. She stood on the front porch, drying her hands on her apron: the floral one she wears when company comes calling.

My mother, a tall drink of water, was in great physical shape for her age. I still had not figured out why I was so short. It was just unfair.

Finn, my parents' black and white border collie, welcomed us with a howl and a series of happy yips. I squatted to the ground as best I could and gave Finn the attention he demanded. A sloppy pink tongue washed my face, bowling me over with love and affection.

I was so pear-shaped I had to press my hands to my knees to lift myself into a standing position. My breasts ached. I was heavy and slow. I had indigestion, and my feet hurt. I couldn't wait for this pregnancy to be over. Did I think that? I was terrified—the outcome of this pregnancy was unknown and inevitable.

"Tomás, how do you like our island? What did the two of you get up to today?" Martha asked again, not waiting for the first answer.

"It's the most beautiful place in the world, Martha," Tomás replied with a huge grin. "Tiegan showed me around the salmon pools today. I can't wait to go back and try my hand."

I smiled to myself. I did not know Tomás was such a sportsperson that he enjoyed fishing. There was still so much to discover about my new husband. When I told him our rivers ran with wild Atlantic salmon, he insisted I take him there. We drove up the Ceilidh Trail, parked behind the hardware store, followed the path through the bush, over the bridge, past the hatchery—first to Slide Pool and then to the Boar's Back, where my father taught me how to fly fish when I was a little girl, to those idyllic Faerie pools, where I would dream all those big girl dreams. While Tomás explored the shallow granite basins, I sat on the grassy bank, dipping my swollen feet in the chilly waters.

"Well, now. We'll have to get you out in the big boat, Tomás. Try your hand at jigging for mackerel or sticking a few swordfish." Without taking a breath, my mother continued, "Tiegan, did you take Tomás to Glenora? He's likely to enjoy a tour of the distillery, given his talents for the craft." Her voice rang with knowing conviction and clear pride in Tomás's talents.

"We're going tomorrow, Mom." I shared my smile with the two of them. My mother was twitterpated with my husband. In her words, Tomás was the bee's knees, and she couldn't find enough good things to say about him, to me, Tomás himself, or anyone who would stop and listen.

"What about the old still in the backlands, sweetheart? You might show your man the way to making the silver. Now he's part of the family." Her gaze lingered on Tomás, her eyebrows rising. "That's moonshine in these parts, Tomás. Tiegan's grandfather had quite an operation back in the day. Now, I've plumb forgot, but Tiegan would mind all those family recipes. She was his right hand for many a year. Och, I'd wager we still have that old black pot ahide in the barn. Howard." Her voice lifted, rising in a crescendo. "The kids are here."

"Moonshine? Tiegan, you didn't tell me that."

There were a few secrets I might not have shared.

The whir of my father's bandsaw quieted, and he stepped out of the barn. My father was a giant of a man, rooted in a gene pool of legends—Fionn mac Cumhaill, the all-knowing and brave warrior, is my father's namesake—though everyone calls him Howard.

Tomás extended his hand in greeting, his shoulders straightened. "Mr. Moss."

"Son, there's no need for that. Howard will do just fine." My father's easy grin admonished his new son-in-law.

My heart melted as I watched the two of them. Tomás was on his left foot, unsure how to respond. I hoped he would reconcile with Joseph, his father. But for now, my dad had taken Tomás under his wing.

"Will ye have a wee dram of whiskey, b'y, while the ladies fuss with their doin's?" My father slapped Tomás on the back, turning toward the barn, Finn yipping at my dad's heels as they walked away in a cloud of dust. My father was a gifted storyteller, a shanachie, as they say in these parts, and I knew he would keep Tomás amused with ancient folktales of the Gael.

I guffawed at my father's comment.

"Dad, maybe Mom would like a wee dram." They both turned, facing me.

My father's face leathered with a teasing smile, and his green eyes twinkled. Then his expression changed, and his mouth gaped open.

Stabbing pains cut through my belly, the death hand pressing down on my uterus—a plug popped, and bright red blood streamed down my thighs.

"Tiegan, *meu amor*, are you all right?" Tomás's voice echoed in the breeze.

"Tiegan, sweetheart?" My father's gruff voice rises. "Martha, call 911!"

———

I remembered little after that, not the ambulance, not the sirens. I woke in a hospital theatre surrounded by nurses dressed in muted pastel shades and poofy bouffant caps—spotlights shining down from the ceiling, a heart monitor bleeping.

"I'm here, Tiegan. I'm right here." Tomás wore blue scrubs and a white face mask. Another voice demanded my attention.

"Tiegan, I'm Dr. Olupona. It's nice to see you awake. How are you feeling?" His gloved hands held stationary in front of his chest—waiting.

"My babies."

"Are doing just fine: good, strong heartbeats."

Tomás squeezed my hand. I focused on him, only him, on the flicker of gold in his chocolate eyes.

"As I told your husband, your uterus has ruptured. There's no need to worry, though. Everything's going to be just fine. But right now, I need you to go to sleep. We need to bring these babies into the world, and we can't wait a moment longer."

Another voice spoke to me—the anesthesiologist positioned behind my head. "Count backward, please, ten, nine, eight, seven..."

I took a deep breath and swallowed my fear.

———

I woke up in a private room, an IV line taped to the back of my hand, my mouth dry and chalky. The lights were low.

Tomás leaned in, and a wave of terror surged through my heart.

"The babies?" My voice squeaked. I was afraid of the answer.

"Are beautiful, *meu amor*—a boy and a girl. Do you want to meet them?"

Tears filled my eyes, tears of happiness, tears of joy.

Tomás pressed a button, lifting the bed. There was pain where the incision was, but I knew it would lessen. I didn't die. The babies didn't die.

Two bassinets sat side by side at the end of the bed. Tomás lifted each bundle and placed them into my arms. A boy with a mop of black hair and a girl with hair kissed by autumn's fire. They looked at me with eyes of dark chocolate flecked with the light of the sun.

"Tomás, they're beautiful."

"You're beautiful, *meu amor*. You've made me the happiest man in the world."

He stood beside the hospital bed, his arms at his sides, his eyes dark and wary. There was something he wanted to say.

"What is it, Tomás? Is something wrong?"

"You need to give them names, Tiegan. Names only you will ever speak, to protect them—from the demons." His throat tightened; his voice constricted as the words rushed out.

"Really?"

"Yes, really..." He stared, unseeing, into the crack of doom.

This was an ancient Roma custom that shielded a newborn's identity from underworld demons and earthly evils. Through the ritual of naming and magical practices involving running water, it safeguarded the newborn from malevolent forces.

I arched my eyebrows, a grin tweaking on my lips.

Eye of newt, toe of frog, wool of bat, and tongue of dog—a hocus-pocus of words, and I could recite them all. Yet none could keep Sylvie's spirit at bay. From beyond the back, Sylvie found me. But I humored him. I touched the soft, silken face of each babe.

"Okay, Tomás. I will name them."

23

"A house is made of walls and beams;
a home is built with love and dreams."—Unknown

Tiegan
"Are you ready?" Tomás appeared in the doorway of our bedroom in the villa by the sea, wearing just a pair of jeans. His toned chest glistened from his workout.

The Algarve sun streamed through the floor-to-ceiling windows, and the salty breeze wafted through the open sliders. Gulls screeched as they soared across the blue sky while the cat lay in wait beneath grapevines heavy with fruit. Harvest time was approaching.

"I think so. Did you pack the diapers and the wipes?" I looked up from the suitcase, packed with enough clothes for the week's holiday.

"Everything's in the backpack." He ran his hand through his wet hair, a grin lighting his eyes.

"What about Patrick's pacifier?" I folded a black T-shirt and added it to his pile of clothes.

"Yes." He walked up behind me, wrapping his arms around my waist.

"Rosalia? How is she getting to the airport?" My eyes drifted shut, engulfed in his scent, minty froth, and pine shavings.

"Anca has everything arranged." His warm breath ruffled my hair.

"Did you take your pill?" I murmured, turning into him and catching his lower lip. We had overcome his fear of flying with one simple prescription pill.

"I don't like meds. I'm fine." His tongue slid against mine, flicking the roof of my mouth and sending a line of fire to every pleasure point.

"Tomás. You know you need them." I melted into his sculpted chest as the embers ignited.

"I need you, *meu amor*." His hand skimmed my throat as he deepened the kiss, his tongue stroking mine while his hands drifted. "I need to taste you."

In one quick motion, he backed me onto the bed, his hands resting on either side of my knees.

"Now?" I leaned on the heels of my hands, anticipation coiling inside me.

His eyes flashed as he knelt before me, his hands skimming my inner thighs and lifting the skirts of my sundress.

His hungry gaze set my heart on fire. The feel of his soft lips made my skin dance. My need chased his tongue as it separated the folds of my sex, stabbing the inner channel and then swirling over my clit.

My fingers curled into the folds of the duvet as I rode the waves of pleasure. When he raked his teeth over my clit and suckled the hooded bead, my mind left me, my thighs trembling as orgasm struck. Wet heat flooded my core as he held my sex open, ravaging my flesh like I knew he would.

My need for him was explosive. Sex was a word with a new meaning. It was nothing like it was then. It was more.

I gazed at him, my need ratcheting higher as he slid the leather belt from the bronze buckle and unsnapped the button of his jeans. He edged closer, resting the wide crown of his cock on my clit.

His eyes were half closed, the muscles in his chest rippling as his cock glided over the heated bead, tantalizing every nerve ending I possessed.

A song played on the wind, dancing with the voices in my head. Yeah, she was there. This was for her as much as it was for me. Sylvie lived and breathed in my soul. It was our secret, hers and mine.

When his hips pressed against mine, I almost lost my mind. I curled my calves around his, the friction of his heavy shaft too much to bear. I was close, so close.

"Come for me, *meu amour*." He dipped his head, trailing his tongue along my jugular and nipping my earlobe, all the while his cock stroked my clit.

"Yes. Yes." My hands tangled with his as the flames rose between us, as his cock drove my climax home. He entered my wet channel with one heated thrust, filling me. My pussy pulsated, clutching the hard column of steel. There was so much heat.

A grin lifted his lips as he stared into my hungry eyes.

There was. No such thing. As enough. I bucked into him, taking him to the end of me. His resolve was a thing to be envied. He made me work for it. His hands clasped to mine so I couldn't touch him, his stance wide, his throbbing cock grazing all the right places.

"Come for me." He was breathless in his need. At least I had that.

My mind went numb, and my thoughts slammed shut.

There was no one but him. Heat surged down my spine like wildfire, a wave of electricity and flickering sparks. I cried out, my voice rising higher with each jolt.

"Beautiful. You are so beautiful." He lifted me then, his hands clasping my bottom, my skirt crumpled in his arms. I was lax, sated with pleasure, and completely undone. He crossed the terrace, setting me on the chaise lounge beneath the pergola.

Dappled sunlight danced in the breeze. The ocean roared.

I reached for him then, cupping his ball sack, his throbbing shaft in my hands, a soft smile playing on my lips. My tongue swirled over the wide crown, tasting him.

A groan prowled from his throat. I would have my way with him.

I dug my hands into his jeans, his buttocks hard beneath my grasp, his cock stretching my lips as I worked his shaft with a lapping tongue.

He gave into his desires, as I knew he would. One hand rested on my shoulders, the other cupping my breast, pinching the arrowed peak, striking a line of fire through my core.

He thrust deeper and deeper, my lips wrapping his shaft as his need reached its peak, whispering my name, almost reverently, as his cock jerked, flooding my mouth with the salty-sweet taste of him.

I could never get enough.

Our life had been a whirlwind. On the brink of the sun-drenched cliffs, we wintered in the Algarve of Portugal, where Tomás would oversee Bianca's and Casa Rosalia's operations. The craft brewery had flourished—the Sea Witch and Knotty Buoy brands were on supermarket shelves throughout the region.

On the opposite coast, on Cape Breton Island, sat our second home—where we would spend the summer months. Big enough for the four of us, the sprawling farmhouse on the shores of Mabou Harbor, complete with a large family-sized kitchen. We converted a barn into a studio for me to paint, and when the babies weren't demanding his attention, Tomás was free to tinker with silver and gold while he fulfilled his duties abroad.

It had been a year since the babies arrived since we vowed to be husband and wife, the old way—the Romani way. Today was the big white wedding, although I was not wearing white. Today was for family and friends—celebrating our life together—a time for both families to become one.

"You look beautiful, sweetheart." My father's eyes shined.

"Thanks, Dad. You're looking pretty dapper yourself." I placed my palm on the lapel of the black tuxedo.

"Are you ready?" His face scrunches into a million smiles.

"I'm ready." I wore a crimson red satin gown, an off-the-shoulder design embroidered throughout, with beaded hems and a corset back—my hair braided with strings of pearls. I carried a bouquet of black lilies—for Sylvie.

My father cut a striking figure in his black tuxedo and red cummerbund, complemented by silver cufflinks that belonged to my grandfather.

The sweet strains of a violin accompanied Anca's haunting voice, calming the butterflies in my stomach and encouraging my feet to move. When I told Anca I wanted to walk down the aisle to this song, my father's favorite Irish hymn—she insisted she would sing.

I moistened my lips with the tip of my tongue and clung

to my father's arm. As I walked down the aisle, slivers of green grass tickled my toes. I reached for my medallion and took comfort in its warmth.

The sun shone on the faces watching me. It was a small wedding, but those in attendance were the ones who counted the most.

Tomás's mother, Angelina, who is gentle and kind, smiled, looking at me with warm eyes. Next to her, Joseph sat close by, no longer distanced from his family. He tipped his flat cap and smiled at me.

Rosalia and my mother sat side by side, each with a chubby baby on their lap. Baby Patrick chattered a blue streak while baby Rose studied everything and everyone. They wore amulets made of fossilized bone, crafted by their father—to keep the dark spirits at bay.

Rosalia and I had arrived at a truce of sorts. She taught me how to cook and prepare every family recipe, from roast *bacalhau* to seafood *cataplana* to Tomás's favorite paprika stew. We named our daughter Rose.

My aunt and uncle waved as I walked past, my aunt dabbing at her eyes with a handkerchief, the same pattern as my mother's apron.

Vera, my maid of honor, smiled not at me but at Tomás's best man, Eli—who looked sharp in his Hawaiian shirt.

And Derek—even Derek made the trip to the Island of Cape Breton to be part of our special day.

———

Sylvie

S I would sometimes awaken in the dark hours of the night, a sensation racing through my heart: a scatter of lightning, a shimmer of light, a thread of gossamer silk flowing to my fingers and toes.

My breath sawed in and out, inhaling the heady musk of wisteria. The dirge of a banjo floated on a miasma of mist, calling to me. I would wander there, lost to the brackish waters, my heart singing to the tinkle of hollowed-out bones.

I would reach for Tomás and take what we both needed. We were together then. We were one.

"Life is a one-time offer, use it well."—Unknown

"Dearest Tiegan,

I hope your flight landed safely and you're both having a right fair time away. Don't worry about the wee ones. Your Aunt Carol arrived yesterday, and we are having balls of fun.

Your father and I have mapped out your journey on the big atlas. My goodness, the Taj Mahall…Kathmandu…the Himalayas… Send us a photo of Shangri-La when you find it.

Does Tomás like his new hiking boots? Young Jordan across the way has the very same ones, and he says they're just the cat's meow.

Be sure to tell Tomás his family are off the island and on their way back to Portugal. We saw them to the airport after a fine lobster supper at the public hall. Lovely folks, I must say, even though they come from away.

We had a large day before they left. Your father and I toured the highlands with Roselia, Angelina, and Anca for some sightseeing. Well, we even had a visit to the Fairy Hole.

Your father was after telling Rosalia of Glooscap's Cave, and she was after a gander, right insistent she was too. Well, the tides were coming in, and they were calling for a breeze, so we had to hurry them along, and there Rosalia went fair ahead of the rest of us, wading through the waters, scrambling up the scree and into that cave. I was quite taken aback with that one, she so reminds me of your grandfather... all that talk about sacred mountains and such.

Well, I must be off now, sweetheart. The wee ones are fussing after their nap. Give Tomás a hug from us, and have a wonderful time away.

Love,

Mom

Xoxo

PS. I mind forgot to say. We're after having a fine kitchen party before the folks set out. Well, it struck me what a right smart idea it would be to invite the widow woman Marjorie Jones. Do you remember Marjorie? Well, here's the pickle! Your Derek and our Marjorie came from the same village when they were just wee, back in the old country. Well, they knew one another right away and set to talking, and if the two of them didn't hit it off right smart. Your father's after calling me a matchmaker, that's for darn tootin'."

ABOUT THE AUTHOR

Awards:

Mary Christmas, a Steamy Small-town Romance.
N.N. Light's Book Heaven 2024 Book Awards
First Place for Best Holiday Romance
Unwrapped in Roros
Passionate Ink - 2023 Passionate Plume - Finalist
Finding Tiegan
American Book Fest Awards 2023
Winner - Romance Erotica.
Paranormal Romance Guild
Second Place 2022 Reviewer &
Reader Choice Award
Contemporary Romance Writers
Stiletto Contest Winner 2022
N.N. Lights Book Award 2021.
Best Erotic Romance
Sorrento Seduction
Passionate Ink - 2022 Passionate Plume - Finalist
N.N. Lights Book Award 2022 - Finalist

Hanna's Story:

I began my writing career in the pre-dawn of a winter morning while my husband snored like a train. We could call my husband the catalyst. If not for him, I would never have gone to the kitchen to make coffee, feed the cat, and sit on the loveseat in front of the fire. In those moments of wondrous quiet, it was there that I did something I had never thought possible. I opened my laptop, and while the coffee went cold, I wrote a story. My husband had no idea that these sojourns to the loveseat in front of the fire would become a daily occurrence, that writing would become an obsession, but the cat knew. She knows everything.

I write stories that make you laugh, make you cry, and make you love. Thank you, friends, for reading!

In the beginning, there was an empty page.

I am a writer who lives in Muskoka, Canada, with a husband who snores, a hungry cat, and an almost perfect canine––he's an adorable little shit.

Visit Hanna Park at

https://www.hannapark.ca

ALSO BY HANNA PARK

The Scald Crow

Mary Christmas

Unwrapped in Roros

Sorrento Seduction